Dreaming Vienna

Advance Praise for This Book

Dreaming Vienna is thematically complex, its sentences thoughtful, often melancholy, lyrical.... Conley knows when to end sections and begin new ones so that a reader can stop and reflect.... The pacing [is] designed to whet the appetite. Characters are well developed, and [even] the exception–Herr Professor Doctor Wagner, whose portrayal veers into caricature–[shows clearly] that caricature is a valuable form of art. *Dreaming Vienna* ... is meant for people who are comfortable with ambiguity and open-endedness, for people who appreciate having something to chew on, something that will make them do a little work.

–Christian Hatala, Independent Scholar

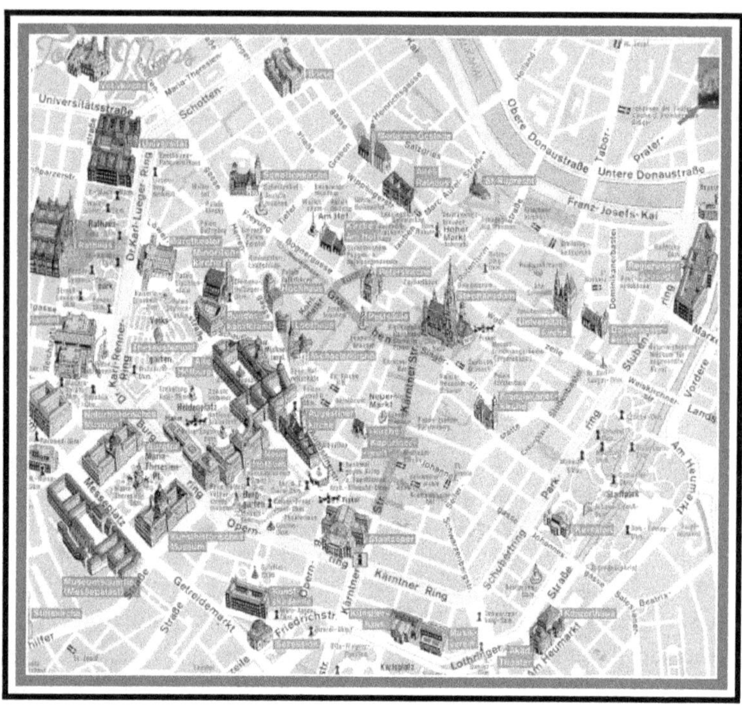

Tourist Map of Vienna

Dreaming Vienna

by

Timothy K. Conley

Golden Antelope Press
715 E. McPherson
Kirksville, Missouri 63501
2023

ISBN: 978-1-952232-89-3

Library of Congress Control Number: 2023945480

Published by:
Golden Antelope Press
715 E. McPherson
Kirksville, Missouri 63501

Available at:
Golden Antelope Press
715 E. McPherson
Kirksville, Missouri, 63501
Phone: (660) 229-2997, (660) 349-9832
http://www.goldenantelope.com
Email: ndelmoni@gmail.com

For Susan

A man who is not born with the novel-writing gift has a troublesome time of it when he tries to build a novel. I know this from experience. He has no clear idea of his story; in fact, he has no story. He merely has some people in his mind, and an incident or two also a locality. He knows these people, he knows the selected locality, and he trusts that he can plunge these people into those incidents with some interesting results. So he goes to work. To write a novel? No—that is a thought that comes later; in the beginning he is only proposing to tell a little tale; a six-page tale. But as it is a tale which he is not acquainted with and can only find out what it is by listening as it goes along telling itself it is more apt to go on and on and on till it spreads itself into a book. I know about this, because it has happened to me so many times.

–Mark Twain "Those Extraordinary Twins"

Preface

In 1900 Sigmund Freud published the first edition of *The Interpretation of Dreams* in Vienna. Among the dreams Freud discussed were the following:

Elephants; numbers and calculations; deceased relatives; swimming; fire; narrow alleys; burglars; being chased by wild animals; being threatened by knives, daggers, and lances; hunger, thirst, comfort; landscape and locations; a modified staircase; rescue; urethral stimulus; dental stimulus; pulling teeth and teeth falling out; parturition; missing a train; punishment; convenience dreams; anxiety dreams, examination dreams, consolation dreams, emission dreams; traversing narrow spaces, staying too long in the waltz; and falling, hovering, floating.

What follows is a consideration of the implications of dreams, death, and desire on the meaning of the universe in more recent times.

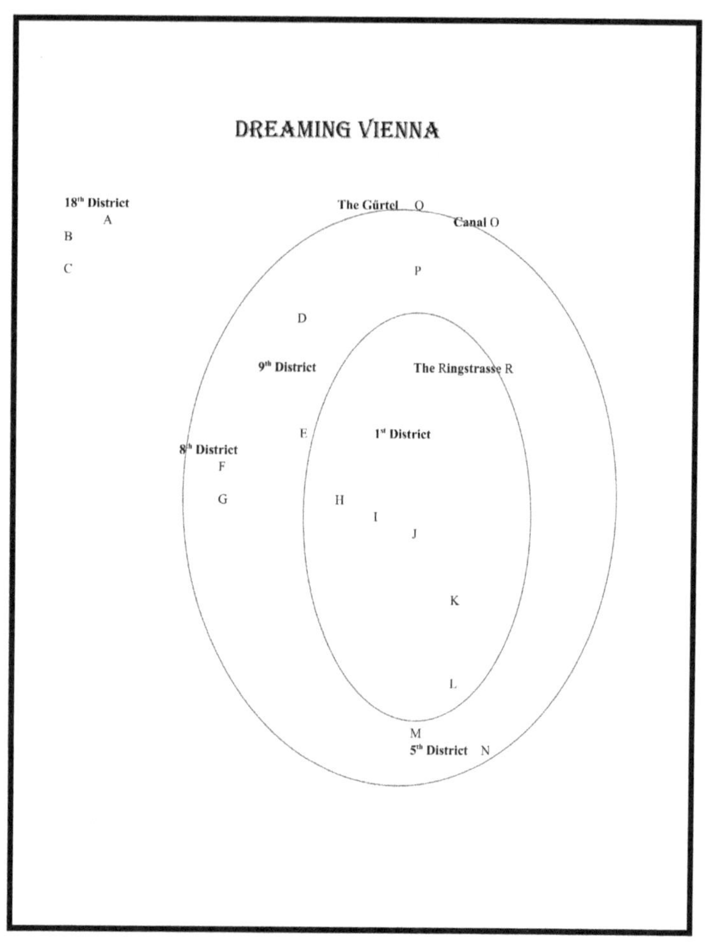

Approximate Locations of the Actions

- (A) Pötzleinsdorf end station: where Felix begins his tram ride and next to where Maria Schmidt lives

- (B) Schlosspark: where linguists get lost, apple falls on Professor Schneider, and Victor sees children sledding

- (C) Schafberg: where Victor hopes to reach & where Professor Schneider has his garden house

- (D) Klaus Weber's apartment: where he is haunted by ghosts of Mauthausen

- (E) Schottentor: where Felix's magical ride ends

- (F) University: where Wagner's Institute is located

- (G) Café Regina: where Anna is hired as waiter/dishwasher

- (H) Café Landtmann: where Professors Wagner and Schneider meet

- (I) Café Griensteidl: where Anna washes dishes

- (J) St. Stephan's Cathedral: where Mozart's Requiem is performed

- (K) Café Hawlka: where Professor Wagner meets Felix

- (L) Vienna State Opera: where *Don Giovanni* is performed and where Anna gazes on the beautiful women

- (M) Naschmarkt: where Amalia sells her rugs

- (N) Amalia's apartment: where Amalia entertains Anna

- (O) Canal running from north to south: where Wasserman brothers rescue Victor

- (P) Augarten: where Laura Stone meets Herr Winkelmann and Wasserman brothers

- (Q) The Gürtel; outer ring road encircling the city's districts 2-9

- (R) The Ringstrasse: the inner ring road encircling the 1st District/Inner City

Contents

Dreaming Vienna

Chapter 1
The Whimsical Life and Magical Death
of Felix Kulpa the Younger
St. Louis, 1953-1981

October, 1981–The Passing of Felix Kulpa

The garbage truck swerved to avoid a collision with the BMW, rented by a family from the northern part of south-central Germany. The orange-clad sanitation worker slowly descended from the truck and turned to curse the German family, and so he did not see the streetcar, strassenbahn #41, on its glorious ride toward Schottentor, the end station where so many tram lines meet. Nor did the worker hear the bell, despite Felix's fantastical clanging. Some Viennese believe the collision was accidental.

"It was very unusual," the last member of the Volksoper chorus to leave the dressing room, told the police. "Only that one car, coming very fast toward Währingerstrasse. The night was so quiet—just that bell." She paused, as if to find the right words. "It seemed to be seeking clarity." The police took no notice of her statement. "A member of the chorus," the official report stated. "She provided no useful information." What happened to Felix, it seems, had been waiting to happen for a long time.

November, 1953-April, 1963–Youth

At his birth, no one questioned whether Felix Kulpa was short or tall; as an adult, Felix Kulpa was not a short person. Nobody called him a short man, and Felix was certainly not a short man. When he was young, however, friends of the Kulpas never asked, "How tall is young Felix?" They always asked Felix's parents "Just how short is that young man?" And his parents would always tell them "Felix is not a short young man." And he wasn't. But he always was well grounded.

When Felix was only ten, he heard that he could use a school trombone if his parents signed a contract and if he took after-school lessons. He took those lessons and thrust the trombone slide as far as his arms could reach. After two months, he insisted to his trombone teacher that he could learn the music for the regional school music competition. It was, as Felix told his parents, a "Back-roll," a simple melody from some opera, or so Felix thought.

He practiced for a few hours before the day of the contest and knew that he could win, or at least do fairly well. He was the second-to-last of twelve grade-school trombonists, thumping their way through Offenbach–da da-da da; da, dada, da da, da-da-da da-da, DA (three times each); ten grade-school trombones, ten grade-school sets of arms, ten intense faces, ten hopeful lungs and lips, all before Felix took his turn. And Felix thumped and thumped his way through. When he finished, the judge smiled the same smile she had smiled for the last 35 minutes. When all had finished their thumping, she posted the scores outside the classroom. "Felix Kulpa—satisfactory." Felix was not upset, but neither was he content.

Grade school, 1963–Shadowland

Young Felix was teased at school because his shadow was longer than his person.

"Watch out, Nancy," Phil the Bully yelled, "You're stepping on Felix."

"Oh Felix, I'm so sorry," said Nancy. "I hope I didn't make you shorter."

Felix said nothing. He only hoped that someday he might hang Phil the Bully from the school's flagpole.

"Do you know the names of the Eight Dwarves?" Phil asked Nancy.

"There's only seven," said Felix.

"Oh no. There's Happy, Dopey, Grumpy, Bashful, Sleepy, Sneezy, Doc, and Shorty," Phil insisted.

"There's no Shorty," Felix told him.

"Really? Why don't you just look in the mirror?"

After each taunt, he turned and tried to realize the possibilities for extension. During recess Felix would stand by himself and try to reach out to make his arms match his shadow. After school, as he walked home across the railroad tracks, he became obsessed with shadow figures who lived in a shadowy world. But finally he realized that shadows always remain flat and cannot ascend as he yearned to do.

Summer, 1963–Beneath the Bed and Up the Tree

Felix' parents were both identical twins: his father (Felix Not Yet the Elder) and his uncle (Francis); his mother (Gertie) and his aunt (Sandra). After the first Identical Twins Convocation, Felix (Not Yet the Elder) married Gertie, and Francis married Sandra. They were always very close, and they always gathered for a group vacation each summer. At the earliest family vacation which Felix thought he remembered, the family had a grand party, but Felix was too young to stay up for the finale. He was also too tired to climb into the attic bunk bed he shared with his cousin, and so he snuck into his parents' room, or perhaps it was to his aunt's and uncle's room, and slid under the bed and went to sleep. But he soon awoke to a sagging bed and moans or perhaps laughter above him. It sounded like his father (Felix) and his mother (Gertie), but it could have been Felix and Sandra, or Francis and Gertie. It could have even been, thought Felix, Felix and Francis, or Gertie and Sandra. Or just Felix the Elder. Felix was confused, but he also was enchanted with the painful joy, and so he lay still and listened carefully until the sound died down and he went to sleep. When he woke up the next morning, the room was empty, and no one talked about the finale.

Felix was feeling a bit ill the next Sunday morning, and so he slipped off his robe, lay in bed, and sucked on a menthol cough drop. But then he remembered the tragic story of his Uncle Tyler, who died after he too sucked on a cough drop while he lay in bed. Felix tossed the cough drop toward the waste can, which he kept by his bed, just for such instances.

But Felix missed the trash can, and the cough drop rolled under his bed, gathering dust from all that Felix had hidden or forgotten . . . but Felix would not search beneath the bed.

Oh, thought Felix, "another one."

Behind the Kulpa back yard, Mister Charlie Hicks had an apple tree. When he was old enough to push the lawnmower, Felix mowed the grass—once a week in August and September. Mr. Hicks, however, was not a kind man, nor was he a happy man. As Felix mowed one September afternoon, Old Man Hicks sat rocking on his porch, smoking a cheap cigar. On that sweating September afternoon, Felix looked up to the top of the apple tree, overloaded with that sweet red fruit. Old Man Hicks, however, never moved an inch from his porch to pick the apples from that golden tree.

Felix climbed the limbs of that apple tree, trying to reach as far as he could. But yellow jackets always came out about the start of the fall to suck the sweetness of that apple tree, and they got a trifle upset when anybody tried to reach for their fruit.

But Old Man Hicks never moved from his porch. He just kept sucking on his cheap cigar, sending his smoke up to heaven while he rocked his life away.

Felix climbed the tree and grabbed an apple and started on down, but those yellow jackets were not at all pleased. "A boy shouldn't climb up our apple tree and reach out to take fruit that doesn't belong to him," they sang to one another.

They stung Felix's face and arms, making their point about climbing too high. Old Man Hicks just kept sitting on his porch, puffing on his nickel cigar. He smiled at Felix's pain and laughed at Felix as he scrambled and fell down that apple tree. Felix swore that day that he never again would mow that grass or get near that apple tree.

A year later, Charlie Hicks was laying in the ground. That September, Felix looked up to the apples at the top of the tree and he thought he could still see the cigar smoke moving up to the clouds. But he never tried to climb that tree again.

May, 1965–Dreams

Felix was twelve when his older cousin, Sandra (the daughter of Sandra and Francis) asked Felix's parents if she could have a party in the family basement, a party with boys and girls, with soda, pretzels, and music, perhaps even dancing. The night before the party, Felix dreamt again of a unicorn but that night the unicorn became a spear and then a drill. When he awoke, Felix knew what he must do: drill a hole in the floor of the closet of his bedroom. Such a hole, reasoned Felix, would enable him to look down from above on the dancing boys and the dancing girls. The hole had to be big enough for Felix to see the magic below; even more the hole must be secret.

"Felix," his mother asked, "what are you doing in the basement? We must get ready for the party."

"Just so," thought Felix, as he searched for the wood drill, "we must get ready for the party."

He found his father's manual wood drill, hidden. He tucked it safely under his shirt as he walked past his mother. "I think I need a short nap," Felix told his mother, as he headed to the bedroom. "Just a short nap," he said.

Felix closed the bedroom door, quietly opened the closet door, found what he thought to be the best viewing point, and began turning and churning the drill, boring down toward paradise. Unfortunately, Felix had not realized how thick the floor was, and so what he called his short nap took most of the early afternoon. But at last he broke through and could look below to the basement floor, or at least to the shreds of crepe paper strung across the iron beams. "At least I'll see something or someone," thought Felix, who returned the drill to his father's work bench and waited for the party to begin.

The girls came first, and then one by one the boys shuffled in, trying to look older and trying to seem uninterested.

Felix was watching them all, all of them, although he wasn't sure which head belonged to which body or which shoulder belonged to which neck. But Felix had needed a long afternoon nap, and so he soon fell asleep in the closet, once again denied knowledge and fulfillment.

No one ever discovered the hole.

November, 1964-January, 1965–Holidays

Every Thanksgiving, just after the mashed potatoes ran out but before the minced meat pie, the stories would begin, the same stories, just told to remind the Kulpa family that they shared family memories. Cousin Frank would tell about the time at Christmas his chair exploded right under him. Then Grandma would tell everyone to quiet down while she told the story of her grandmother, who came from Ireland because of the famine. But Felix always waited for Aunt Mae and the sad legend of Uncle Gus, who disappeared on a sunny May afternoon.

Mae was known for her skill in making arrangements, but on this occasion, she had no time to prepare. "We had no warning," Mae always said, with just a glimmer of a tear. "Why wasn't there a warning?"

"That happens," Father told everyone, every year. "Sometimes they just appear, without a warning."

"He just was out mowing the back lawn," Mae reminded us. "He wasn't out there more than 15 minutes, just mowing the lawn."

They all had seen copies of the *Central Daily Journal*: Gus was the lead story for a day or two. "LOCAL MAN SNATCHED BY TORNADO!"

> Witnesses testify that they saw a body twirling in the sky above the city. "It's not entirely unheard of," according to local meteorologist John Goodbody. "Tornados are unpredictable. They

come and go on their own. Sometimes on a bright sunny day, with no sign of clouds or wind." Sheriff Claude Swifter and a team of volunteers are still searching for the body of Mr. Terwilliger.

Mae went out with searchers for the first three days, but then everybody got tired of looking. They did find the lawnmower, one of those old-fashioned rotary mowers. Gus was obsessed with keeping the grass trimmed. Everyone in the family knew he mowed faster than anyone else, even after that time a twig got caught in the blades and the handle knocked the wind out of him.

There was a memorial for Gus a week after he disappeared. "Everybody in the neighborhood turned out for that service," Mae repeated each Thanksgiving. "Everybody." It wasn't a closed casket service. In fact, there wasn't a casket because they still hadn't found Gus, only the lawn mower. Father Bischoff gave the eulogy and said that Gus lived a blameless life. "There were rumors," Father Bischoff added, "but then there are rumors about all of us."

Ten days later Mae convinced Sheriff Swifter to hire a team of bloodhounds from the state police. He and Mae circled the neighborhood and the nearby woods for a day or two on their own. Four days later and almost three weeks after the mystery twister swept Gus away, they found a body. "We couldn't say it was Gus," Mae said, as Mother swirled whipped cream over each piece of pie. "But we couldn't say it wasn't Gus."

Mae would always pause then and take a bite of her pie. "He had sort of a grimace that looked like a grin, or maybe it was the other way around. We just couldn't tell."

After everyone had finished their pie but before Mother cleaned away the dishes, Mae always had the last word. "There wasn't a warning, and I couldn't make the arrangements," she said. "Why wasn't there a warning?"

At Christmas when Felix was ten—and then when he was eleven and for the next two years–after his third glass of wine,

Grandfather Kulpa would always lament his fate. With sentimental tears gliding down his face, he would say: "Well, everyone, this might be my last Christmas. I hope you all remember me when you open the presents." When Felix was 16 no one sat in Grandfather's place. But they all drank an extra glass of wine.

Every New Year's Day when Felix was young, even younger than his trombone days, his mother insisted that they all have a plate of herring and sauerkraut, as his parents listened to the Vienna Philharmonic's concert. If his father had recovered and if his mother were willing, Felix the Elder would take Gertie in his arms, and they would waltz across the living room, bumping into chairs, sometimes knocking over the glasses.

And Felix the Younger would listen, and he would imagine a world of order and grace, a world secure in its rhythms and beauty.

When the Philharmonik played "The Radetzky March," his mother and father would stomp through the halls and the sound would fill the house, rising through the floors, up the chimney, into the clouds.

December, 1966—An Unfortunate Incident

Although the Kulpa family was not known for their religious devotion, Felix did enjoy the privilege given the Holy Innocents Parish Knights of the Altar. If they served Mass during the school weekdays, they could be late for their first class. If they were selected to serve at a funeral mass, they could miss an entire morning of classes; more importantly, they were allowed to keep the money given by the bereaved families for the knights' services. And, if they were diligent in studying their catechism and reliable in serving at the 6:00 a.m. mass, they might be chosen as the Supreme Grand Knight. Perhaps the Supreme Grand Knight's greatest honor was to carry the statue of baby Jesus on the Christmas Eve midnight mass and to place the infant in the manger.

Felix no longer dreamed of achieving glory and recognition on the trombone, and he had never been good or tall enough to excel on the Holy Innocents boys' basketball team. He knew, then, that if he were to rise above his classmates, he could only do so by becoming the Supreme Grand Knight. To everyone's surprise, everyone except Felix's, he scored higher than any other boy on the eighth-grade catechism test and he volunteered to serve the early mass each Sunday for the entire summer. By all appropriate measures, then, he ascended to the rank of Supreme Grand Knight, at least for the first half of eighth grade. An unfortunate incident at the Christmas Eve midnight mass led to his premature downfall.

Just at midnight on the 24th of December, all the lights in Holy Innocents church were turned off as the entire assembly of knights walked slowly in procession, each one holding a lit candle and each one trying to keep the wax from reaching their cassocks. Felix was the final knight in the procession, just before Father Bischoff, the pastor of Holy Innocents parish. Felix held the infant Jesus as tightly as he had ever held his family's most beloved heirloom (his grandmother's grandmother's flower vase), and he counted each step, keeping in time with the congregation's singing of "Silent Night." All went well until Felix reached the manger: after taking his final deep breath, he lay the infant Jesus in the crib of hay. He stepped back, relieved of the burden and proud of his success. When Father Bischoff stepped toward the manger, solemn and devout as any pastor would be, he stopped suddenly and glared at Felix. "You damn idiot," he whispered loudly enough for the first ten rows of the congregation to hear, "you put baby Jesus in upside down! Damn you, Kulpa."

Felix sank into himself, not certain what to do but certainly afraid of Father Bischoff, who was known for the force of his holy anger. Felix did not rush to join his parents, as he longed to do, nor did he flee from the church. When the mass ended, Father Bischoff summoned Felix to come to the rectory the following Saturday morning. Felix, however, did not obey his pastor, and so Felix no longer was the Supreme Grand Knight.

September, 1971–The Education of Felix Kulpa the Younger, Part One–Shadowy Truth

When he finished elementary school and no longer was tormented by Phil the Bully or Father Bischoff, and after he left high school and was no more required to wear a tie each day, Felix was no longer short, although he was not yet tall. Yet still Felix sought knowledge, as much as he sought a higher vision. When he enrolled at the university, he felt that such wisdom must be housed in the Department of Philosophy, or at least near the Department of Philosophy. He only took one course in the Department of Philosophy, but in that one course, Felix found what he thought to be the meaning of the universe.

Introduction to Ancient, Medieval, and Renaissance Philosophy, with an instructor whose name Felix never could quite recall, began with Plato's *Republic*, and Felix tried to read thoughtfully, as he believed to be most appropriate. Felix tried to follow Socrates' arguments, but he sympathized most with Glaucon. Felix tried to show the instructor whose name he could not recall that he had closely read the assignment by using Glaucon's own words in class. "I really do not understand," Glaucon told Socrates, and Felix told the instructor, "and therefore beg of you to assist my memory."

However, the instructor missed the point of Felix's question, and so only repeated what the instructor felt to be the key passages in Plato. "Those who see the absolute and eternal and immutable may be said to know, and not to have opinion only." Felix did not entirely follow the instructor's explanation, but he did agree that he sought the absolute and eternal.

"Ahhh," Felix replied, "I understand, but could you clarify the exact number of Platonic archetypes?" Felix was not quite certain what a Platonic archetype might be, but the question seemed to emerge from somewhere deep inside his troubled spirit, somewhere in which chaos and serenity were intimately embraced.

The instructor was not accustomed to questions and even less to interest, and so he was eager to continue. "Philosophy, you must realize, is the noblest pursuit of all, but it is not likely to be much esteemed by those of the opposite faction." Felix nodded and looked intently at the instructor, for he did not want to be considered among the opposite faction.

The instructor believed that he had found at least one true believer among the dozens who sat sleeping in the classroom, and so he felt secure in repeating words he recalled from his own Introduction to Philosophy class. "Philosophy is the pursuit of wisdom, understood as a scientific knowledge of the supreme principles and causes in various orders of being." The instructor looked even more intently at a spot somewhere above the heads of the students. "The basic concerns of philosophy are the efforts of human minds to reach some permanent truths; and the history of philosophy cannot be a graveyard because in philosophy there are no dead. All great philosophers are still alive."

Felix felt that he dealt too often with death and the dead, who still haunted his memories and his nights. Perhaps philosophy might provide an escape to permanent truth.

"The true lover of knowledge," the instructor continued, "is always striving after being—that is his nature." Felix always felt himself to be a true lover, although he began now to slip into dreams of climbing the mountain of desire rather than following the instructor's explanation, which ran on for several minutes. Felix missed the first five minutes of the instructor's introduction to Plato, but Felix was recalled to the present when the instructor entered Plato's cave, speaking of "... the forms which they draw and make, and which have shadows or reflections in water of their own ...."

For Felix, shadows were a way to extend himself, not imperfect reflections but the manifestation of his ideal self. He believed that he must escape the cave to reach reality, to touch truth, to ascend. Felix hurried away from the Introduction to Ancient, Medieval, and Renaissance Philosophy, secure for at least that afternoon in his sense of the world.

Felix slept through the two classes on Medieval Philosophy, but he awoke in time for the instructor's sessions on the Renaissance. When the instructor introduced Marsilio Ficino as "the guiding spirit of Renaissance Platonism who offered a defense of personal immortality," Felix was entranced. According to Ficino, the instructor explained, in the afterlife each one of us will receive our heart's desire to the full, and thus the order and rationality of the universe is preserved. For Felix, who sought clarity and desired permanence, Ficino justified believing in truth and in enrolling in the course.

Felix fell asleep reading the instructor's summary of selections from Pietro Pomponazzi. The next morning, however, he remembered that Pomponazzi mentioned shadows or savorings of intellect and what he called the immateriality of the human soul. Felix too believed in shadows and was not comfortable about his own materiality. Immateriality, he thought could be more helpful. Before start of the next philosophy class, Felix asked the instructor to briefly explain Pomponazzi.

"Pomponazzi? Of course, Pomponazzi. Pomponazzi was within the metaphorical, Platonic tradition of participation and contact. According to Pomponazzi, the human soul is immortal in an essential way. Yes. Pomponazzi. Very important minor figure of the Italian Renaissance, Pomponazzi. Is that clear? Good question."

As he mused on such possibility, Felix missed most of the instructor's lecture on Italian Platonists, but he awoke from his daydream to hear that "Renaissance Stoic writings can enkindle once more in the human heart a respect and love for practical wisdom, which is the mother of all virtue. Any questions?"

There were none. But as the classroom emptied, Felix needed to ask one more question. "Excuse me, sir, but did Pomponazzi believe in practical wisdom?"

"Pomponazzi? Yes. Pomponazzi. He did divide the intellect into the speculative, the productive, and the practical. According to Pomponazzi, humanity is rendered unqualifiedly good only through practical intellect, which is the final end for the human race. Is that clear? Good. I must go."

Felix thus believed he only had to use practical wisdom to ascend to a view of the world, a view above but part of an immortal universe. He would dedicate himself to the pursuit of the absolute in the ephemeral, as viewed from the skies. Yes, thought Felix, I need to rise and then look down.

September-December, 1973–The Education of Felix Kulpa, Part Two—Civilization

Felix thought it best to balance philosophy and the pursuit of true wisdom with psychology and the meaning of personality. The Psychology Department, located not far from the Philosophy Department but in a different building, had room for Felix in just one course, Introduction to Freudian Psychiatry, which had many seats still available.

The instructor, who never gave her name, began the first meeting by assigning everyone one text by Freud for the final project—a summary and critique of Freud's writing. Felix was assigned *Civilization and Its Discontents*. She then told everyone that the class would not meet again until the beginning of April for their reports.

Of course, Felix had heard of Freud: he knew that sons loved their mothers, feared their fathers, and dreamed of spears and snakes and caves. Felix was also fairly often discontent, but he had no real concept of civilization, other than what it was not. When as a child he licked the margarine from the knife, his mother would call him "uncivilized." When as a teenager, he slept past nine, he was also "uncivilized." But his mother was no longer there to tell him what was not civilized, and so, perhaps, he thought, Freud might help. If he knew what civilization meant, then he would know what to look down upon.

He looked for what he believed to be the most important concepts, which, for Felix, were the most useful, the most practical. He did not include references to the father: Felix believed that Pomponazzi would not approve. Felix also believed that Pomponazzi would not approve of Freud's equation of religion with an oceanic feeling which originated in the infant's sense of helplessness. But Felix himself had often felt helpless, even beyond infancy. Felix likewise felt justified in skipping Sunday services when he read that religion depressed the value of life, distorted the picture of the real world, and demanded unconditional submission. And yet, Felix thought, the music could be so sublime.

Music often comforted Felix, particularly the arias of romantic opera. He had never seen an opera in person, but one Christmas his parents gave him a recording of *The Royal Family of Opera*, and he was forever enchanted by the voices of desire, even as they succumbed to consumption. They seem to die happy, Felix thought. Yet Freud wrote that the program of becoming happy cannot be fulfilled. The Royal Family, however, believed in love, and so Felix looked to Freud to discover the secrets of such passion.

"Thou shalt love thy neighbor as thyself," according to Freud, "but only if my neighbor deserves such love, if he is like me (I therefore love him as self) or if he is more perfect (therefore I love him as ideal self)—but such a precept is unreasonable." Felix agreed with Freud that many strangers might not be worthy of love and, even more, that he would forgive his enemies but only after they had been hanged. But then Felix realized that he might find love among strangers and that he no longer wished anyone to be hanged. Freud, it seems, was not offering consolation. Felix would include his reservations in his final report.

He also knew that he must include Freud's definition of civilization: the professor would expect at least some analysis, or at least a summary. "Civilization," Felix read, "is a process in the service of Eros, whose purpose is to combine single human individuals, and after that families, then races, peoples and nations, into one great unity, the unity of mankind." Felix longed to be in the service of Eros, although he wasn't certain what such service would require, and unity seemed to lead to clarity, as Felix would likely state in his conclusion.

But then Felix found what seemed to be a contradiction in Freud's theory. "It is always possible to bind together a considerable number of people in love, so long as there are other people left over to receive the manifestations of their aggressiveness." How could civilization serve Eros and seek one great unity while it also sought antagonists? And how could Felix reconcile Freud with Pomponazzi? Pomponazzi seemed to believe in the divine and the eternal, whereas Freud seemed to believe in the savage and the past.

"Men are not gentle creatures," according to Freud, and "the inclination to aggression is an original, self-subsisting instinctual disposition in man." Felix did not think he was aggressive, but perhaps he should simply acknowledge his common humanity and seek out enemies.

May 1975–The End of Education and the Beginning of Wisdom

Felix took no more courses in philosophy or psychology, and he wrote no more of glory or love. At the university, in fact, he had been taught doubt and the art of forgetting, yet he still dreamed at night of Platonic ideas. Each day he remembered without knowing, and so he too soon forgot what he had learned. Unfortunately, he too soon became immersed in his daily routines and discontented with the world. When he finished his studies in managing communication, he took the only job offer he had: an assistant to the public relations liaison for a mid-major university. "I have some skills," he assured the personnel officer at his interview, "and I am able to deal with mediocrity." The university had no other candidates, and so they were forced to hire Felix. Each year he was told that it was impossible, for the time being, to rise to the position of associate public relations liaison. And so, Felix remained.

June 1981–Arrangements

One Sunday in June, 1981 in the sixth year of managing communications, a knock at the door awoke Felix from his daydreams. "I'm afraid I have some bad news for you," the officer began. "There's been an accident. At the railroad crossing." Felix was heartbroken but not surprised, for he knew that his grandmother assumed that traffic signals, speed limits, and warnings were merely recommendations, not requirements. But he struggled to suppress his tears, and his parents, on the Alaska cruise they had always dreamed of, were not there to help. Felix alone had to identify the body at the county morgue. He returned to the empty house and called Aunt Mae, who had dealt with all the complications and all the sadness of sudden death. She came the next day to help Felix make the arrangements.

Felix knew that his grandmother had always said she could not bear to lay forever underground: she would ascend to heaven, his mother told him, where she could look down and protect young Felix. Mae understood, and so she made the arrangements for grandmother's cremation. "You could keep the ashes near you," she told Felix, "or you could scatter them wherever you think best." But at the funeral home, Felix could not focus on the ashes, only the smoke.

Felix returned to his parents' house. He retraced their New Year's Day dances, sat at the family holiday table, and remembered his grandparents. In the back yard, he looked out at Charlie Hicks' apple tree, which was bare of any fruit and seemed much shorter. In his bedroom, he looked inside the closet with the hole in the floor, and on a shelf above the remaining hangers, he found his notebooks with his scribblings on Renaissance philosophy and Freudian psychiatry. He also found a note left by his grandmother, who apologized for not being a good grandparent and wrote that Felix must not resign himself to a life of accommodations and regret. "Take a year away from your work," his grandmother wrote; "Go somewhere, be someone, rise up in the world, assert yourself." At the reading of his grandmother's will the next week, Felix learned that she had provided enough money for Felix to take a year off for travel. "To expand your horizons," she had written, "so that you might achieve your heart's desire."

Summer 1981–Revelations and Resolve

To make such a discovery, Felix knew he must reconcile what he had learned five years earlier in his philosophy and psychology courses with his sense of uncertainty and his memories. He tried to read through his notes, but he could only understand the words which he had underlined in his courses, and he couldn't tell which words belonged to which courses. He decided to make a list of all those terms which he could decipher:

> Absolute, eternal, supreme principles, permanent truth, shadows, personal immortality, order and rationality of the universe, savorings of the intellect, immateriality, essential, monism, practical wisdom, civilization, love, hate, aggression, Pomponazzi, Freud, discontent.

Felix wasn't certain how the list could help him achieve his heart's desire, but he had no other guide. He also knew that he must find that place which offered both dislocation and familiarity, somewhere which provided difference but also looked a bit like home. Felix was befuddled.

And then, from the radio near his bed, the sounds of romance and clarity and order—the Radetzky March, and New Year's Day, and Vienna. "Of course," Felix realized, "I must go to Vienna, the city of opera, and Strauss the Elder and Strauss the Younger, of Freud, of beautiful people." Felix looked for his most recent copy of *Travelling the World in Style and Grace*, which had named Vienna "The Most Livable City in the World," and he knew that he too must be among the most livable.

Of course, Felix knew little about Vienna and knew no German. He did not know that Vienna became a city without Jews or that beneath its beauty at times lay a world of repressive order, a shadowy world with rules he could not understand. To Felix, Vienna was irresistible, and so in the last weeks of August he set out to learn what he could, including the language.

To prepare for his days of glory in the City of Dreams, Felix found a comprehensive, but inexpensive, guide to Vienna's history and culture, and language tapes at the second-hand store, tapes which promised him mastery of elementary German in three weeks. "Bitte," he heard was essential: "bitte" could mean please, welcome, excuse me, and he would need such terms for any encounter. He also learned how to ask for and give directions: if someone would ask for help in locating the nearest bus stop, "Wo ist die Autobushaltestelle?" they always ask. He should reply: "Erste Strasse links, und dann geraudeaus," the bus stop was on the first street to the left and then straight ahead. If someone would ask for the time, he would reply "Zwolf Uhr"—if it was noon or close to it. Felix could then himself ask for directions to the bus stop and could learn if he was late for the bus.

Felix felt prepared, and so he booked a one-way ticket to Vienna for the second week in September, 1981. He could not delay, for revelation awaited him in Austria.

September 1981–Felix and his Flight to Vienna

On the plane to Vienna, Felix tried to impress the attendants by asking for a copy of *Die Presse*, the only German-language newspaper available on the plane. But the effort to read German exhausted Felix, and he soon could no longer avoid sleep. Just as he pretended to read the newspaper, so dreams pretended themselves to Felix ... and in his world of dreams, he rode into the City, dressed in the vestments of a knight of the golden fleece, scattering mobs of vagabonds and thieves from the northern provinces.... Felix saw himself on the clouds of beauty high above the City, crowned with gold, diamonds, rubies, one sapphire (it must be a sapphire, but only one), pearls.... He wore the mantle of the Holy Roman Empire, and he wielded the Sceptre of the Ainkhun.... He inscribed the skies with the imperial whale tusk, messages of love and power. He awoke from his dreams as the plane descended to Vienna, with "The Emperor's Waltz" playing on the intercom.

After his bus and taxi rides, Felix arrived in Pötzleinsdorf–a magical realm of the 18th District, overlooking the city from the northeast. He looked on a clear day and an apple tree gently cradling the year's blossoms. Outside the nineteenth-century home in which he would live, Felix saw graceful statues of disrobing maids and happy dogs guarding the entrance. Stairs carried Felix to the front door, and a winding staircase carried him to his apartment. He knew that he would be living in a magical world and that he would meet people unlike anyone he had ever met and that he would see things unlike anything he had ever seen before. From his front windows, he could look to the southeast toward the districts of

Oberdöbling, Brigittenau, and Florisdorf, with what he imagined to be the Hungarian hills in the distance. Felix felt that he was closer to heaven than he had ever been.

When Felix awoke the next morning, he knew that he must do more than simply look down on the city: he must encounter the real Vienna, the material and livable city. He wasn't yet quite sure how the public transportation system operated, and he was afraid in his ignorance that he might offend tradition and decorum and possibly the law. But he was also determined to explore the streets and shops as soon as possible: it was Sunday morning, however, and most streets were vacant, and no shops were open. Felix was both surprised and relieved.

He began walking down Pőtzleinsdorferstrasse, the street which ran from near the hilltop of Schafberg down toward the city center. Felix did not know, however, that Pőtzleinsdorferstrasse somehow turned into Gerstoferstrasse, another street that seemed to head toward the First District. "This is indeed a puzzling city," thought Felix. "It seems to have a structure of its own." He soon found himself in Tűrkenschanzpark. There did not appear to be any Turkish restaurants nearby, and so Felix knew that the area had some link to the past. He then was on another street with another name, then a smaller street with yet another name, although he did not see any signs with any such names. Ten minutes later he came to a bridge across the Danube River, or across what he thought was the Danube River but which actually was the Danube Canal. Strauss was irresistible on such an occasion and at such a location, and so he hummed a waltz which reminded him of skating rinks at home.

When he finished his waltz and reached the opposite side of the Danube Canal, Felix sat on a small bench and considered what he seen and what he should do next. Suddenly, he was startled by a weak cough and a question: "Entschuldingun. Wo ist die Autobushaltestelle?"

Without hesitation, Felix replied: "Erste Strasse links und geraudeus."

"Viel Dank," said the man in the grey coat, who followed Felix's directions and, just as he turned left at the next street, waved a second thanks, which Felix returned.

"My first Vienna morning," thought Felix, "and already I have demonstrated practical wisdom, in German, and have helped someone in need. This is indeed a magical city." Felix quickly realized that the closest bus stop might not in fact be to the left at the first street and then straight ahead, and so he felt it best to retrace his steps across the bridge. This time, however, he did not hum any Strauss tune.

As he tried to remember how he had reached that bridge, he became a bit confused. He wasn't certain if he was walking back to Pőtzleinsdorf or heading to the city center and the cathedral of St. Stephan. He knew he must visit the cathedral for Sunday mass and perhaps a few souvenirs, but he did not know how to get to the Inner City or how to return to his apartment. It was noon, and so he could now watch the strassenbahn moving along the city streets and taking in those who made it to the tram stop in time.

He did not know, however, what one needed in order to enter and ride these wonderful cars. No one seemed to control the doors or the speed of the strassenbahn, the city's wonderful trams: they simply seemed to move on their own, merely announcing their presence and power by a clanging bell. Three people waited for the next arrival, one of whom was a young woman in a bright blue dress and white tunic. As Felix walked past, she turned and smiled, and her golden smile seem to promise to Felix that he would find wonder and adventure in this magical city. The smile carried Felix into districts and streets unknown, and so he did not reach his home until four hours later.

Felix waited another day before trying to explore the city and, most importantly, to find Freud's home. Felix walked from Café Maximilian to Schottentor, where he asked for directions. Felix knew that Freud lived at 9 Berggasse, or a street with a similar name, but Felix mistook Burggasse for Bergasse, and so he never found the house. But when he returned to Schottentor, nearby he saw a statue of Freud, and Felix reasoned that a bust would be sufficient.

"What would you suggest, Professor?" Felix asked the memorial stone opposite the church of failed assassinations; "What should I do?" Of course, Sigmund Freud seldom advised lovers or fools, but on this occasion, perhaps he made an exception. Just as Felix spoke to Sigmund, a lone trumpeter practicing for Sunday Mass stepped outside the Votive Church and sounded one note to scare off the pigeons. Felix turned, only slightly, at the noise, and then walked to Schottentor and took strassenbahn 41 to the end station.

As he slowly continued up the hillside above Pötzleinsdorf, he was passed by a carriage driver also heading home. The driver gently urged his horse up the incline, and then drank once again from the schnapps he kept beneath his seat for just such occasions. It was time to get home ... clip-clap, clip-clap, clip-clap.

That night, Felix once again dreamed, and in his dreams he recalled the trumpeter, and he envisioned his mission in the City of Dreams and Freud. He saw himself as a street musician on Kärtnerstrasse, the avenue of exclusive shops and expensive tastes. Yes. He saw himself playing his favorite arias at night near the State Opera House on his childhood trombone. Even in his dream, Felix assured himself that he would only perform Puccini arias, and perhaps a selection from *The Royal Family of Opera: La Traviata* or *Madame Butterfly* or, if he felt expansive, *Carmen* or *Les Contes d' Hoffman*. He only felt invigorated by certain operas, and he refused to compromise his standards.

In his dream, Felix knew that he could draw people away from the puppet master with the dancing clowns and the accordion player in the baroque wheelchair. Felix awoke, and then he had a vision, a vision of the world as it should be. He was playing "O soave fanciulla" on Kärtnerstrasse, near the Aida bakery, and a crowd gathered. They begged him for more, and he played "E lucevan le stelle," and everyone cried and asked him for more. He played, from *Butterfly, Tosca, La Boheme*, and still the crowd called for more and more and more. Felix played on his golden trombone and angelic notes came from heaven. Finally, Felix saw himself carried by the crowd to the State Opera House, and the ushers cheered his entrance and begged his forgiveness for their earlier rudeness, and the conductor waved his baton and the Philharmonik stopped, stopped in the midst of *Turandot*. Pavarotti stopped in the midst of "nessum dorma," and no one objected.

All eyes turned to Felix and his golden trombone, and he went to the stage and accepted their applause–again and again and again–and he bowed graciously, and he accepted the bouquet brought by the woman with the golden laughter, and the world was as it should be, and he smiled graciously. Such was Felix's first vision.

Felix awoke and went to the window, and he knew now there could be a time when he would dance in Vienna. If he could look past the building opposite his bedroom window, he felt that he could see the woman with the golden smile move to the edge of a balcony to catch the moon in her silver mirror.

The blue moon had risen fully above the fog as other dreamers awoke in the midst of their own dreams. It seemed to be a time when magicians could carve golden temples upon cherry stones.

On the morning of his second week in Vienna, Felix himself had to dash to catch the streetcar, strassenbahn #41 at the Pőtzleinsdorf end station. As he walked down the hill to the stop, he saw the tram pull around the circle and make its brief stop before heading toward the Inner City. Felix had nowhere in particular to go, but if he sprinted then others would assume he had important appointments. And so he ran, and jumped aboard before the door closed.

At the next stop, the woman with the golden smile slowly walked in and sat opposite Felix, who hoped she would ride all the way to Schottentor. But she stood up in time to exit at the Gűrtel, the outer beltway around the city. As she stepped toward the door, she smiled again at Felix and handed him a small card. Felix thought he must leave the tram and follow her as she walked toward the market. But he could no longer see her in the crowded street market, and so he looked down at the card.

Explore the World of Male Fantasies
For English Speakers
Call Hanneliese
19:00-19:05
543-237-863

Felix was not certain he had any male fantasies, but he did know that prostitution was legal in Vienna, and he had not yet made any Austrian friends. "Perhaps," he thought, "I might encounter someone interesting."

That night, exactly at 7:00, Felix dialed Hanneliese's number, hoping her voice would be as golden as her smile.

"You have reached The World of Male Fantasies. Please give us your name and nationality."

"My name is Felix Kulpa, the Younger, my father was also named Felix but he was the Elder. I grew up in ..." Unfortunately, he was cut off before he could adequately reply.

"What has brought you to Vienna?"

The voice sounded familiar—golden, perhaps, but certainly familiar.

"I came to Vienna because ..."

"It is required that you clearly state your current status."

"My status? Well, I'm not sure I know what you mean? Could you give me some..."

"Where are you living in Austria?"

"I've rented a room in a private home in a very nice part of Vienna. It's not far from ..."

"What are you fantasies?"

"Well, I'm not certain. I would like to meet you, I think. I saw you on the strassenbahn, and I was hoping that we might..."

"I am sorry but your time is nearly complete. Please call again so that we may schedule your appointment."

The line went dead. Felix put the phone down and considered whether he should call back immediately or wait until the next day. He called again, and again, but Hanneliese, or the voice of Hanneliese did not answer.

As he got ready for sleep, Felix reconsidered the questions, his answers, and the voice. And then he realized why that voice was so familiar: it was the voice of public transport, the voice which announced the next stop on the strassenbahn. Each day he had been listening to the voice of Hanneliese, calmly, wisely telling him that soon he would approach "Währingerstrasse-Volksoper" and finally "Schottentor— End Station." Hanneliese had spoken to Felix since his first day in Vienna, spoken with confidence and serenity. And now he could turn to her to help him explore the world of male fantasies.

Felix knew he must prepare more diligently for his next call to Hanneliese for his time was certainly limited. He wrote down all her questions and the next night he was ready to answer so that he could arrange for a rendezvous in person.

"You have reached The World of Male Fantasies. Please give us your name and nationality."

"Felix Kulpa. I am an American citizen."

"What has brought you to Vienna?"

"I hope to attend the State Opera and visit the home of

Sigmund Freud."

"It is required that you clearly state your current status."

"I am currently on leave from my job."

"Where are you living in Austria?"

"I have a room in a private residence in Vienna."

"What are you fantasies?"

"I dream of fame as a musician. I also have fantasies about making love to you on a speeding tram. In that dream, we are..."

"Your time is nearly complete. Please call again so that we may schedule your appointment."

Once again, the line went dead, and Felix could not call back that night. He went to sleep and dreamed of a chorus line of Viennese women, kicking their legs above his head.

A mid-autumn cold spell had little effect on Felix's dreams; it did, however, bring on a brief pause in his pursuit of Hanneliese. He was not running short of inspiration, but he was running far short of funds: despite his lack of skills and his ignorance of all but the most basic German, he needed to find a job. He spent most mornings in Pötzleinsdorf considering how he might find something to do, and he spend most afternoons in cafés, hoping to be discovered.

He knew that Freud's favorite was Café Landtmann, which Felix visited one October morning. Café Landtmann, as Felix discovered, is a rather formal, reserved, and very orderly café, one not quite ready for a young man such as Felix, who was not yet certain of either his place in the world or his German. But Felix found an empty table and sat waiting for someone to ask him what he might want that day. Immediately to his right sat two middle-aged gentlemen, looking both professorial and preoccupied and very much as if they deserved a table at Café Landtmann. Felix sat patiently, as he knew he must, but after fifteen minutes, he thought that perhaps he did not deserve a place at Landtmann. "I should leave, quickly," he thought, "before they ask me to leave." Felix stood up, looked both left and right, and then hurried out towards the door on his right, but he stumbled into the table with the two gentlemen sipping their morning coffee. "Sorry, bitte, sorry," he mumbled.

Safely outside Landtmann, yet still wanting to look as if he belonged in a Vienna café on this chilly October morning, Felix once again was befuddled, but determined to find somewhere he could be secure, safe, perhaps, in the rear of a small café. Today, however, he thought it best to return to Pőtzleinsdorf, where he could be protected from forces he was not yet prepared to confront. One afternoon a week later, he began his search in First District, not knowing where he should go. Just then some god of fantasy and delight intervened on behalf of Felix, as he found Café Hawelka, where one open table remained, at the very back of the café. Felix sat by himself, half hidden by the smoke from dozens of European cigarettes.

Felix had been sipping his coffee mélange for about half an hour when what seemed to be the same two gentlemen dressed in slightly worn black suits approached what remained the only vacant table in the café and asked if they might join him. "Bitte, frei?" one of the men asked, as he pointed to the empty chairs. They seemed just a bit tipsy and perhaps a bit too academic, but Felix felt that perhaps they might pay for a glass of wine, and so he politely told them they were most welcome to join him. Felix also hoped they would understand English. After several drinks, one of the gentlemen, who introduced himself as Professor Doctor Wagner, asked Felix if he would join his staff. "From how you've spoken," the professor told Felix, "I can detect that you are a native speaker of English, perhaps an American. Am I not correct?"

"You are correct, Professor Wagner. I have always been a native speaker."

"Then I may have a position for you, one that pays a modest salary. Are you interested?"

Felix did not want to appear desperate, and so he hesitated before speaking.

"Yes. I may indeed be interested. What would I be doing?"

"You would be required to visit my Institute three evenings each week so that you could review the work of my assistants, none of whom is a native speaker such as yourself."

"But they are very ... gifted," said Wagner's colleague.

"I believe I could do such work," said Felix.

"Excellent! Here is the key to my office. Please come in promptly at 18:00 next Tuesday so that we may discuss details. You will find the Institute on Doppelganger Strasse, in the Eighth District."

Felix tried to disguise his surprise at being given a key to any office, but he began to think that perhaps such things happen in Vienna. "This is a wonderful city," he thought, "a truly magical city." He called on his training as a Knight of the Altar to be reliable and respected by authority, and he believed that he could use his familiarity with Freud's writings (as distant and limited as was that familiarity) to guide his relationship with Professor Wagner.

On the following Tuesday, Felix left Pőtzleinsdorf at four o'clock, knowing that he would need at least two hours for the strassenbahn ride and the probability that he would get lost in the Eighth District. Yet he also knew that Hanneliese's voice would call to him before each of the tram stops, even if she could not guide him to Doppelganger Strasse. He reached Schottentor in twenty minutes, walked past the University and into the Eighth District, and began searching for the Institute. An hour later he found the brass plate announcing the Institut fűr Linguistik und Nominification on the third floor. Although he was an hour early for his meeting with Professosr Wagner, Felix knocked on the Institute's door, heard no response, and waited.

Felix had been taught by his mother that patience was its own reward, and so he was reluctant to use the key which Wagner had given him. "It's best that I not act too aggressively," he thought, "I've read that Austrians prefer leisure and indirection." And so, Felix waited.

An hour later, Professor Wagner had not yet arrived, and Felix began to doubt that Wagner had in fact offered him a job. Yet, he had that key, which perhaps, he thought, he should at least try to fit in the door and see if he had the right Institute and the right door. "Ah," Felix said aloud, "the key turns the lock!" Just then Wagner emerged from across the street, in a sort of slow but frantic rush.

"Ah, young man, you have found my Institute. Forgive my tardiness, meetings, you must know, so many meetings."

"Good day, Professor Wagner. It is good to see you again."

"Of course, young man.... Frank, is it?"

"No, professor, my name is Felix, Felix Kulpa."

"Quite sure? Well then, you must know your own name, mustn't you?"

"Yes, I believe so."

"Well, Felix, I am sorry to tell you that I am late for an important engagement and must hurry off. Just take your time and become familiar with the organization. And please lock the door when you leave."

"But Professor ..."

"No time for conversation today. Must leave. Lock the door."

Felix had not yet entered Wagner's Institut für Linguistik, but now he felt it his duty to see what he might actually be doing and how he might do it. He turned on the light switch and looked to his right, where he saw three small desks, each with a name plate affixed to the front: Mag. Johanna Stubblemeier, Beata Fuchstberger and Gunter Stadtbad. Each desk had a small stack of neatly organized papers, but Felix did not think he should look through the papers. "I am supposed to review the work," he thought, "and these people must be Professor Wagner's assistants, but I don't know which work I should be reviewing." Felix, still standing just inside the doorway, turned to the left where rested a much larger desk, an academic altar befitting the stature of a Viennese professor, as the nameplate announced PROFESSOR DOCTOR BERNHARD WAGNER. The desk was littered with piles of papers, folders, envelopes, note cards, binders, pamphlets, books, magazines, journals—each pile leaning against another pile and all piles threatening to collapse. Felix felt it best to leave quickly and quietly, and so he very gently turned the key and locked the door.

Felix did as Professor Wagner had instructed: every Tuesday, Wednesday, and Thursday he visited the Institute, reviewed the height of each stack of papers on the assistants' desks, and left a note on the smallest pile on Professor Wagner's desk. "All seems to be in order," he wrote each week. Taped to the right side of Professor Wagner's desk, Felix found an envelope with his weekly pay (100 schillings) and Wagner's note with the simple inscription, "Continue," which Felix did for the next three weeks.

As the final roses still lingered in the Volksgarten, Felix continued his dreams of love and desire. One late October morning, as he again took tram #41 from Pötzleinsdorf to Schottentor, and heard the voice of Hanneliese announcing each stop, he felt that Hanneliese was speaking only to him, and he hesitated before stepping off the tram. He had no plans for this dreary Saturday, and so he walked to Mariahilferstrasse and took the U4, the subway line, to Hütteldorf, the western end station, so that he could hear her voice again and again. From Hütteldorf he rode the schnellbahn, the city's rapid trains, to Südbahnhof, the southern end station, and then a bus to the Südtiroler Plaza. He still desired Hanneliese, or at least her voice, and so he caught the underground line, U-1, to Karlsplatz and finally U-2 to Schottentor, where the lines converge. Throughout the morning, Felix had once again been struck by the smoothly efficient schnellbahn and even more by the U-Bahn. Perhaps, Felix thought, it is the transit system itself which runs Vienna and which Hanneliese herself directs.

And then, at Schottentor, Felix heard the voice of the bells, and the answer was revealed to him.

He stood above the underground station, not waiting, for he had nowhere to go that morning, but also not thinking, only joining Hanneliese's voice to Offenbach's barcarolle. He looked to the east, down the Ring, where the tram would emerge from the morning's light rain. Suddenly, strassenbahn D materialized, the driver clanging his bell to alert pedestrians, cars, buses, everyone that they must attend to this presence. Immediately behind D, trams 1 and 2 followed, all the drivers ringing the bells. At that same moment, to Felix's left, 43 came down Universitätstrasse, clanging, relentless–44 was less than a block behind. Beneath Felix, 38 entered the underground circle, and then 41, 37, 40, and 42–a convergence of power, grace, sound, authority. And then Felix knew.

There was no system running Vienna; there was no hidden source of power, no forces of state or religion governing people's lives. There were simply the strassenbahn–ponderously sublime, immune, inscrutable, gliding on rails of power and glory, red and white manifestations of decorum–throughout the city a presence both benevolent and threatening, limited in direction by the rails, but finally omnipotent within their own domain–43 standing room places, 32 seats on each streetcar–eternal, glorious, lovely. And each one guided by the voice of Hanneliese.

Unlike the buses, Felix reasoned, which are bound by the conventions of traffic and driving, unlike the U-Bahn, which are purely abstract means of transport, traveling above or below the life of the city, unlike the schnellbahn, which enter lives too rapidly and disappear too quickly, Felix now believed the strassenbahn themselves to be power and desire incarnate. And the drivers are their agents, he realized, their instruments, their consorts.

Thus, Felix realized the significance of the streetcar drivers: they sit in the position of privilege; they are invulnerable, indulgent, whimsical, powerful but only insofar as they partake of the strassenbahn's energy and desire and as they heed the voice of the serene Hanneliese. And so Felix also realized that, before it was too late, he too must become a driver of the strassenbahn.

To accomplish his purpose, Felix knew that he must uncover the knowledge of the strassenbahn, knowledge, he believed, kept sacred at the Wiener Stadtwerke–Verkehrsbetriebe. For "Wünsche, Anregungen, Beschwerden," Felix learned, he must call 7909/100 and speak with the English-language worker.

He made his first call immediately, from a telephone at the Schottentor U-Bahn station. The answering machine told him:

"This line is not in operation. If you have any wishes or complaints, please call us between 8:00 a.m. and 3:30 p.m. If an emergency has arisen, please attend to the line until an agent has responded."

Thirty minutes later, an agent noticed the blinking red light and reluctantly picked up the phone.

Felix introduced himself, mentioning his admiration for the transit system, and he asked the man from the Wiener Stadtwerke the first of his many questions.

"How many strassenbahn are in operation at the peak times each day, if you could please inform me?"

The man from the Wiener Stadtwerke told Felix that he did not know, and if Felix needed this information, he should write but the answers would be liable for costs.

"And is this information required for an immediate emergency?"

Felix had neither money, an emergency, nor time for an adequate explanation; he only knew that for him this information was required.

After some minutes of friendly argument, the man from the Wiener Stadtwerke told Felix that in the past year on the streets of Vienna there were 592 Strassenbahnen, 326 U-

Bahnen (if one counts each wagon), and 502 buses. Felix reasoned that not all of these cars were in operation–even at peak times–and that some of them would most probably be receiving service. Thus, Felix assumed, 2/3 of the numbers given seemed a fair guess about the number of cars in service during the day. He made the same calculation aloud on the phone, and the man from the Wiener Stadtwerke agreed.

Felix, however, was not yet satisfied.

The man from the Wiener Stadtwerke said nothing. ("How much information does he desire?" thought the man from the Wiener Stadtwerke, "and what might these revelations cost me? Who must approve such action?") And yet ... the agent from the Wiener Stadtwerke felt compelled by the intensity of Felix's voice to reveal even more, and he began to share Felix's thirst for knowledge, although he did not know, as did Felix, that such knowledge would lead to power and love.

"How does one become a strassenbahn driver?"

The agent sighed deeply before answering, for, despite his position as civil servant for life, he detected Felix's passion, a passion which he too had once known.

"First of all," the man from the Wiener Stadtwerke told Felix, "one has to apply for a job at the Gemeinde Wien–Wiener Verkehrsbetriebe, and without Austrian citizenship, connections, and influence, it is very unlikely that anyone could be admitted. After being accepted, the person becoming a driver has to undergo a three-month training and schooling. After these three months, he can drive a strassenbahn on his own. You see," sadly reported the man from the Wiener Stadtwerke, "everyone who gets a job with the Gemeinde Wien must then become a member of the Union of Community Employees."

"Oh, I see," Felix told the sympathetic agent. "Thank you. You have been very helpful. I greatly appreciate your assistance."

Felix knew that he would have to sit and watch, very closely, very intently. He did not have time to wait for an opening in the Drivers' Union, he did not belong to the Union of Community Employees, and he did not have influence to secure a position immediately.

Felix resigned himself to act on his own. And so he spent that afternoon riding the strassenbahn, round and round Vienna, in and out of Vienna, everywhere. He sat near the driver; if possible, he stood directly facing the driver, but most drivers did not allow this intrusion, and so Felix could only imagine how he might slow the carriage and how he might stop it. He rode every hour, all day, making notes on which passengers the drivers would allow in and which they would deny entrance.

Felix was convinced that he now must share his dream with Hanneliese: he would control the tram, allowing no one else to board. Together they would glide through the city. "Love on the Vienna rails," he thought, "Love on the rails."

Before he could seize control, he knew that he must speak with Hanneliese herself, to let her know that he would soon fulfill his wishes and act out his fantasies. And so, again, he called, and again he heard the familiar words spoken by the recording of angelic Hanneliese:

"You have reached World of Male Fantasies. Please give us your name and nationality."

"Felix Kulpa. I am an American citizen."

"What has brought you to Vienna?"

"I hope to attend the State Opera and ..."

"Hello Felix. I've been waiting for your call."

"Hanneliese? Is it really you, in person?"

"Yes. Of course. I'm so glad you called. How can I help you?"

"With my fantasies?"

"Perhaps. If that is what you wish."

"I'm not sure. Well, I suppose I am sure, but I need you to know what we will do."

"I will help you. First tell me what you wish to explore."

"It's the strassenbahn, and you, and your voice, and desire...."

"Felix, you have a complicated fantasy. Tell me again why you came to Vienna."

"My parents, you see, they always listened to the New Year's Day concert, and they gave me *The Royal Family of Opera.* And in college I wrote a paper on Freud. And my grandmother died and left me some money."

"Did they tell you anything about Vienna?"

"No. In the will, my grandmother just said that I should take charge of my life, be aggressive, and not be afraid to seek love."

"And your mother? Did she tell you anything?"

"My mother? She just told me not to forget to water the cactus."

"Felix, what have you learned, and what do you really desire?"

"I don't know if I've learned anything since college. At one time, I believed in Pomponazzi and Bruno, and possibility and practical wisdom, I suppose, but I also believed in conflict, and power, and hanging my enemies. Right now, I only believe in the strassenbahn, and your voice."

"Felix, you've been attending to the wrong voices and exploring the wrong fantasies. Listen to me, now, and listen to your mother."

"What are you saying?"

"Your dream of love on the tram is a silly male fantasy."

"But then what should I do?"

"You cannot replace such a fantasy with wisdom. Perhaps you may only replace this fantasy with joyful folly."

"That's it? That's all you can say?"

"Your time is complete."

Once more the line went dead, and once more Felix went to sleep.

Felix had discovered the source of power and knowledge, and he had listened to the voice of beauty. But his fantasy of love and Hanneliese seemed doomed. He now must decide what he should do to serve love and yet please his parents. Finally, he decided to seize the moment when he himself could become the agent of efficient desire.

The opportunity came that very evening, near midnight on the final run of the #41 from Pötzleinsdorf to Schottentor. Felix had been waiting at the glass shelter in the final glow of the autumn sky. The driver left his position for his final cigarette, and Felix knew that he must act immediately, on that evening, in that tram, or perhaps risk yet another disappointment.

Felix quickly walked past an elderly man who simply nodded at him and seemed to recognize the joyful folly and doom of the evening. "A pity," the man thought as he leaned on his golden cane. "He seems a person without tradition. Such a waste. I should have counseled him."

But Felix had no time that night for counsel, and so he boarded the strassenbahn on the night of his death, and entered the realm of expectation that had for so long awaited him.

Felix moved quickly to the seat, shut the door as the driver turned–startled, the cigarette smoke even on that autumn evening frozen between inhale and exhale–and Felix clanged the bell and headed down Pötzleinsdorferstrasse toward Gersthof. The streets were deserted that Saturday evening, and no one sprinted to catch Felix on his ride of glory. He drew energy from the strassenbahn itself, and together they gained life and speed as they moved like a single body down toward the heart of Vienna–past Erndtgasse and Türkenschanzplatz, faster and faster, the bell clanging the entire way, and Hanneliese's voice announcing the next stop–past Gersthof, Weinhauser Gasse, Aumannplatz–Felix knew he must reach Schottentor, where he would circle and return uphill–he and the tram gained even more speed and passion as they flew past Martinstrasse and

Kutschkergasse, with the Volksoper almost in view and Hanneliese's voice now just repeating, "faster, Felix, faster"–Felix held the arm of the controls yet tighter and he rang the bell in an ecstasy of speed and power, and he very nearly got across the Gürtel.

Before he died, Felix had a vision of the world as it should be. He was far above the city, viewing Vienna as God views it. Felix saw a world without cars and without people–a world of buses and trams, choreographed by the Virgin Mary, moving gracefully through the city while Hanneliese sang the barcarolle– "Belle nuit, o nuit d'amour, souris a nos ivresses; nuit plus douce que le jour, o belle nuit d'amour!" Schnellbahn encircled the city; U-Bahn moved quickly from point to point; buses twisted themselves around tight corners and narrow streets.

But the strassenbahn. Ah! the strassenbahn! They danced waltzes of power and romance wherever they went. Seen from above, they were the life of the city; they were the sublime vessels of love and desire, knowing no one but realizing everything. And Hanneliese smiled on Felix, and God smiled on Vienna and on the strassenbahn and on the passengers and–most of all–on the drivers, for they were fulfilling his purpose.

In this final vision of the world as it should be, Felix had reached Schottentor at a speed beyond belief. He circled below ground and used the Währingerstrasse incline to shoot into space, a glorious constellation in the starried sky. As he rode across the midnight skies above Vienna, he saw his family below cheering him on. Felix shouted out greetings and told them he would soon return home, as he and his tram rode across the Austrian night. Forever. Glorious. Secure.

Chapter 2
Victor
St. Louis, 1981-1982

Christmas Eve, 1981

Word soon reached the Kulpa family of the unfortunate death of Felix. The American Embassy assisted the Kulpas with the repatriation of the remains of their son, whose body was flown to St. Louis for the funeral. "Felix will not be forgotten by those who knew him," said Father Bischoff at the funeral. "I certainly will not forget him." The Kulpa family, including his cousin, Victor Trilling, joined in prayers for the soul of poor Felix. Although Victor was nearly fourteen years younger than Felix, he was often compared to Felix. "Felix always seemed to lead a rather aimless life," Aunt Sandra said. "And this young Victor; well, he's acting just like Felix did at his age." Victor, however, was awakened to a sense of mission just one month after the funeral when he extracted the head of Jesus from beneath the skirt of Virginia Taylor.

Prior to that glorious Christmas Eve, Victor had done little to justify his parents' confidence that he would lead a charmed life. "Oh, my Victor," his mother too often told Mrs. Coldwell who lived across the circle, "is such a gifted young man. He will do wonderful things. Just you wait, Edith, just you wait." Edith Coldwell had little patience for waiting for her own children, and even less for Victor. Mother and Father always believed that Victor had special gifts, although they were not sure what those gifts were. Once Victor had calmed a neighbor's daughter who had fallen into a puddle and gotten mud on her first communion dress. "Don't worry," Victor told the girl. "No one will notice." When Victor was twelve, a classmate broke his wrist after falling from Charlie Hicks's apple tree. Victor volunteered to turn the pages of the boy's History class final exam. The teacher did not think it necessary, but Mother and Father thought the offer once again revealed Victor's special gifts.

And so Mrs. Coldwell tolerated Irene Trilling's praise for the talented young Victor, who had not yet discovered what his mission might be. That is, not until after the midnight mass on that snowy Christmas Eve.

In his only attempt to achieve status at Holy Innocents parish school, Victor had been a knight of the altar since third grade, and he had moved up the ranks through what he thought to be diligent study of his catechism and what others attributed to the lack of ambition on the part of all the other young knights. Thus, when he reached eighth grade, he, like his cousin Felix, became the Supreme Grand Knight, who wore the scarlet robes of the elect for the midnight procession on Christmas Eve. He led the entire corps of knights, followed by the stern pastor, Father Theodore Bischoff, and the girls' choir of Holy Innocents parish. Victor knew from tales of his cousin Felix that his duties were to carry the statue of the infant Jesus from the entrance of the church to his crib in the manger scene in the church sanctuary. Irene Trilling could only smile the benevolent smile of the blessed mothers, while Joseph Trilling constantly cleared his throat to ensure that everyone knew whose son cradled the infant Jesus. "Si-i lent Night," the girls'choir sang, "Ho-o ly Night," as Victor carefully stepped closer and closer to the manger.

All went well until Victor missed the final step, tumbled to the church floor, and heard that dreadful sound he would never forget, the sound of the plaster Jesus breaking into too many parts for the bending angels to heal. "Ohhhhh," he heard from the congregation, and then an even louder "Oh no" from his mother and a terrible curse from his father. Victor found the infant's right arm and then one leg and the headless torso, but the savior's head rolled back down the aisle, past the assembled knights, past the irate Father Bischoff, only coming to a stop beneath the skirt of the enchanting Virginia Taylor, whom Victor secretly but passionately loved.

Victor knew what to do and he did it without thinking, running past the knights, eluding Father Bischoff's grasp, and reaching for the head of Jesus under the skirt of the divine

Miss Virginia. "I have it!" he yelled, expecting to be honored as a hero who had accomplished his sacred mission.

"Give that to me now," said Father Bischoff. "You're no better than that damn cousin of yours. He's burning in hell now, and you'll follow him there as well."

"My damn cousin?" thought Victor, just after Virginia stepped on his grasping hand and just before she struck his head with her dominant right foot.

Victor silently retreated to the changing room of the Knights of the Altar, where he slowly removed his holy day scarlet-trimmed surplice and then even more slowly the scarlet cassock worn only on the holiest of the year's holy days. He had temporary sanctuary from the humiliation he knew he would soon face, but he also knew that he must eventually leave the church and rejoin his family, if they would have him. He waited until just before Father Bischoff gave the final blessing and before the congregation had begun to leave the church on that midnight clear. Only then did Victor rush out the side door to the Trilling car, hoping that the back doors would be unlocked. Those doors, however, were still locked, and so Victor had to endure both the silent glances of mothers and fathers and the repressed laughter of his classmates as they filed past.

Questions Emerge on Christmas Day, 1981

On Christmas morning, Victor's parents carried the disgrace brought on the family by their son with them to the 9:00 Mass. Victor's father would have preferred to stay in bed, but his mother insisted that they would only increase their shame by remaining at home. "Besides," she reasoned, "perhaps no one would notice." No one in the Trilling family, however, believed her.

And so the entire family dressed in their Christmas best and slid into the pew at the back of Holy Innocents church, trying to look as innocent as the sheep surrounding the infant Jesus, whose body had been hastily repaired by the parish janitor. Before the unfortunate fall at midnight, Victor had always looked forward to holy day masses and funerals, when incense could fill the church and create a world apart, a world of grace, not sin, a world of hymns, not curses. As a senior knight of the altar, Victor was often assigned to bear and gently swing the thurifer, releasing the sweet smoke throughout the congregation. Victor believed fully in incense. Father Bishcoff, however, put his faith in fire, not smoke.

Father Bischoff paused before he began his Christmas morning sermon to survey the congregation, finally fixing his glare at the rear of the church. "What a curious and disturbing sign," he said in a most solemn tone, "an infant in a manger. What a terrible sight of utter poverty and abandonment! A child rejected by the world, wrapped tight, ever so tight, as tight as the very skin that bound the brittle bones of that babe, wrapped tight against the winter's cruel, cruel cold and the night of utter and complete sin. What mother wouldn't weep, what father wouldn't cringe, as she lay her sinless babe down on straw in a manger, where earlier animals had been eating...."

While Victor's mother and father listened to that story once again, Victor, by himself in the pew behind his parents, thought of those dogs, those cruel dogs of his youth that chased him twice each day–as he ran past the pen on his way to school and, again, as he ran past on his way home–cruel, cruel dogs that would have torn his skin, ripped his flesh–if only he could run past them and get home, where he could shut them out forever–and when his father came home.... Once, while his father slept, he had washed the car, carefully, he thought, and without any command or suggestion, he was proud of his work, proud that he had so carefully washed the car. "Victor, look at all the streaks," his father shouted. "If you're going to do a job, do it right. Do it right, Victor. If you're going to do a job, do it right."

"... But Mary doesn't weep," insisted Father Bischoff. "No. Mary doesn't weep. She is silent; she adores, she is prostrate with joy! The value of her child, God's child, does not depend on what he does but on who he is–the Son of God. And he lies in a manger, an animal's feeding trough stinking of animal breath and animal sweat, because he will become a meal for us. He will become the Food of Life, the Eucharist, the Bread of Eternal Salvation and Forgiveness for our terrible, terrible sins!"

Victor was yet again reminded of his failings and his damnation, and he sunk into the pew, hoping no one would turn to him.

Father Bischoff only looked directly at Victor's mother, or so she thought, and he seemed to speak only to her. "The Christmas story is beautiful with a terrible beauty, a mysterious beauty, the beautiful terror of the drama of redemption. A redemption we do not merit, a redemption entirely undeserved, a terribly merciful redemption! The sight of a newborn baby, an innocent child, shivering on a bed of cold hay stinking of animal sweat–this sight is a stark and striking reminder of our Sin, the Sin of the world where children are abandoned, and abused, and broken, yes they are broken, where our God is ignored. Yes. The God of Terror and Beauty is casually ignored, but, my children, at what a terrible, terrible price. At what a dreadful price!"

Victor knew that he had begun to pay the price, but Father Bischoff had more to say to him.

"The wrath of our God burns against the sinners, their damnation does not slumber; the pit is prepared, the fire is made ready; the furnace is now hot, ready to receive them; the flames do rage and glow. The glittering sword is whet, and held over them, and the pit has opened its mouth under them.... That world of misery, that lake of burning brimstone is extended abroad under you, Victor." Or so Victor thought he heard, for he knew that Father Bischoff was speaking only to him. "There is the dreadful pit of the glowing flames of the wrath of God; there is hell's wide gaping mouth open; and you have nothing to stand upon, nor anything to take hold of; there is nothing between you and hell but the air; it is only the power and mere pleasure of God that holds you up."

"Yes," thought Victor, "and I must pay that price. Oh, I just wish he would stop."

"Let us pray for a change in our families," Father Bischoff concluded, "in our church, in our country, and in our world. Please do not leave the Infant in the cold, do not leave the infant shattered on the manger floor, like the people of Bethlehem who had no room for him in their busy and materialistic lives. Let us come back every week to be Silent like the glorious Virgin, to Adore like the perceptive shepherds, to Rejoice like the thoughtful Lambs, and to Feed on Jesus, as the eager Cows would have done, to taste the heavenly flavor of this Babe of Bethlehem and the true Son of God."

"Let us pray. Oh my God, I am heartily sorry for having offended Thee, and I detest all my sins, not only because I dread the loss of heaven and the pains of hell, but most of all because they offend Thee, my God, Who are so good and deserving of all my love."

"I am so heartily sorry, very heartily," thought Victor, a bit more sincerely than anyone else on that Christmas morning, when the Infant lay pieced together by the parish janitor.

January, 1982–Felix Kulpa the Damned Cousin

A week later, as always, the Trilling family gathered on New Year's Day to listen to the Vienna Philharmonic concert, just as their cousins the Kulpas did, and so recover from the previous night, and eat herring for good luck. Victor and his parents had always been joined by Uncle Felix and Aunt Gertie Kulpa, who were grieving for the death of their son and so did not join them, and Great Aunt Mae Terwillinger, who each year revealed family secrets. After the concert ended and after the herring ran out, Aunt Mae would call everyone to attention while she reviewed the past year and recalled the years before. Until Victor had shattered baby Jesus, he had always been ready for Aunt Mae to end her talk and slowly drift into sleep. This year, however, Victor needed to find out more about his cousin, the one whom Father Bischoff had damned to hell.

To Victor, Aunt Mae had always been old, but not aged. For years she seemed, at least to Victor, to remain the same grey-haired, slightly stooped great aunt, a relationship which Victor knew of but did not quite understand. She always dressed in black, although for holidays like New Year's she added a small red carnation pinned to her dress. She also always seemed on the verge of a smile, as if she knew something which others might not find humorous but which she thoroughly enjoyed.

On the New Year's Day after the incident at midnight mass, after everyone had their good-luck herring, after the dishes were cleared off the table, and after everyone had settled down in the family living room, Victor's father asked what he always asked at this time: "Well, Aunt Mae, what news of the family in the past year?"

Aunt Mae always looked surprised at the question, but she always was ready with an answer. "Not a great deal," she always said, "just the usual."

"Nothing remarkable this year?" Victor's father asked.

"Well, you probably all know about my cousin's rheumatism and John's recovery."

"Yes, Aunt Mae," Victor's mother said, "John's recovery was so wonderful. I hope he continues."

"He might," said Aunt Mae, "he might, but we mustn't try to hurry him along."

"And poor Felix and Gertie," Mother added. "They must wonder what happened to Felix. Why did he have to die?"

"Oh the Kulpas," said Aunt Mae, "don't get me started on them."

"Why Mae," Father said, "it was a tragedy. Felix's grandmother died; she wasn't that old. And then poor Felix. That family suffered too much this last year."

"Well, Grandmother just drove too fast, and Felix ... Felix was a troubled young man, a talented but very troubled young man. He went off and left for Europe after his grandmother died, and then ... well then he just ... he just had that accident. I hope he found happiness somewhere, but he's never to be heard from again. You know he wrote to me from Austria— postcards and a few letters, but I never could figure out what he was doing. A troubled young man."

Victor's father knew that was the signal for the evening to end, for everyone to say good night and wish all a Happy New Year. He turned off all the lights in the living room, except for the one on the table next to Aunt Mae, who had slowly drifted off to sleep.

"Come on Victor, time for bed."

"I will. Just let me stay up for a few more minutes."

"All right. Just don't disturb Aunt Mae."

Victor waited quietly in his chair, until everyone else had left the room, then tip-toed over to Aunt Mae and whispered to her. "Aunt Mae, are you awake?"

"Of course I am, Victor, how else could I be talking?"

"I'm sorry if I woke you. I just wanted to hear some more about Cousin Felix."

"Ah, poor Felix. What else would you like to know?"

"Did he ever get in trouble with Father Bischoff?"

"Trouble? Not exactly, as I recall. There was that one Christmas Eve, the midnight Mass, when he led the procession just as you did this year."

"Did he drop Infant Jesus?"

Aunt Mae's smile emerged, not as laughter at Victor and his unfortunate fall from grace, but more at the seeming irony of the boys' unfortunate fates.

"No. He did not drop Infant Jesus. He just put the statue in upside down in the manger."

"You mean Jesus was face down?"

"Yes, Victor, and Jesus remained face down throughout the mass."

"What did Father Bischoff do?"

"There wasn't much he could do during mass. He simply kept on with the service, although every so often he would look at the manger, and then at Victor, who tried to avoid Father Bischoff's gaze."

"Did Felix get in much trouble?"

"I don't believe he did. From what Francis told me, Father Bischoff asked Felix to see him in the rectory about two days after Christmas, but he never did. After that Felix said nothing at all about the incident, and neither did Father Bischoff, who seemed to have forgiven Felix and have forgotten about the entire episode."

"But at the midnight mass, Father Bischoff said that Felix was damned. He seemed very angry at me and at Felix."

"Father Bischoff is a good man," said Aunt Mae, "but at times he does seem to lose control. But he forgives and forgets. Now, get to bed."

"Yes. Thank you, Aunt Mae. Good night ... and Happy New Year."

"Yes. Happy New Year, Felix."

January, 1982–Father Bischoff and his Unexpected Invitation

Three days after the family gathering, Victor received a note from Dorothy Taylor, Virginia's mother, who worked as a receptionist at Father Bischoff's rectory.

Victor,

Father Bischoff requests that you meet with him at
the parish rectory on the morning of next Saturday,
to discuss matters of great importance. Please call
me at the rectory so that I may let Father Bischoff
know that you will come.

Mrs. Taylor

Victor knew immediately what those matters of such importance were: the shattering of the holy statue of the infant
Jesus. Of course, he called Mrs. Taylor that same day and
learned that Father Bischoff would be expecting him at 10:00
on Saturday. He did not tell his parents about the meeting:
they need not be reminded of the incident.

Victor slept little that Friday night, and he awoke at 6:00
on Saturday morning, four hours before he would meet Father
Bischoff. As was their custom, Irene and Joseph Trilling did
not come down for breakfast until 8:00. When they opened the
kitchen door, they found that Victor had put away the dishes
from Friday's dinner, set the table for breakfast, and had hot
water ready for their morning tea.

"Why Victor, you've done so much already this morning.
How long have you been up?"

"Not long, Mother. I just wanted to have everything ready
for you and Father."

"Thank you, Victor, This is very considerate."

His father opened the morning newspaper while his mother
sipped her chamomile tea. Victor stood nearby, waiting as
long as possible before he left for the rectory.

"Victor, why don't you sit down?"

"Oh, I've already had my cereal, and it's almost time for
me to leave."

"So early? Where are you going?"

"There's a basketball game at school. I don't know who's going to be there, but it should be a big crowd."

"On Saturday morning? Oh well, go and have fun. Just be back in time for your chores."

"I will."

January, 1982–A Sanctuary for Sinners

Victor knew that Father Bischoff would give him a stern lecture on the proper handling of holy objects, a lecture Victor also knew that he deserved but which he dreaded. All the more reason, so Victor reasoned, to leave home an hour before the meeting so that he could walk away his anxiety. The rectory was only a quarter of a mile from the Trilling home, and so after he crossed Laclede Station Road, he needed to walk past the ranch houses on Verbena Drive, the opposite direction from the rectory, and then turn at Highland Avenue, cross the railroad tracks, and then see if any stores were yet open on Merchandise Road. None were yet open. "Good," thought Victor, "no one will see me and ask why I'm walking about on Saturday morning." He then retraced his steps and headed toward the rectory on Verbena Drive, only pausing to see if Virginia Taylor might still be in her bedroom, but the curtains were closed.

Despite his efforts to rid himself of guilt and anxiety, Victor still hesitated before he knocked on the rectory door, expecting Mrs. Taylor to answer. But today Father Bischoff answered the door and whispered to Victor to take off his shoes and socks and leave them outside by the door. "No need to track in dirt, my son, no need at all."

"Is Mrs. Taylor ill today?" asked Victor.

"No. I have given her the day off. She deserves at least one weekend free from tending to my needs. But I did request that she bake some of her special chocolate chip cookies for you. Come, let's have a treat in the kitchen."

Victor knew that his stomach would not tolerate cookies of any kind this morning, but he took one and sat in the kitchen chair reserved for him. "Victor, you're only nibbling at the cookie. What's wrong today?"

"Oh nothing, Father Bischoff," lied Victor, who knew that soon Father Bischoff would begin his lecture and would then most likely give Victor a severe penance. "I'm just not hungry this morning."

"As you wish. Perhaps then we should address the reason why I asked you to come."

"I'm sorry, Father, for what I did on Christmas Eve."

"Yes, my son, that was a very serious sin. But there are ways for you to make up for that transgression."

"Anything," thought Victor, *"just so that I can do my penance and then leave."*

"Victor, you must come with me to a holy place here, one in which penance is available to all sinners."

Father Bischoff pointed to a hallway at the back of the reception room, a dark hallway without windows. "We must visit the shrine, my son," said Bischoff, "the shrine at the end of the hall. Please walk ahead of me."

Victor had never seen the hallway before, but he felt that it was his obligation to follow Father Bischoff's directions, and so he slowly walked down the hallway to a doorway, which seemed to be locked.

"Victor, my son, you may open the door. It is not locked for now."

As Victor turned the handle and slowly pushed open the door, he saw a small figure standing on a pedestal at the back of the room, with candles on either side and a spotlight illuminating the figure's head, a sort of halo projecting streams of light from behind the figure's head. The figure, a porcelain young child, was dressed in the garments of a bishop, a scarlet tunic trimmed in gold, with a small cross hanging as a pendant from the Infant's neck. The Infant held a small globe in his left hand; he held up two fingers of his right hand, either as a blessing or a warning. The Infant's face was surrounded by golden curls, perhaps those of a young girl or a young boy, but the face showed no emotion, as if frozen in blessed sanctity beyond the understanding of mankind.

"What you see, my son, is the most holy Infant of Prague, who looks over children and sinners."

"We are both sinners, my son," Father Bischoff whispered," both of us, and we must both pray for forgiveness." Father Bischoff motioned for Victor to kneel in front of the shrine to the Infant of Prague and remove his shirt. Father Bischoff then began the prayers to ask for forgiveness.

"O Jesus, who has said, 'Ask and you shall receive, seek and you shall find, knock and it shall be opened,' through the intercession of Mary, Your Most Holy Mother, we knock, we seek, we ask that our prayers be granted. O Jesus," Father Bischoff continued, "who has said, 'All that you ask of the Father in My Name, He will grant you,' through the intercession of Mary Your Most Holy Mother, we humbly and urgently ask your Father in your name that our prayers will be granted."

Father Bischoff stood next to Victor and again told him to pray that his sin be forgiven.

"O Jesus," Father Bischoff's voice seem to grow more intense, "Who has said, 'Heaven and earth shall pass away but My word shall not pass away,' through the intercession of Mary Your Most Holy Mother, we feel confident that our prayers will be granted."

Father Bischoff took off his shirt and stood immediately behind the kneeling Victor.

"Divine Infant Jesus," his voice grew both softer and more threatening, "we know You love us and would never leave us, and I will never leave you, my son; we thank You for Your close Presence in our lives. Miraculous Infant, we believe in Your promise of peace, blessings, and freedom from want. We place every need and care in Your hands." Father Bischoff placed his hands on Victor's naked back and whispered, yet more softly and yet more intently, "Lord Jesus, may we always trust in Your generous mercy and love. We want to honor and praise You, now and forever. Amen. You will be forgiven, my son, but first you must submit to your punishment."

"Father Bischoff, please don't touch me, don't hurt me."

"I would never hurt you, my son. You only must make amends for your sin."

"Father Bischoff, you are making me feel uncomfortable. I want to leave."

"Stay, I warn you, or your sin will not be forgiven."

Victor stood up, frightened but not willing to remain. He grabbed his shirt and ran down the hallway toward the rectory door.

"Damn you, Trilling, come back here." Bishoff now shouted and began to sob. "Just like your damned cousin. Come back here now!"

Victor quickly picked up his shoes and ran down the back stairs.

"Don't you tell anyone, Victor Trilling, please, Victor please." Father Bischoff stood in the doorway to the shrine, as he pleaded and cursed. "Tell no one, or you'll spend eternity in hell. Please, Victor. Please." The Infant of Prague looked on, neither approving nor judging, as if the weight of the clerical robes on the infant's small body enforced a saintly repose, exterior to time—the enigma of forgiveness and salvation.

January, 1982–Days of Forgetful Regret and Ambiguity

Father Bischoff waited two days before he visited the Trilling home. He carried with him Victor's socks: "I found these on the school playground," he told Mrs. Trilling, "and one of the boys thought they might belong to Victor."

"Father Bischoff, we are so pleased to see you and so honored that you have taken the time to visit," Mrs. Trilling told the priest. "I was afraid that you might still be upset by Victor's clumsiness on Christmas Eve."

"Of course not, Mrs. Trilling. We all make mistakes."

"Mr. Trilling isn't at home right now, and I'm sure he will miss seeing you.

"Mr. Trilling is a good man," whispered Father Bischoff, "but I have come to see Victor."

"Let me get Victor," she said. "He will be so happy to see you."

Mrs. Trilling went to Victor's bedroom, where he had heard the knock on the door and Father Bischoff's voice. "Victor, dear, Father Bischoff has come to see you, and he's brought with him those socks you said you left behind at the playground."

"I'm not feeling good, mother. I don't think I should come down."

"You could at least say hello to Father and thank him."

"No. I'm really feeling sick."

"Well alright, I'll let Father Bischoff know. I'm sure he'll be disappointed; he's such a thoughtful person—strong yet considerate, don't you think?"

"Yes mother."

Mrs. Trilling explained to Father Bischoff that Victor was a bit ill this morning, and so he didn't want to expose Father Bischoff to any germs. "That's very good of him," said the priest to Victor's mother. "Yes, very good of him. Please give him the socks and tell him that I am praying for him and his health."

"Thank you, Father. Thank you for coming and for your prayers."

"Goodbye, Mrs. Trilling."

January 1982–Regret and Sorrow

Even before school began again after the holiday break, Victor had entered the age of uncertainty: he did not know if he should tell his parents about Father Bischoff, he did not know if he could remain a Knight of the Altar, he did not know if he could ever go to mass at Holy Innocents church, and he did not know if he would spend eternity in hell. He only knew that it would be difficult to return to school.

"I'm not feeling well, mother," Victor complained on the morning of January 4th. "I don't think I should go to school today. I might infect someone else."

"Well Victor, let me take your temperature." Irene Trilling firmly believed in the Catholic school system and the accuracy of thermometers.

"No fever, Victor. Perhaps you just slept funny."

"No, mother. I really don't think I should go to school today."

As he passed Victor's bedroom on his way to breakfast, Victor's father heard the boy's complaint, a complaint for which he had no sympathy.

"Victor, you can't miss the first day back after the break. Get dressed and come down for breakfast."

Victor knew then that his case was hopeless, and so he slowly dressed and joined his parents in the kitchen. "But I don't want any breakfast, mother. Could I just have some tea and toast?"

"That's not enough," his mother said. "But you can't force food down a boy's throat, can you?"

Victor silently finished his toast and tea, slowly put on his shoes, and silently left the house for the walk to school. During religion class, he sat quietly in the last row while Sister Mary Rosetta reviewed the question for the coming test on the catechism.

"Virginia, what is the tenth station of the Cross?"

"Jesus is stripped of his clothes, Sister Rosetta.

"Excellent, Virginia. Now, Edward, what are the five Glorious Mysteries?"

"The Resurrection, the Ascension, the Descent of the Holy

Spirit, the Assumption of the Blessed Virgin Mary, and ... and
... "

"Yes, Edward, what is the fifth Glorious Mystery?"

"I remember, Sister Rosetta," interrupted Virginia Taylor.
"I know the answer."

"Virginia, please give Edward time to answer. Edward, do
you know the fifth Glorious Mystery?"

"The Crowning of the Blessed Virgin Mary!" Edward
shouted. "The Crowning of Mary!"

"Correct, Edward, but you do not need to shout. The
Church is built on grace and mercy, not on enthusiasm."

"Yes, Sister Rosetta. I'm sorry."

"Now, Victor, what are the Seven Deadly Sins?"

To become the Supreme Grand Knight, Victor had months
earlier memorized all the answers to the test, but today he said
nothing.

"Come now, Victor, I know that you know the answer.
What are the Seven Deadly Sins?"

"I don't know, Sister Rosetta. I'm sorry. I just can't remember."

"Anyone else?"

Before anyone else could raise their hand, Virginia shouted
out, "I know, Sister Rosetta, I know."

"Alright Virginia, tell everyone what the Seven Deadly Sins
are."

"Pride, Anger, Lust, Envy, Gluttony, Avarice, and Sloth,"
said Virginia. "Those are the Seven Deadly Sins."

Victor no longer wanted to hold Virginia's hand. He
silently sat in the back row, not even hoping that anyone
would ignore him.

When he returned home that afternoon, Victor's mother
asked him how his day went. "Did you tell everyone what
you did over the holidays?" his mother asked. "Did you tell
them about our New Year's Day party?"

Victor shook his head, put his school bag on the hook to the kitchen door, and retreated to his room. He did join his parents for dinner, but as soon as he had dried the dishes and taken out the garbage, he retreated to his bedroom and hid beneath the covers. Sleep came, reluctantly, and dreams followed. He looked on as the Infant of Prague and the baby Jesus merged into one image, an infant's head stitched together on a bishop's body. Victor seemed to be pushed closer and closer to the infants until he saw scars below the infant's neck. "See what you've done," a voice called out. "See what you've done." Victor woke up, turned on the lamp next to his bed, and waited for the sun to rise.

February, 1982—Disappointment

A week later, Victor received a note from Virginia Taylor, asking if they could meet after school. "I have something important to tell you," the note read. Victor was waiting on the corner across from Holy Innocents school when Virginia emerged from the front door of the school.

"Hi Victor. What's new?" Virginia and Victor had been together in school all day, and so Victor had no idea what could be new.

"Not much."

"What are you doing this weekend?"

"Not much."

"I'm having a party."

"I know. I heard about it."

"Well, that's why I wanted to see you. I have an apology to make."

Victor thought that perhaps Virginia might finally apologize for kicking him at midnight mass. Or maybe she knew about Father Bischoff; maybe her mother said something. But Virginia shouldn't apologize for that. And besides, he thought, I don't want her to know, and I don't need her apology.

"It's about my party. My party this week."
"Well. What about your party?"
"I can't invite you Victor. Mother said I can't invite you."
"Why not?"
"Mother said we won't have room for everyone. I told her that you wouldn't break anything, but she just said we don't have enough room."

Victor would not have gone to Virginia's party, but he did want to be invited. He was angry and sad, disappointed but glad that he did not have to refuse an invitation. He tried to control the tears, but instead he simply said. "That's ok. I couldn't come anyway."

"I'm sorry Victor. I'm really sorry."
"That's ok. It's really ok."
"Thanks Victor. But we'll still be friends, won't we?"
"Sure."
"See you in school tomorrow."
"Yes. I guess so. See you tomorrow."

Chapter 3
Nobody
St. Louis, 1982-1983

Summer, 1982—Nobody Emerges

The Preston family lived on the same circular street as Victor and his parents. Their only child was named Grace, and her best friend was called Nobody. Grace Preston was not yet five years old, and she lived in one of the ten neat suburban houses on Sherwood Circle, just beyond the city limits of St. Louis. Until she went to Holy Innocents kindergarten, Sherwood Circle was Grace's entire world. Although she seldom spoke unless someone spoke first, she knew everyone in the neighborhood, and everyone knew her. "That Preston girl," Mrs. Taylor called her, "she's a strange one, isn't she?" Neither Mae Terwillinger nor Irene Trilling thought her strange, and they looked forward to seeing Grace play by herself in the small park in the center of Sherwood Circle. "She always seems to be creating her own little world," Mae told Alice Preston, "a world that we shouldn't try to invade." James, her father, taught elementary school in the city; Alice, her mother, kept a clean house, baked excellent apple pies (although she burnt the crust of even the best pie), and watched over Grace, who had a habit of losing the dimes her grandmother gave her and forgetting where she had placed her eyeglasses. Alice, however, was a steady and gentle mother to her only child, and James believed in Alice.

Alice always told Grace on which side of the plate the fork should go, what time was best for her to go to sleep, and how she should treat her friends (with kindness and respect, if they also placed the fork in its proper place). Alice believed in telling the truth, and Grace believed in her mother. "Limits now, and happiness later," her mother told Grace, and so Grace accepted the kindly discipline of the Preston household.

Nobody, however, had no such limitations: Grace could call on Nobody at any time, any place, and Nobody would always appear. Nobody had no other friends, but, with Grace, Nobody did not need any other friends. Nobody was particularly fond of evening talks with Grace, beneath the covers of Grace's bed. Nobody was faithful, sincere, and honest.

It wasn't clear to either James or Alice when Nobody joined the family. They only knew that one evening in mid-July Grace told them that Nobody would join them for dinner.

"Thank you, Grace," Alice said, "but then nobody was invited today."

"No, Mother, that's not what I mean. Nobody is my new best friend, and she would like to sit next to me."

"Nobody?" her father asked. "What an unusual name. How did you meet Nobody?"

"I didn't meet her, father. Nobody just ... just came to me, in a dream. And she wants to stay."

"Well then," said Alice, "we should probably add a chair at the table tonight. Will Nobody like anything to eat or drink?"

"Don't be silly, Mother. Nobody doesn't eat or drink unless it's just the two of us. She would just like to sit here next to me."

"Here's a chair, Grace," said her father. "I hope it's the right size."

"It looks good, Father. Thank you."

For the rest of that summer, Nobody always had a place at the Preston dinner table. On most days, Grace and her other friends played Forbidden Island in the Preston backyard, creating a magical tent under the pin oak tree with blankets and towels from the Preston laundry. Nobody looked on, but never joined the girls, who had not yet been introduced to Grace's best friend. When Janet and Kathleen went home for dinner, Grace asked Nobody to join her in the tent, where she served tea and biscuits which her mother had baked that morning.

"Would you like to dance, Miss Nobody?"

"Of course, Miss Grace, if it is a waltz."

"Why, you know I only do the waltz. I've heard it's the most romantic dance."

"After you, Miss Grace."

Together Grace and Nobody waltzed through the woods of Forbidden Island, as the birds hummed the Blue Danube and the flowers applauded.

"Grace, dear, it's time to come in for dinner."

"Yes Mother, just one minute."

"Miss Nobody, I know you understand. We must go inside."

"Of course, Miss Grace. I do understand. Thank you for a lovely afternoon."

"Grace, it's time for dinner."

"Yes Mother. I was just telling Nobody that we must go inside."

Grace slowly left Forbidden Island, with Nobody at her side. Grace washed her hands, instructed Nobody to do the same, and together they sat down at the dinner table.

"Well, Grace, I hope you had a good time with Sarah and Kathleen."

"And Nobody, Father."

"Oh ... Nobody was there as well?"

"After Janet and Kathleen left, Nobody and I danced—a waltz, just like you and Mother have done."

"Excellent, Grace," said her mother. "A waltz is so romantic. We always hoped to waltz in Vienna, but we haven't had the chance, have we?"

"No, we haven't ... but soon, perhaps."

"Will Nobody and I go with you, Father?"

"I hope so, Grace. Yes. I hope so,"

September, 1982—Kindergarten Questions

At the end of each day's classes, Nobody met Grace across the street from Holy Innocents'parish school. Together they slowly walked home, while Grace told her what had happened and what had not during the day. On Tuesdays in September when the days were still warm and the honey bees still friendly, Grace and Nobody stopped at the abandoned house of Old Man Hicks. No one lived there, not since Old Man Hicks had died on his front porch, leaving no wife, no sons or daughters, and no friends—just the smell of cheap cigars which seemed to be his one gift to the neighborhood. Grace and Nobody never tried the doors or windows, and they always walked carefully through the knee-high grass to reach an apple tree where they sat on Grace's school books and discussed their plans.

Grace had ideas for their future together, and Nobody would often, but not always, agree.

"We should talk to Mother and Father about Halloween costumes."

"Of course. Halloween is my favorite holiday."

"This year, I want to be a Persian queen who rides over the city on her magic rug. And you should be a ghost, a very friendly ghost."

"I don't think that's a good idea, Grace. No one would believe that I'm a ghost."

"Well then, what do you want to be?"

"I would like to be a tiger, a Bengal tiger, with great wide orange and black stripes and huge teeth."

"That might be difficult for Mother to make. Why don't you just be a ghost?"

"I don't want to be a ghost."

"Well, let's not talk about that anymore. We still have weeks before Halloween ... but Oh! Who's that?"

"Hello Grace. Just what are you doing back here today?"

"Oh, hello Sheriff Swifter. I didn't hear you coming."

Claude Swifter, a large man in his early fifties with a smile for anyone he knew and anyone he arrested, had been county sheriff far longer than Grace had been alive and certainly longer than Nobody had joined her.

"You should be careful about hanging out here, Miss Grace. It's not a good place to set up camp."

"Well, Sheriff, Nobody and I were just stopping here on our way home from school."

"Nobody?"

"She's my best friend."

"Where is Nobody just now?"

"Well, you can't really see her. I'm the only one who can see her."

"Oh ... I see. You just make sure Nobody knows that you could get in trouble at the Hicks house, and if you do, I might have to send you both to jail."

"Really? Would you send us to jail? Where?"

"Well then," said the sheriff with a smile, "to Nowhere, I suppose."

"You're kidding us, aren't you Sheriff Swifter? You wouldn't send us to jail."

"No, I wouldn't Grace. You and your friend should just be careful. Go on home now, and say hello to your parents."

"I will. Goodbye Sheriff."

"Goodbye Grace ... and goodbye Nobody."

Grace and Nobody slowly walked home, but they didn't tell their mother about Old Man Hicks' apple tree or about Sheriff Swifter. Some things just shouldn't be shared.

On their walk home a week later, Grace heard the church bells ringing in a slow pattern she had never heard before. "I wonder why the bells sound so sad today. Don't you wonder, Nobody?"

"It is odd, Grace. I don't know why the bells ring so slowly. Look: there's Mrs. Trilling. Maybe she knows."

Irene Trilling lived three houses from Grace's house, and she always waved hello when Grace and Nobody walked past. She had a son, Victor, who was nine years older than Grace and last year was the Supreme Grand Knight of the altar. Grace thought Victor would make a fine prince on the Forbidden Island, but she never told anyone, except Nobody, of course.

"Hello, Mrs. Trilling."

"Hello Grace. It's good to see you. Is school finished for the day?"

"Yes. We're on our way home. Is Victor home yet?"

"No Grace. He isn't."

"We didn't see him at school this week. Of after school either. Is he sick?"

"Well no, Grace, he isn't."

"Is he somewhere else this week?"

"Yes, Grace. He is ... he is going to another school. A better school for him. Not far away."

"That's too bad. I miss Victor."

"Yes, Grace. I miss him too. But this school ... this is better for him."

"That's good. But he'll be back some time, won't he?"

"Yes, Grace. Victor will be back."

"That's good."

"Yes ... it's good."

"We have to get home now. Mother is waiting for us. Goodbye Mrs. Trilling."

"Goodbye Grace. Be careful."

"Oh, we will. We're always careful."

Grace and Nobody took four steps, when Grace turned around and called to Irene Trilling. "Oh Mrs. Trilling, can I ask you a question?"

"Of course, Grace. What would you like to know?"

"Why were the church bells ringing so slowly today?"

"Well, Grace, you see, there was a Requiem Mass this afternoon, and when the mass is over, they ring the bells."

"What's a rakem mass?"

"A Requiem Mass is for ... someone who has passed away, someone who has died, someone who won't come back."

"Victor will come back, won't he?"

"Yes, Grace. Victor will come back."

"And there won't be a rekem for him, will there?"

"No. Not now."

Grace and Nobody turned to walk home, just as a procession of three cars passed down the street. Grace saw a white car with its lights on and only the driver inside, a large black car with its lights on, and a small blue car, also with its lights on. Grace waved to the two people in the blue car, but no one waved back.

"Is that a parade, Mrs. Trilling?" Grace called out.

"It's called a funeral procession, Grace. The person who's gone is in that big black car, and all that person's friends are going with him to say goodbye."

"All the friends?"

Irene Trilling watched the procession until it turned at the next corner, heading for Resurrection Cemetery. "As many as could come, Grace."

"That's sad, Mrs. Trilling."

"Yes, Grace. It is sad. But not for you, Grace. Hurry home and tell your mother hello for me."

"I will, Mrs. Trilling. Goodbye."

"Goodbye Grace."

Grace and Nobody talked about requiems, parades, and Victor as they finished their walk. Just before Grace opened the kitchen door to their house, Grace looked closely at Nobody: "Well now, Miss Nobody, isn't that something?"

"Yes indeed, Miss Grace. We've learned something special today."

"Nobody."

"Yes."

"Will you come to my rakem?"

"Of course I will, dear Grace. And somebody else will come as well."

"That's good. Let's go have some cookies."

October, 1982–Disguises

As Grace spent more and more days at school, she had less and less time to play with Nobody. Most days, in fact, Grace spent more time with Janet and Kathleen and a new friend, Sophie, who had just moved to the neighborhood. The four girls talked about school, the boys who misbehaved, and Halloween costumes. When Grace went to her bedroom each night, however, she always had time to talk with Nobody about the three other girls and what they had done each day.

"Tomorrow, dear Nobody, is school colors day and we're all supposed to wear green and white. What will I wear, you should ask. Well, I don't really like green or blue, but I do have green socks and white socks. Maybe that will be enough."

"I'm not sure that's enough, Grace. Don't you have a green and white sweater?"

"I do, but I don't like it. People always stare at me when I wear it. I don't want people to stare at me. It makes me feel bad."

"Just wear a jacket over the sweater and don't take it off until you're in school."

"Well, that might work. I'll ask Mother. Thank you, Nobody ... and good night."

"Good night, Miss Grace."

The next morning, Grace put on one green sock and one white sock and found the sweater at the back of the lowest drawer in her clothes cabinet. At breakfast she asked her mother if the sweater was ugly.

"No, dear, that sweater isn't ugly. Your grandmother gave it to you last Christmas. You liked it then."

"I know I did. But when I wore it outside, people stared at me."

"They stared at you? Are you sure?"

"Yes. People stared at me at the store. One man looked right at me in the cereal aisle."

"Grace, he probably was looking for his favorite cereal, not at you. The sweater is perfect for green and white day, and you should wear it."

"Well, if you don't think it's ugly. Father, what do you think?"

Grace's father was just finishing his second cup of coffee before he left for his school. He put down his cup and looked carefully at the sweater.

"Actually, Grace, I'm not too fond of green or white, but your grandmother did give it to you and it's still almost brand new. Why don't you just cover it up on your walk to school and only let anybody else see it inside the school? What does Nobody think?"

"Father, Nobody isn't awake yet, and besides, she doesn't care about green and white day."

Grace sat without saying anything while she considered what to do. She didn't like the sweater, but it was green and white day, and Janet, Kathleen, and Regina would certainly wear those colors.

"Yes, Mother and Father. That's what I was thinking. Yes, I'll just wear my jacket over the sweater and only show it at school!"

"Good decision, Grace," said Father, "Good choice."

And so Grace wore her jacket buttoned tightly on the walk to school. When Regina asked why Grace hadn't taken off the jacket inside school, Grace just told her that she had forgotten. "Don't you have any green and white?" asked Regina. "Well of course I do," Grace told her. "Here look at the sweater, my grandmother gave it to me."

"It's very pretty, Grace," said Regina, "and it's perfect for school color day."

Grace wore the sweater all day, proud of her colors. On the way home, she fastened only the bottom three buttons of the jacket.

October, 1982–Costumes

Grace had not forgotten about her Halloween costume: as Halloween grew closer, each morning, and many afternoons, she asked her mother how she would make the queen's costume and, just as important, the magical rug. Most days Grace did not talk with Nobody about the ghost costume, but at night, just before going to sleep, she reminded Nobody about the ghost costume. "Mother won't have time to make a second costume," she argued, "and besides no one can see you; you're almost a ghost now." Nobody finally agreed.

While Alice Preston worked on the queen's robes, Grace cut up old t-shirts into ragged strips, coiled each strip as tightly as she could, and tried to weave them together. Grace knew they didn't look much like a magic carpet, and so she asked Mother to do her best to sew them together. Alice had not heard Grace talk about Nobody for more than a week, but she knew that Grace had talked about a ghost costume.

"Grace, dear, will Nobody need an old sheet for her costume?"

"No, Mother. Don't be silly."

Alice finished the queen's robes and crown two days before Halloween, and she fashioned the t-shirt strips into what might have looked like a discarded floor mat, but Grace felt it looked exactly like the magic carpet she needed.

Alice and James did not want Grace to go out by herself, but Grace insisted that Nobody would be with her—she insisted so often that her parents reluctantly agreed that she could go out without them accompanying her (although they would walk a dozen feet or so behind, across the street from her). Grace could only go to houses on their street and had to finish an hour before dark.

Grace put on her royal robes and crown and carried her candy bag in one hand and the magic carpet in the other. She told Nobody to be quiet and stay close to her. "Just watch what I do," she whispered to Nobody as they left their house, "and don't scare anybody."

Grace first went to Mrs. Trilling's house, knocked on the door, and said in a queenly voice, "Trick or Treat, Mrs. Trilling!"

"Why Grace you look so wonderful. You must be a queen."

"I am, Mrs. Trilling, and this is the magic carpet I ride on."

"That's quite a carpet, Grace. Did you make it?"

"I helped Mother, but I haven't tried to fly."

"Well, that will come. But right now, here's your treat."

"Thank you, Mrs. Trilling. Could Nobody have some?"

"Nobody?"

"Nobody's my invisible friend. She's a ghost for Halloween."

"A ghost—what a wonderful costume for an invisible friend. Here, have some candy for Nobody."

"Thank you, Mrs. Trilling."

"You're very welcome, Grace."

"Mrs. Trilling?"

"Yes."

"Did Victor come home for Halloween?"

"No, he didn't Grace, but his spirit is with me."

"Just like Nobody!"

"Yes, Grace, just like Nobody."

"Good night, Mrs. Trilling."

"Good night, Grace. Stay safe."

Across the street, Alice and James thought that Grace was taking too long at the Trillings' house, but they had known Mrs. Trilling for years, and so they did not worry. Next door was Mae Terwillinger, who had lived in the neighborhood longer than anyone else, even after her husband had died; and Alice and James knew that she would want to see Grace in her costume. Grace looked across the street and waved to her parents, who nodded their heads yes as they pointed to the Terwillinger door.

Grace swung her candy bag with one hand and shook her magic carpet with the other as she walked to the Terwillinger front door.

"Trick or Treat!" she shouted as she posed as well as she could as a queen of the night.

"Well hello and happy Halloween," said Mae Terwillinger. "What a fine costume! Now, just who are you?"

"I'm Grace Preston from down the street, but tonight I'm a queen with a magic carpet."

"So you are. You make a fine queen."

"And my invisible friend, Nobody, is dressed as a ghost!"

"Well, now. Nobody makes a very good ghost."

"Could we both have some treats?"

"Of course you may. Here's one for you and one for Nobody."

"Thank you, Mrs. Ter'inger."

"You're very welcome, young Grace. Just don't fly too high tonight!"

"We won't. Good night."

Mae Terwillinger slowly closed the door and thought of the ghosts whom she lived with and silently wished them well.

It was beginning to get dark, and Grace knew that she could not stay out much longer. "Only two houses," she whispered to Nobody. "They gave us a lot of candy, but only two houses." She began to walk more quickly, hoping to get as much as possible before she had to go home. Alice and James saw her running down their street, and they knew that they had to move just as quickly. Alice caught up with Grace who had just passed two houses without their lights on.

"Grace, dear, not so fast. Just stop for a minute."

"But Mother, there's not much time left."

"I know, Grace, but see these next two houses don't have their lights on. Come on, now, it's time to go home."

"Just one more, please."

"Grace . . ."

"Just one more. Look, there's a house down the street with its lights on."

Three houses down lived the Taylors, whom Alice and James never particularly liked but who the Prestons knew would have candy for children from the neighborhood, children whom the Taylors recognized and could trust. "Good Catholic boys and girls," Mrs. Taylor had once told Alice. "You know what I mean." Alice wasn't quite sure she knew what Mrs. Taylor meant, but she was hoping that Grace was a good girl.

"Alright, Grace. One more house, the Taylors. Father and I will stay right here, and you must come right back."

"Thank you, Mother."

Grace skipped as well as a queen should skip and knocked on the Taylors' front door. "Trick or treat!" she said.

The Taylors had two daughters–Virginia, in high school, and Gloria, a few years older than Grace, but, in Gloria's view, much more refined and intelligent. Virginia opened the door with one candy bar in her hand. "Well, what are you supposed to be?" she asked Grace, as Gloria looked on from behind a curtain in the living room.

"I'm a queen who rides on this magic carpet."

"That doesn't look much like a carpet, but I guess that's ok. Here's your candy."

"Could I have one for Nobody?"

"Who's nobody?"

"My invisible friend."

Virginia laughed and called back inside her house.

"Mom, come listen to this. She says she has an invisible friend, and she asked for candy for that friend. Nobody, she calls it."

Mrs. Taylor came to the door and looked down at Grace. "Kids will try just about anything these days." She motioned Virginia inside and closed the door. Gloria looked out to see what kids might be trying to do, but her mother swept her away from the window and closed the curtains. Grace stood outside the house until her mother joined her, took her hand, and told her that it was time to go home.

November, 1982—Nobody Disappears

Once past Halloween, All Saints and All Souls Days, Grace spent even more and more time with her friends and less and less time with Nobody, even at night. After Virginia Taylor's laugh and Mrs. Taylor's words, Grace felt that an invisible friend might be even worse than silly. Only when Grace had a bad day at school or when Mother served cauliflower at dinner did Grace ask Nobody for help—and she only asked after her bedroom lights were turned off. She only mentioned Nobody to her parents if she spilled orange juice on the tablecloth ("How did this happen?" her mother asked; "Nobody did it," said Grace) or if she forgot to water the cactus ("Do you know why the cactus is so dry?" asked Alice; "Nobody knows," Grace replied).

Both Alice and James were pleased that they no longer had to set a place for Nobody at each evening's dinner table, but they were puzzled why Grace kept using Nobody as an excuse and as an imaginary friend over whom she had no control. They finally decided to end what they saw now as a childish fantasy which might hurt Grace. After a Saturday dinner, without cauliflower, they asked Grace to stay at the table for "just a few minutes," as Alice said.

"Grace, dear, how are your friends at school?" asked Alice.

"They're fine, Mother. We have fun together."

"Good. It's important to have friends you can play with," James added.

"Yes, Father. I know that."

"And it's important," said Alice, "that you have ideas and dreams."

Grace didn't reply: she knew that it was important to have friend, ideas, and dreams, and she knew that her mother and father knew that she knew. "What do they want to tell me?" Grace thought. "Am I in trouble?"

"It's also important that you know when to stop a ... a game, Grace," said Father. "All games must finally stop; you need to know what's real and what's just a game."

"Like checkers?" Grace said.

"Yes ... like checkers," James told her, "and like Nobody."

"But Nobody's different...."

"Yes, Nobody is different," said Alice, "but Nobody isn't real: she's just a character you made up, a fiction. It's probably time that your game with Nobody ended and that she ... leaves for a while."

Grace knew that she believed it was time for Nobody to leave, but she didn't want her parents to make her leave, and thinking about life without Nobody made Grace sniffle and cry and run to her bedroom. "It's just not fair," she cried as she left the dinner table. "It's just not fair. Nobody wants to stay."

An hour later, James and Alice went to check on Grace, whom they found asleep under her covers, still in her school uniform. They turned off the lights and hoped that Grace would forgive them in the morning. At breakfast the next day, Grace did not forgive them, nor did she say anything to them, except to ask for a second pancake. She walked to school by herself: as she said, "I don't need anyone's help this morning, Mother."

Before he left for his own school, James told Alice that there probably wasn't anything to worry about or anything that they should do. Alice, however, was not convinced, and so she made an appointment to talk with the school counselor to find out if Grace had any problems at school. Claudia Smith was able to meet with Alice two days later during Grace's reading period. "It's better if the child does not know her parents are meeting with me, at least for the first visit," Ms. Smith explained, "and at 10:00 Grace will be busy with her reading assignments."

Alice was careful to arrive at the school only minutes before 10 and even more careful to walk quickly away from Grace's classroom to the counselor's office.

"Mrs. Preston?" said Ms. Smith.

"Yes, I'm Alice Preston, Grace's mother. Thank you for meeting with me."

"It's good to meet you. Please sit down."

Alice sat at the only adult chair in the room and waited for Ms. Smith to begin; Claudia sat behind her desk, waiting for Alice to begin.

"You see ... Grace is ... My husband and I are just a little concerned...."

"Grace is a fine young girl. I've checked her grades, attendance, and behavior checklist and she seems to be doing quite well. Is she having troubles at home, if you don't mind my asking?"

"No. Not really. It's just that since last summer she has had an invisible friend; she calls her Nobody ... and she keep blaming Nobody for any trouble she gets into, and she talks every night to Nobody, after she's in bed."

"Every night, Mrs. Preston?"

"Well ... I suppose not, at least not recently. But my husband and I thought it was time to stop believing in this Nobody and so we asked her last Monday to let go of Nobody. She cried and ran to her room. Since then, she really hasn't talked with us."

"Has she been talking with this Nobody?"

"No, at least not as far as we can tell."

"Are you worried about Grace?"

"Yes, we are. We just don't know what to do. Do other children have invisible friends? Do they cause problems?"

"Mrs. Preston, we have had children–not so many but quite a few, actually—who claim to have friends that only they can see and talk with. Most of them grow out of it, but a few need some professional help."

"Professional help? Do you mean a psychiatrist?"

"Some professionals specialize in helping children and young adults deal with similar problems. Perhaps you would like me to recommend someone?"

"I don't know. I would have to talk with my husband.... A psychiatrist, for someone as young as Grace.... She isn't a difficult child...."

"Of course not, Mrs. Preston. I was not suggesting that Grace causes any problems. We just want to do all we can to ensure that no problems come about ... now or in the future."

"Yes, yes, of course. Let me think about this."

"Well, if you do decide to seek professional help, here is the card of someone who deals with young people. Her name is Doctor Laura Stone. She grew up in St. Louis, but she does not live in town these days. She has her office and home in Peoria, three hours from us. However, she regularly comes to meet with her clients and their parents. In fact, she will be here next weekend to help a young man and his mother. They're having some serious issues, much more serious than an invisible friend—I hope you don't mind my saying that— and perhaps she could meet with you as well. After you speak with Grace's father, please call her at the number on her card and see if you can arrange a meeting."

"Thank you very much, Ms. Smith."

"You're very welcome, and please call me Claudia."

"I will Claudia. Thank you again."

"Good day, Mrs. Preston ... and good luck."

"Good bye, Claudia."

When Claudia spoke with James about an appointment with Doctor Stone, he was initially more than a bit skeptical. "A psychiatrist? For Grace?"

"For all of us, James, that's what Claudia recommended."

"Who's Claudia?"

"Claudia Smith, she's the counselor at Grace's school."

"Is she qualified to offer such advice?"

"She's been a counselor for ... years, I believe, and she said that Dr. Stone is seeing another young person and his mother this weekend. We could call and at least meet her. We don't have to commit to any more than that."

"What's her name again?"

"Dr. Stone, Dr. Laura Stone."

"Doesn't sound like a good name for a child psychiatrist."

"Well, Claudia recommended her. She's from St. Louis, but now she's out of town.... She doesn't know anyone here, and no one we know would recognize her."

"Where's her office, in town, I mean."

"She uses the office of another psychiatrist; I have a card with the address. ... Please, James, we have to see if Grace needs any special help."

"I suppose it can't hurt, just to meet her. Ok ... go ahead and call her. See if we can see her on Saturday morning,"

"Good! Thank you. I'll call tomorrow morning."

Neither Alice nor James said anything to Grace about Dr. Stone. They just said good night and turned off the lights in Grace's bedroom. Nobody did not visit Grace that night.

After Grace left for school and James left for his classes, Alice called the number on Dr. Stone's business card. A receptionist answered, checked Laura Stone's calendar for the weekend, and told Alice that the only opening was at 10:00 Saturday morning. "First appointments, especially at such late notice," Alice was told, "last only for fifteen minutes. Dr. Stone has a very busy schedule, and so you must be on time."

"We will. Thank you."

Before dinner that night, Alice told James that she had arranged a meeting with Dr. Stone for the coming Saturday. "That's good," he said, and then under his breath added "at least it's only fifteen minutes." At dinner James told Grace that they were going to meet with a person who could help Grace to do even better at school. Grace looked up from her plate of spaghetti and simply said, "Ok." That night, Grace fell asleep, and again Nobody did not visit.

Saturday morning, the Prestons left home at 9:00 for the ten-minute drive to the psychiatrist's office. As they drove into the parking lot, Grace saw two people walking toward the front door of the medical building and pointed toward them: "Look, Mother, isn't that Mrs. Hopewell? ... And that's Jonathan."

"Don't point, Grace," Alice said. "It's not polite."

"But that's Mrs. Hopewell and Jonathan." Grace sat up and waved to them from her backseat,

"I don't think that's..."

"No, she's right," said James. "I'm sure that's Felicia and Jonathan."

"Oh ... no," Alice said. "Let's park on the other side of the lot. I ... I don't want to disturb them."

"Why would we disturb them, Mother? Let's be friendly."

"Well," said James, "sometimes people need to be by themselves."

"In a parking lot?" asked Grace.

James turned the car to a far corner of the parking lot.

"What should we do, Alice? Do you want Mrs. Hopewell to see us here?"

"No I don't," she said. "No ... it would be awkward."

"What's awkward?" Grace asked.

"Nothing dear. We just ... well I just remembered that today I must go shopping this morning. We need food for the weekend. Yes, I'm afraid we'll have to cancel our meeting."

"What about help for me in school?"

"I'm sure we can find another helper. James, let's just go home."

After Mrs. Hopewell and Jonathan entered the building, the Prestons drove slowly away. They assumed that Mrs. Hopewell and Jonathan were seeing Dr. Stone, but they did not want to ask about the meeting. "Better just to let it pass," James said. "Let's not intrude."

On Monday morning, Claudia Smith called Alice about the appointment. "How did your meeting with Dr. Stone go, Mrs. Preston?"

"Well, we uh...."

As Alice tried to think of what she should say, she could hear a knock and then a door open. A man's voice interrupted the conversation.

"Hello. I'm here to service your photocopy machine."

Claudia held one hand over the phone and sounded more than a little upset.

"Who are you? Why did you barge into my office?"

"I'm Anthony Ignazio, from the Burlington Photocopy Company. Your copier is scheduled for maintenance."

"I don't have a copier here."

"Isn't this the principal's office—a Mrs. Turnbuckle."

"Does this look like a principal's office? Please, I'm on a confidential phone call. You must leave."

Alice could overhear Claudia's conversation, but Alice was patient—and puzzled. She thought about hanging up, but that, she reasoned, might be rude; so, for Grace's sake, she stayed on the line.

"I will, but please tell me where I can find Mrs. Turn-buckle's office."

"There's no Mrs. Turnbuckle at this school. You have the wrong office, the wrong school, and probably the wrong city."

"I don't think that's possible, but . . . "

"Please leave now.

"I am leaving, I am. Very sorry for the confusion."

"Good bye."

Anthony Ignazio tried to close the door as quietly as pos-sible, but Anthony was more sincere than careful, and so the door slammed shut. Claudia tried to regain her calm when she tried to speak once again to Alice.

"Mrs. Preston? Alice? I'm sorry for the interruption."

But Alice did not answer.

"Hello, Alice? Are you there?"

Alice had finally decided that she did not want to wait and, even more, that she did not know how to tell Claudia Smith that they had not met with Dr. Stone. Claudia twice called back, but no one answered. An hour later, Alice did call and told Claudia that "we must have been disconnected."

"Oh yes. That's right," said Claudia. "I'm very sorry about that interruption."

"I understand. Of course, sometimes such things happen."

So tell me, how was your meeting with Dr. Stone?"

"My husband and I, and Grace, did drive over to see her, but we must have misread the card. We ended up at a parking lot for a discount clothing store."

"Oh, I'm sorry. Perhaps you could try to arrange a meeting with Dr. Stone on her next weekend visit?"

"We'll try, but, you see ... the holidays are coming up, and our weekends will be quite busy. We'll have to see about early in the new year."

"Well that's unfortunate, but I understand. Please let me know if I can help you and Grace in any way."

"Thank you very much, Claudia. We do appreciate your help."

Alice did not enjoy making up such a story: she felt dishonest about the pretense, but she also felt relieved that Claudia did not ask her any more about Dr. Stone, Grace, and Nobody. After Grace had gone to bed, she told James about the incident and about the story she'd told Claudia Smith. He said very little, other than that she'd done what had to be done. He did not tell her that he was glad that he did not have to speak with Claudia. "Alice just does such things much better than I do," he thought. Grace never found out about the phone calls, about Dr. Stone, or about the Hopewells' meeting. A week later, Grace told her parents that Nobody would not join them for Thanksgiving. "Nobody will be gone for a while," she explained.

December, 1982–Dreaming

James had been raised Catholic, but after four years at a Jesuit high school and four years at a Jesuit university, he became more and more skeptical of the church.

"I don't think churches work," he often told Alice. "They just seem to offer consolation and hope, but they don't really tell us the truth. Don't you think so?"

"Perhaps, James, but so many of our friends are good Catholics, and they seem to be leading good lives." Alice's parents had insisted that Alice attend the neighborhood Catholic grade school, but they had never taken her to Mass. She learned order, discipline, and good manners at school and at home; they hoped that in college she would learn understanding.

Everyone on Sherwood Circle attended Holy Innocents Church, and everyone had their children attend Holy Innocents School—everyone, that is, except the Prestons, who did enroll Grace in the church's kindergarten but who did not go to Mass. Yet Father Terence Murphy, the newly appointed pastor of Holy Innocents,had met the Prestons and thought that they were, in his words, "good people, people whom we should welcome." They weren't surprised, then, when they received a Christmas card from Father Murphy, who preferred that everyone call him Father Terence.

Included in Father Murphy's card was an invitation to join him and other good people on a two-week tour of the great cathedrals of Europe. "Please join us," the brochure read, "on our pilgrimage to the holiest churches in western Europe. In each city we will have tours of these remarkable sites, with expert guidance supplied by priests who have been trained at the Vatican on liturgical history and who have been designated official cathedral envoys." The schedule included stops in Luxembourg and Bavaria, with extended visits to Paris ("the City of Lights"), Rome ("the City of Faith"), and Vienna ("the City of Dreams"). Father Murphy added a personal note to the Prestons: "James and Alice, the tour will make an ideal Christmas gift for your entire family; I'm sure Grace would learn from the experience."

At the bottom of the invitation was an endorsement from Father Murphy's recently promoted predecessor, now Monsignor Theodore Bischoff, whose pastoral duties as adjutant bishop of the diocese precluded him from joining.

Alice and James had long wanted to tour Europe: a boat ride on the Seine, espresso in an Italian café, a waltz in Vienna, but they never had the money even to leave the neighborhood for a week. Alice tossed the card and the brochure on the hallway table, where Grace saw the shiny pages with color photos of St. Peter's, Notre Dame, and St. Stephan's cathedral in Vienna. "What's this, Mother?"

"It's a travel brochure, Grace."

"A travel brocher?"

"Yes, dear. Father Murphy is going on a trip in the summer, and he asked if we would like to go with him."

"Can we go?"

"No, dear. We can't."

"Why not?"

"We have to save money, Grace ... for next year, your school, and other things."

"I could save money to help."

"I know you could, Grace, but we need much more."

"Can I just keep the travel brocher?"

"Well, I suppose so. Just keep it in your room."

"Ok! I'll put it in my hiding place, where nobody else will see it."

Grace ran to her bedroom and slid the papers with those shiny photos of the great cathedrals of Europe under her bed. "There," she said to herself, "it will be safe."

Alice and James did not join Father Murphy's tour as a Christmas gift for the family, but they did hang their stockings on the mantel, with their names paper-clipped to the top of the stockings, "so that Santa will know what to put in each one," Alice told Grace. Alice had added a fourth stocking this year for "Nobody," the tag read. When Grace saw the extra stocking with Nobody's name on the tag, she took it down and threw Nobody's name tag in the trash can.

"Why did you do that, Grace?" Alice asked.

"Nobody is a fiction Mother. You told me so."

Alice said nothing to Grace.

Three days before Christmas, James asked Alice if they might go to midnight Mass at Holy Innocents on Christmas Eve. "Mrs. Hopewell has said they have a wonderful service, with everyone holding candles in the darkened church as the altar boys carry Jesus to the Nativity scene. Everyone sings Silent Night during the procession, and then the lights come on for the Mass. We wouldn't have to stay for the entire service.... What do you think?"

"Could Grace stay up that late?"

"With a late-afternoon nap she could. At least we could try."

"Grace, what do you think? Do you want to stay up late and go to church and see the procession?"

"Will Janet and Kathleen be there?"

"I think so, if their parents let them stay up late."

"Yes, Mother. Let me go."

"We'll see. You just have to promise to take a nap, a real nap, in the afternoon."

"I promise."

Grace kept her promise: she was in her bedroom for two hours on Christmas Eve, and she did try to go to sleep. The Prestons went to the midnight service, and Grace stayed awake until the church lights were turned on.

December 31, 1982–January, 1 1983–Celebrations

Neither Alice nor James Preston would be considered socialites: they had neither the desire nor the money to go out each weekend or to entertain friends for dinner. But each year, they hosted a small New Year's Eve party with the same guests: Felix and Gertrude Kulpa, Felix' twin brother and his wife Sandra (the twin sister of Gertrude), Felicia Hopewell and her troubled young son, Jonathan. Alice and James did not particularly enjoy either of the Kulpa brothers and sisters, but they had grown used to their company at New Year's Eve. They knew that recent years had been difficult for the Felix and Gertrude Kulpa: their son had gone to Austria in 1981, and died in a traffic accident. Throughout 1982, they seldom spoke of their son, and no one asked. At one time, Felicia Hopewell had been a close friend of Alice's; but since Felicia's divorce, her son Jonathan had grown more and more difficult. Alice, however, convinced James to include her in this year's party. Before they arrived, Felix and his brother Francis had had several drinks ("Don't remember how many," Francis told James Preston when he met the Kulpas at the door).

"Hello there, young Grace. Happy New Year. Say, I hear that Nobody is your friend, Grace," said Felix. "Is that true?"

"Stop it, Felix:" Felicia Hopewell said. "You'll hurt Grace's feelings."

"No, Mr. Kulpa. Janet, Kathleen, and Regina are my friends at school."

"But I've heard the same thing, Grace," added Francis Kulpa. "I've heard kids talk about Nobody."

Felicia took Grace's hand, and stood between her and the Kulpa twins. "Just stop it, both of you."

"That's ok, Mrs. Hopewell," said Grace. "I don't mind."

"But I do, dear. Let's find Jonathan and see if he knows any good jokes." Grace and Felicia walked through the living room, then the dining room, and finally into the kitchen, where Alice told them that Jonathan had said he was feeling ill, and had left the party.

"He should have told me," Felicia said to everyone and to no one.

"I'm getting tired, Mrs. Hopewell," said Grace. " I think I should go to bed."

"You're right, Grace," said her mother. "I've just lost track of the time. Say good night to Mrs. Hopewell. I'll tell your father and the others that you've gone to bed."

"Good night, Mrs. Hopewell. Thank you."

"Good night, Grace. Sleep well."

Felicia stayed in the kitchen and told Alice what the Kulpa twins had said to Grace. Alice simply shook her head and went back to washing the party plates.

In the living room, however, Felix and Francis could not let go of Nobody. Each had a third Manhattan, and each found himself extremely clever.

"I wonder what kind of friend Nobody is. What do you think, Felix?"

"A friend your wife will never see!"

"That's a good one! How about a friend who always goes with you for a beer?"

"Even better, a friend who wears the same color sox as you do."

Francis poured himself a fourth drink and stumbled back to Felix, laughing aloud as bourbon splashed to the floor.

"A frien' to young girls and old men."

"Tha's a goo' one. How 'bout a frien' who listens to you?"

"A frien' nobody sees ..."

"Wai ... nobody is its name."

"Oh yeah ... a frien' everybody never sees."

With each comment, the voices of the two drunk twins grew louder until they shouted with one voice, "A frien' of frien' forever!"

James had been in the far corner of the room, trying to talk with Gertrude and Sandra about their years together as young girls when he heard the loud voices across the room. Both Gertrude and Sandra had seen their husbands at other parties and in other rooms, and so they simply looked at each other, rolled their eyes, and asked James to excuse the twin Kulpas.

"Of course I will, but why are they talking about friends? What friends?"

"I'm afraid they began when they were teasing young Grace about her invisible friend," Gertrude explained. "We heard weeks ago that Grace had a secret friend whom she called Nobody."

"Well, she's past that," said James, "and besides, they shouldn't make fun of my daughter."

"We know that, James," Sandra said, "and we can only say that we're sorry."

"Perhaps it's time for everyone to go home," James told the sisters. "It's not yet midnight, but we've all had a long week."

"Yes, I think you're right, James," added Gertrude. "I'll get Felix's attention."

"And I'll do the same for Francis," said Sandra.

"Please do, or else I might do something we would all regret."

"Don't worry, James. We'll get the boys' coats and head them out the door," said Gertrude.

"And please give our thanks to Alice," added Sandra.

"I will ... thank you.... And Happy New Year."

"Happy New Year, James," the twin sisters called out in unison.

Gertrude knew that their husbands wanted to keep up their silly game and, even more, wanted to continue drinking, and so she explained to Felix and Francis that Alice wasn't feeling well and that the party was over. "We all need to go home," she told them. "It's time to go home."

"Al right, Gertie," slurred Felix. "But jus' one mo' frien'ly drink?"

"Tha's right, ol' Felix. Tha's a good one, You tell 'em."

Sandra brought all four coats from the closet: Gertrude's long black overcoat, Felix's dark blue parka, Francis' matching blue parka, and her own green overcoat. The sisters first put on their own coats and then tried to help their husbands.

"Careful, now Sandy," said Felix, "you're hurtin' my buddy."

"Your buddy? Hey brother, you're my fra'ernal frien!"

"Come on, Francis, put your arms through the sleeves,"

"And you do the same, Felix," added Gertrude. "And act your age."

"Can't act my age, sweetie, it's not yet New Year's."

"It will soon be the end of it, Felix. We need to go home. We all need to go home."

The twin sisters managed to get the twin brothers out of the door and into their cars. As Gertrude drove away, Felix rolled down the front window and yelled back at his brother's car: "'Appy New Year, you and nobody else!"

Once the Kulpas had left, James picked up the half-emptied glasses, turned out the lights in the living room, and went to the kitchen. Alice was facing him; Felicia had her back turned and seemed to be sobbing. Alice simply nodded to James to leave them alone, and so he quietly left the room and went to see if Grace had yet gone to sleep. She did not move as he tucked the white comforter under her chin and wished her a very happy new year.

While Alice and James washed the party dishes and cleaned up the spilled drinks, Grace hid under her blankets and listened to the sound of fireworks. She soon fell asleep and dreamed of flying above Sherwood Circle on her magical carpet and softly landing in her bed to the sound of violins.

Hours later, "Wake up, Grace," Alice whispered. "You don't want to miss the concert." On the first day of each year, Alice and James listened on the living room radio to the New

Year's Day concert from Vienna. For the last two years, Grace had insisted the night before that they must wake her so that she could dance across the room with Father while Alice reminded her of their good-luck foods.

"You don't need to eat the sauerkraut this morning," Alice told her, "but you have to eat just a bite sometime today."

"And the herring," Father added. "Don't forget the herring."

"I don't like sauerkraut, and herring tastes like fish."

"Herring is fish, dear," Alice said. "And you don't have to have much. James, whoever told you that herring brings good luck?"

"Don't remember. Herring fishermen, perhaps."

All the while, the Vienna Philharmonic played on: waltzes and marches by the entire Strauss family and their friends. Grace sat on the living room couch, counting to three while James moved across the floor, holding the hand of an invisible partner.

"Come join me, Alice. Come quickly before they stop."

"Just a minute, James. I'm cooking."

"No time to waste, Alice, they've begun the Emperor's Waltz."

"Have Grace dance with you."

James turned to Grace, bowed deeply, and asked if the young lady would care to dance with him. Grace left the couch and took her father's hand. "Just count to three and listen to the music," he told her, "and don't think about herring." James smiled, Grace counted, James hummed, and together they waltzed across the living room floor.

"I wish we could go to Vienna, Father."

"So do I, dear, so do I."

Chapter 4
Laura Stone and The
Wassermann Brothers
Vienna, 1983

St. Louis, Chicago, and Vienna, 1983

The note left by Jonathan Hopewell did not mention Dr. Stone by name, but she knew that five years of therapy did not finally enable Jonathan to survive. Laura Stone, tall and dressed in a fashionable black outfit, met Jonathan's mother at the funeral home. After two hours spent consoling others over the loss of her son, Felicia Hopewell finally sat down in the chair reserved for the family. She tried to compose herself for the next friend or neighbor, and she did her best to wipe each tear from her face. Laura stood patiently in line, knowing that she should find the words to offer Felicia some peace, some sense of hope. But Laura could only say that she was sorry. Jonathan's life should not have ended, Laura tried to assure Mrs. Hopewell, who sat quietly without facing her. "He left an unfinished story," Jonathan's mother said. "A story which should have a different ending." Laura was not invited to join friends and family for the meal after Jonathan's burial.

When Laura returned to her parents' house after Jonathan's funeral, she thought first of Mrs. Hopewell, and then she thought of her own dead son, who lived only four hours. While Laura recovered in the hospital's bereavement room reserved for grieving mothers, her husband dealt with the burial. Laura remained in bed, uncertain and exhausted. When he returned to Laura, he repeated what the assistant funeral director had told him.

"It's a rather interesting fact," the man in the black suit had told Laura's husband, "but did you know that the infant's coffin often weighs more than the infant itself." That was all the man in the black suit told Laura's husband, and those were the last words Laura's husband told her. After four weeks of silence, he packed a few clothes, and left Laura and grief. The story of their marriage had ended, two years before Jonathan's suicide.

Laura seldom thought of her former husband, but she could

not escape Jonathan's shadow or her own dead son. After three weeks of excuses, delays, and postponements of her clients' sessions, she realized that she must leave the city and her practice for more than an extended weekend.

Laura told all her patients that she was taking a year's sabbatical and would first take a temporary lease on an apartment in Chicago. "To refresh myself," she said, "to learn current advances in therapy." Although everyone agreed that she had earned such a break, many silently welcomed the news and sought another therapist. She packed as few clothes as possible and, two days later, took the bus from Peoria to Chicago.

A woman in black stepped carefully to the third row of the bus, just across the aisle from Laura. As she leaned forward to remove her coat, a gold pen fell to the floor and rolled beneath the seat in front of her. She heard the pen fall, but did not see it slide across the aisle as the bus turned sharply left out of the Peoria terminal. An hour later, the woman in black realized that she no longer had her pen. Her black cape slipped off her shoulders as she looked beneath both seats in her row and then beneath those in front. As she moved into the aisle, the bus turned sharply right, and she fell into the vacant seat next to Laura. The pen rolled back across the aisle, two rows to the front. "Oh, I'm sorry," she said to Laura. I seem to be having a bit of difficulty."

"Yes. I see. May I help?"

"I have lost my pen. A gold pen. It must have rolled underneath my seat. Did you see it?"

"No. I was asleep. Or I was trying to sleep."

"I'm sorry if I . . . "

"Oh no. I haven't really slept since we left Peoria."

"Peoria? Where are you going?"

"Chicago."

"Really? So am I. I hope I can find the pen before we get there."

"I'm sure we will."

Laura never did learn the name of the woman whose pen she snatched a bit later as it rolled down the aisle toward the driver. But she was glad that she could help someone without any regrets. She simply gave her the pen, had little else to say. She closed her eyes and tried to dream of late spring snows. By the time the bus reached Chicago, she had lost the possibility offered by the golden pen, and so she could only smile weakly as she walked away into the chill of an early October evening.

As she stepped into the street outside the bus depot, the clatter of hooves on pavement startled Laura. She quickly stepped back, as the carriage rolled past, carrying quilted lovers on a thirty-minute tour of the Loop. They looked so ridiculous, thought Laura, yet probably felt so privileged. She would have followed them to offer advice, if the sidewalks weren't so crowded and the suitcase so heavy. But then she realized that she had nothing to offer them. Instead, she hailed a cab, which took her to the apartment she had sub-let for a month.

For the first few days in Chicago, Laura welcomed the release from obligations and from the hours of listening to the tales and dreams of her patients in St. Louis and Peoria. She valued each person and regretted the year she would be away, but she also reasoned that most would never abandon their weekly sessions. If she were to find even a few weeks of quiet, she would have to give them up fully. Laura needed a destination.

On the third night in Chicago, Laura attempted to recall her own childhood and her parents, who had died years ago in St. Louis. Laura thought of those Saturday afternoons in the winter when her father would play the bagpipe record, louder and louder, and together they would march from the living room through the kitchen and dining room, and then back in triumph to where they had begun and where they would begin again. They would gather in her mother on their second march through the kitchen, where she would be making Saturday chili and praying for the armistice to end the war. The parents' arms wrapped tightly around Laura, and their feet stomped across the kitchen floor, a sound as grand and majestic as the rush of Scots to defend their homeland. The pipes were too loud to be simply music, and they knew the pipes were too loud to endure for long. But on those Saturday afternoons in her childhood, the sound passed beyond hearing and went directly to their hearts or souls or collective memories and drew them into glorious battle. And then, just for those few minutes, Laura and her parents were more than they were: they marched with the ghosts of proud warriors, and the pipes sent the British back in disgrace across the Irish Sea.

"I've not heard bagpipes for so many years," thought Laura. "I wonder what ever happened to that record?"

The memory quickly passed, as Laura tried to decide what she must do and where she could do whatever she decided to do. She knew that she must move again, but she was not certain where she might go. She had friends in Boston who would welcome her, but not for a year. She had collaborated with colleagues at universities in St. Louis and Cincinnati, but she had not seen them for years. "Perhaps," she said to the mirror, "I might return to my graduate studies or to Doctor Fitzpatrick." But she knew that she had not looked at her research nor had she had spoken with Fitzpatrick since she finished her degree. Fitzpatrick had convinced her that Freud was a charlatan and that psychoanalysis was useless in clinical practice. Laura took his word and so never had read anything by Freud other than *The Interpretation of Dreams*. Although she remained convinced by Fitzpatrick's reasoning, she remembered that Freud's book fascinated her and, on occasion, she had asked clients about their dreams.

No destination seemed ideal for Laura's sabbatical, but Vienna increasingly seemed possible. "Why not go to Freud's city," she wrote to a friend in Minneapolis. "Why not go to Vienna and see if the city itself might provide a way to end my sorrow."

"I might as well be alone in a city where I've never been," Laura wrote. "Perhaps I'll learn more if I must learn everything anew." Perhaps, she thought, I really should go to New York, or Boston, or somewhere entirely new, perhaps in the mountains, Vale, but that might be too expensive. Perhaps I really should go to Europe—Paris or London, where Freud sought refuge. But Vienna, Freud's home, the City of Dreams—still seemed almost irresistible, at least for a few months. Laura decided that she would go to Vienna and spend perhaps two, possibly three weeks there to escape the reminders of Jonathan's death and her son's short life, deaths which seemed to have the terrible power to be unforgettable. She would then return to Chicago and write a journal to help her cope with responsibility. "I will allow the days to forget me," she told herself.

Although she was the first to find the boarding area Laura was the last of all passengers to board the Austrian Airlines plane at O'Hare, bound for Vienna. She excused herself, pardoned herself, apologized for being so late, "Sorry, sorry, sorry. Excuse me. Pardon me."

Laura knew that she must get to sleep as soon as possible after the evening meal was served: after her second glass of red wine, she fell into a deep but troubled sleep. She first dreamed of entering Vienna on a golden coach, driven by an elderly man with a grey beard and unlit cigar. But into the skies above Vienna, rode another figure from another dream, a dreamer sitting restlessly next to the Emperor of the Skies, a dreamer cursing even in her dreams ... nails and pinewood splinters were driven into his toes, a thorn and a blessed tooth skewered his heart.... Laura saw herself buried in a child's casket of silver, lined with green velvet and white silk ... and she saw her father's face above the cradle, mother-of-pearl, copper-plates covered with velvet and her mother's tears ...

and the child drove a wooden stake snatched from the heart of the true cross into her father's heart ... and Laura awoke, trembling, hoping that she might finally have another glass of wine. She slept no more that night.

As the plane descended, slowly rolling through the clouds which always seemed to obscure Vienna's skies, Strauss waltzed through the cabin, and the flight attendants moved in time with the Danube, collecting headphones, pillows, the last cup from the last meal–and then ... the passengers seemed to move their heads, tap their feet, and taste strudel and Sacher torte and café melange ... and even Laura, it seemed, could not resist the waltz. Even Laura. Laura closed her eyes and smiled at the vision of life in the Vienna Woods. When Laura looked toward the windows, she saw swirling dancers, in love with each other and the dance itself, and it would never end–retreat a bit, slowly, slowly, and then crescendo through time and whipped cream and ... then back off–just a bit–just a bit slower–just so that they could show everyone that they knew the music, that the music knew them, was created for them, forever.

The plane landed just as "The Emperor's Waltz" ended, and Laura quickly gathered her luggage and found the cab waiting area. Laura knew enough to take a taxi directly to her apartment.

Laura's apartment was on Theresiengasse in the Eighteenth District, and so she would live on the margins, just outside the Gŭrtel, that noisy outer ring of the city. Laura did not know that she was closer to the city hospital than to the red-light district. When she finally entered her apartment—tired from the overnight flight and still haunted by memories of Jonathan—she simply felt empty and glad to be somewhere else.

Laura had no plans for her first days in Vienna. She knew that some plan would be required, some way to fill her days and perhaps to forget, but for now she simply wanted to sit in peace, undisturbed and quiet. She had read that Vienna cafés offered such security.

Laura had read that Freud's favorite café was Landtmann, a café which valued quiet conversations and which was scented throughout with respectability. Laura, however, was not yet ready for an encounter with Freud's ghost. And so on her first day in the city, Laura went where so many other visitors go: Café Central, where the waiters always seemed busy but seldom nearby, and yet where she could sit with one coffee and not seem alone. Laura read whatever English papers she found and listened to waltzes on the piano. Occasionally she wrote a few lines on the margins of the café napkins, and she looked at the tourists as if she were not among them. After an hour at Central, Laura walked slowly through the First District hearing snatches of conversations in English while she looked without interest at store windows.

"Can you believe what that man said?" one woman in a bright red tunic seemed to say to a friend. Laura thought she heard the friend respond: "I'm not surprised."

But the two passed on without stopping, and so Laura could only wonder what the man had said.

Two blocks and twelve small shops later, Laura heard many voices, but only one in English. "...Yes. How did it happen?..." What could have happened? Laura thought, what could possibly have happened?

The morning seemed to last longer in Vienna than at home, perhaps because Laura had no destination, no timetable, no one to see this morning, and no one to help.

A man brushed past Laura, excused himself, just as he said to the man with him, "She should have known...." Laura could only whisper, "Of course," not in agreement but as a courtesy. Laura had somehow walked in a long loop, and found herself once more at Café Central. Just outside the entrance, a small family waited to go inside. A woman who seemed to be the mother of the two children with her turned to what seemed to be her husband and said in a voice loud enough for Laura to hear, "No, that can't be possible...."

Laura was not yet sure what was and what was not possible in Vienna, and so she kept walking past the café and returned to her apartment, where she closed the curtains, drank two glasses of red wine, and tried to sleep.

On the morning of her second day in the City of Dreams, Laura remained in bed, past all her nightmares. She lay still, as the whine of the drill pierced her ears, and the BOOM! BOOM! BOOM! BOOM! struck the inside of her temple, again and again, relentless, indomitable assertions of building Vienna. Laura's father, she knew, would tell her to go for a walk, a long, slow walk. Her father had often done this himself after a difficult night, and many of his nights were difficult. Two nights before he died, when he could no longer walk, Laura's father had seen the angel of death, who stood above his bed, dressed in gray robes and piercing his side with a golden lance, as a stream of blood filled the room and covered his face. He awoke in terror, Laura's mother said; she awoke immersed in sweat and tears. But on this morning in Vienna, Laura awoke only in disgust.

BOOM! RAT A TAT A RAT A TAT A! BOOOM! BOOM!

"Damn."

Laura slowly sat up, propped her body on one hand and tried to silence the construction workers with her other hand. "I'll get up. I'll brush my teeth. I'll go for a walk."

BOOM! BOOM! BOOM! BOOM!

Laura walked carefully those five steps to the bathroom, where she washed, brushed her teeth as if she could scrape away regret, and walked slowly to the chair next to her bed. On days when she met her clients and even on weekends, Laura always dressed carefully, professionally. But today she put her arms into the same shirt she had worn since she left

Chicago, and onto her distant legs pulled the same pants which she had worn with that same shirt.

BOOM! BOOM! RAT A TAT A RAT A TAT A! BOOOM!

Laura carefully opened the apartment door to a street which seemed busier than it should be and shuffled downhill along the Gürtel toward Nussdorferstrasse. From there, she took Alserbachstrasse, past the Franz Josefs train station....

"And now I've got to cross the canal..."

She walked across the Danube Canal on Friedensbrücke, the Peace Bridge, and then turned...

"and now I've to walk along the canal and look out for dogs...."

After three or four blocks, Laura turned left and went along Obere Augartenstrasse, the Upper Augarten Street, until she came to the entrance near a palace. But even after walking from her apartment, Laura wasn't rid of the wine, which lingered bitterly in the recesses of her mouth, and so she sat down at the first bench, just inside the gardens, where she could see the blossoms, and in the background those Nazi flak towers left behind at the end of the war. Everywhere, she saw dogs.

"Dogs," thought Laura. "More cats in Vienna than dogs, at least according to that guidebook, but dogs and dog excrement everywhere. Perhaps the cats never recovered from the war. But the dogs—just yesterday there were dogs at the café, muzzled and leashed dogs, strassenbahn and U-Bahn dogs, and little dogs that fit into those old lady baskets. Just so they don't have to buy tickets for the train."

Laura, however, would soon learn that truly magical dogs romp through the gardens at Augarten, and the game they play is a game of wonder. Most dogs in Vienna do not bark, and so in fact Laura only heard one dog bark at Augarten that day. Dogs which have not been trained to resist biting or barking are muzzled and leashed. However, the magical porcelain dogs of Augarten may roam at will, and Laura was about to hear about these magical dogs from the man with the golden-tipped cane who approached her as she entered the palace grounds and sat down on a nearby bench.

He might have been a retired priest, or perhaps a teacher. He was old, very old, and he walked very carefully, lightly tapping the ground with his wonderful cane. He walked so slowly . . . he must have begun his morning walk around the gardens hours ago, perhaps years ago. Dogs cut back and forth in front of him, but he just kept walking, walking to Laura's bench, as if he had something to say which made his march seem so necessary. But when he finally reached the bench, he simply sat at the other end and said nothing. Laura could not tell if he were resting or quietly dying.

And then, two men emerged from the Augarten maze, two men carrying sheets of paper and arguing with each other. They knew the old man with the golden-tipped cane: they came to the bench and sat between the old man and Laura.

"Greetings, dear Uncle."

"Good day, Fritz Wassermann. And to you as well, Franz."

Even though Laura thought the two men might be only slightly younger than she was, Fritz and Franz seemed to act much younger; perhaps it was their arguing. The Wassermann twins, it seemed, looked so alike yet acted so differently. Fritz smiled at the old man and at Laura; Franz scowled at the roses.

"Good day," Laura nodded to both Fritz and the old man.

"Good day."

"Yes, a good day to you."

The old man seemed content to be at rest, and the brothers looked a bit hung over, perhaps chronically hung over, and so the four of them sat quietly on the bench, trying not to disturb the spirits. But at last the old man spoke, and though Laura attempted to ignore the language she could not yet completely understand, she found herself mentally translating his words:

"You boys know that the Wassermann Family has long held a special place in the hearts of all Viennese. Your stories for your English studies, your stories from Währing–our beloved Eighteenth District–should likewise hold a special place in the hearts of all. Our tradition is one of memory, not forgetting, of patience, not anger. You must stop quarreling and finish the tales. In German and in English! I have said enough."

With that, the old man rose slowly, smiled at the brothers, tapped Laura's leg with the golden-tipped cane, and pointed to a group of dogs, playing with a small bone. One would walk with the bone, and the others would run about, hoping that the dog would drop the bone. The dogs were not leashed, nor were they muzzled, and no owners appeared to control them. They ran back and forth across the field, again and again. The man with the golden-tipped cane smiled at the dogs and at Laura.

"Fritz, Franz, till we next meet. And you madame," he said, turning slowly to face Laura and speaking in English, "I hope and wish that you can make the time to browse through, explore, discover, and enjoy all of the Eighteenth District on your own and to keep active sightseeing and leisurely contemplation in a pleasurable harmony. I wish you nothing but blue skies, apricot schnapps, and memories for your future! Till we meet again."

As the old man with the golden cane stepped carefully, slowly, regularly on the garden walk toward the Augarten maze, Laura felt she should say something, but not too loudly and certainly nothing provocative. She thought it best if she first asked the brothers if they spoke English.

"Ja. A little," said Fritz. "My brother speaks even better. We are both students in English at the University. We work with Professor Wagner. You have heard of him?"

"No. I haven't, but I just arrived in Vienna. Are you both related?"

"Bah!" replied Franz.

"No. I mean to the old man."

"He took care of us after the war, after our parents were

killed in the bombings," said Fritz. "Herr Winkelmann is our uncle and our guardian."

"I see. And those papers? Your guardian said that they are part of your English language studies."

"Yes," said Fritz. "I write my stories in German, and my brother translates them into English; my brother does the same for his stories, which I translate into English. We do this to improve our English."

"My tales; his fancies. Read them yourself." Franz was not growing friendlier.

"Please excuse my inexcusable brother. I am, madame, Fritz Wassermann; this is my brother, Franz. We have written tales about Vienna's Eighteenth District, tales we believe would be of interest."

"My tales are of interest. Yours are careless sentiment."

"Franz, please. Perhaps, madame, you might be interested?"

Despite Franz's words, it seemed to Laura that they both wanted someone to listen to their words, which it seemed she must, and someone to read the tales they wrote about Vienna.

"Yes. I am interested. Please tell me more, but quietly, please."

Fritz said that they spent most mornings at bookstores in the First District, reading books about Vienna–guide books, travel books, histories, maps, books by visitors–and at museums and churches, reading brochures, pamphlets, and guides–

"But you never have enough money to buy any of the books," Franz interrupted.

Each afternoon, Fritz continued, after they had stopped at the hot sausage stand on Währingerstrasse for a frankfurter and beer, they would try to reconstruct what they remembered about the books and what they themselves had experienced in Vienna.

"We often argue," said Franz, "for my brother is an idiot."

"But," added Fritz, "we write it all down, and, if you wish, we would like to share it with you."

"Yes–please. Tell me one of your tales."

"Franz, I believe she might appreciate the tale of the dogs of Augarten."

"Bah! The dogs' tale–my tale, your tale. Tell her, Fritz. But do not expect me to correct you."

Fritz closed his eyes, so that he could remember correctly, he said, and began the tale of the Dogs of Augarten:

"Elisabeth knew of the magic of the dogs of Augarten," Fritz told Laura, "and so each October morning, she went to Augarten with her umbrella in search of the magic. Elisabeth loved dogs almost as much as she loved porcelain, especially porcelain dogs...."

"Bah!" interrupted Franz Wassermann, "Elisabeth lived in the flak tower and stole porcelain figurines from stupid tourists...."

"Franz, please do not interrupt."

"Go on, Mister Wassermann," said Laura.

"Yes. On one October morning, Elisabeth once again went to Augarten with her umbrella and bought a porcelain dog. Elisabeth then took her porcelain dog to the garden, took it out of its box, unwrapped it, and very carefully placed it next to a rosebush . . ."

"Once again, Fritz, you cannot recall the tale correctly. Elisabeth sat waiting in the Augarten maze until the woman dressed in fur and golden bracelets put down her package securely wrapped in Augarten ribbons...."

"No. Franz, you are mistaken. Elisabeth sang the song her mother had taught her, the 'Song of the Emperor's Lost Child.'"

"'The Song of the Wicked Child's Terrible Disgrace,' and the furry woman shook her golden chains in disgust and fear, for Elisabeth's voice growled like the devil's. The wealthy woman ran from the bench, leaving behind her precious porcelain hound...."

"Madame," said Fritz to Laura, "you must forgive my unruly brother. You see, he writes stories about his own life. However, in the authentic tale of the Dogs of Augarten, when Elisabeth sang 'The Song of the Emperor's Lost Child,' the dog came alive and began barking and jumped on Elisabeth. Naturally, Elisabeth was overjoyed."

"Fritz, you reduce horror to cheap sentiment. You see, madame," said Franz, who seemed to grow friendlier and friendlier even as Fritz became more and more agitated at the interruptions, "the dog did indeed become alive, but it snapped at Elisabeth, and then ran across the rose gardens, frightened children and cowardly retrievers...."

Fritz scowled at his brother and gripped the bench, it seemed, to avoid attacking Franz. He spoke louder and faster, trying to outpace Franz, trying to complete the tale as Fritz knew it should be completed before Franz could change history:

"Elisabeth and the dog ran throughout the park and played with the children until the sun began to set and the fog fell from the skies, when Elisabeth knew that she must return to her home...."

"Elisabeth whipped the dog and cursed the children. Elisabeth and her devil dog trampled on the blooms of Augarten–frightened parents tried to comfort their weeping children...."

"Elisabeth ran to the rosebush, called to her dog, and once more sang the . . ."

"'Song of the Wicked Child's Terrible Disgrace' . . ."

"'Song of the Emperor's Lost Child.'" Fritz stood up and fired his words directly at Franz, who slowly rose to accept the challenge. "The dog turned back to porcelain," said Fritz.

"The dog turned to porcelain," Franz agreed.

"and Elisabeth put it back into the box . . ."

"and Elisabeth put it back into the box . . ."

"which she tapped lightly with her umbrella. Elisabeth and her porcelain hound went home."

"which she tapped lightly with her umbrella. Elisabeth returned to her home in the flak tower and dropped the box from atop the tower, shattering the porcelain dog of Augarten."

Fritz and Franz stood only a few feet from each other–Fritz trembling, shaking, his face transformed from pink to red to crimson; Franz smiling, satisfied, triumphant.

"That is a remarkable tale," Laura told them. "Do you have others?"

The Wassermann brothers seemed to be repeating a scene they had often rehearsed, alone, perhaps, or for another stranger who had come to Augarten to see the dogs run and the flowers bloom before the killing frosts.

"You are a boor, Franz, a lower-class, drunken Viennese boor!"

"Fritz, dear brother, you are a sentimental fool."

"Perhaps I should be leaving?" said Laura. To the Wassermanns, to all Augarten and all Vienna, Laura was as irrelevant as spoiled mayonnaise. But she could not resist the urge to speak to them, to try and prevent a scene, a fight, a duel– at least to silence them. She told the Wassermann brothers that indeed she would like to read their tales, but she could not, just then, read them immediately. She tried to urge calm, dignity.

Franz calmly walked away from his brother; Fritz followed closely, shouting that Franz acted shamefully. "You betray everything the family stands for; Franz you are a pig, an ape dressed in beggar's clothes!"

Franz responded, but in words Laura could no longer distinguish. The two of them, arguing still, walked into the Augarten maze, where, it seemed, they disappeared, leaving behind a stack of papers. Laura was uncertain whether she should leave the tales on the bench for the Wassermann brothers to retrieve, or if they intended to leave them for her to read. Fearful that a breeze might simply scatter their work across the Augarten lawn, she carefully gathered the papers and returned a bit puzzled to her apartment.

On her third day in the City of Dreams, Laura was content to remain in her apartment, once again organizing her clothes and resisting plans and memories. She carefully folded her scarves, sorted through her papers on the table facing the one window in the apartment, and, for the second time that morning, arranged the little food she had bought in the refrigerator. Finally tired of ordering her life, as the skies darkened she turned to the tales the Wassermann brothers had left.

"Thank God, they're in English," thought Laura. "I am too tired to read in German."

Laura found that the tales were all short fables, or perhaps fantasies, or even transcripts of a person's dreams, and so she could easily read through most of the stories. She found them at times cheerful and at other times gloomy and depressing. "It's easy to see which ones Fritz wrote and which ones Franz composed," said Laura to the apartment walls. "At least they all have an ending."

Josef

Josef lived his life as the catacomb sweeper of St. Stephan's. Josef worked very hard, but he had little money. Each morning before the sun arose, he disappeared deep into the catacombs to clean them. He only emerged when the tourists had departed and after the sun had set, when he went to Karlsplatz, where he spent the night. On one cold December day, Josef went deeper and deeper into the catacombs, where he discovered a cave which no one had seen for hundreds of years. In one recess of the cave, Josef discovered a nest of frozen scorpions, left by the Turks. The bishop of St. Stephan's had ordered his soldiers to bury the scorpions, but Josef thought that the scorpions should breathe once again, and so he carried them out of the catacombs. When Josef emerged from the cathedral, the sun was shining brightly and many tourists were walking about Stefansplatz. The warm sun brought the scorpions back to life, and they thanked Josef by kissing him again and again on his arms. Because Josef had never seen Stefansplatz in daylight, he was entranced and so did not feel any pain from the scorpions' kisses. The people in Stefansplatz could only stare at Josef and the scorpions; however, the crows from the Vienna Woods saw the scorpions and flew to Josef's arms to eat them. The scorpions would not let go of Josef's arms, and so the crows carried the scorpions and Josef into the hills above Vienna.

"Josef," Laura thought, "you should have stayed in the catacombs, where the dead lay quietly. Silly man."

Laura put the tales down on the table next to her bed and tried to avoid nightmares in her third night in the City of Dreams. She slept for a few hours, but too soon she imagined a shadow of herself, lost in an endless labyrinth and pursued by a faceless man, whose footsteps pounded against the stone floors of the passages which she could not escape. She suddenly awoke, as once again the sounds of nearby construction rattled the windows of her apartment, which seemed wrapped in a dense haze.

On the morning of this fourth day in Vienna, an early November fog had come tumbling down the hills of the Vienna Woods—grey, thick, circling all in its embrace, offering—or so it seemed—anonymity and security to the innocent and the guilty.

Even in the intimacy of fog, however, Laura knew she could not speak to anyone about the infant son whom she had lost, only hours after his birth. A regretful body called her son, a weight, a burden once held and then released for burial, entombed in the vernacular of death. She visited the grave at the beginning of each November, stone angels' wings forever resisting flight. Perhaps, she believed that her husband, her ex-husband, might spend a few minutes at the gravesite, but it seemed unlikely—and she would never know if he ever thought of their buried son or of her. Laura thought as well of Jonathan Hopewell and even more of his mother.

It was not a morning to walk the streets of the city or to stroll in the Augarten maze and search for the porcelain dog. It was a day to remain secure in the apartment and find refuge in a cup of herbal tea. "Perhaps," thought Laura, "perhaps one of the tales might distract me."

Peter Widders

Peter Widders loved Bertha Waage, and Bertha Waage loved Peter Widders. However, the parents of Peter and the parents of Bertha did not want their children to marry. And so Bertha's parents moved to a house on the other side of Schafberg. Every night Bertha wept for Peter, and every night Peter searched the woods for a path to Bertha's house. On a cold night in November a terrible fog descended on the woods, but Peter still searched for the path. He wandered for many hours in the woods, but he never found it. Finally, he sat by a giant oak tree and fell asleep. When the fog disappeared, Peter also disappeared. Bertha heard that Peter had disappeared, and so when the fog next returned, she snuck out of her house to look for Peter. She searched the woods for many hours, but she never found Peter. And so she sat by a giant oak tree and wept. Peter was on the other side of the oak tree, and when he heard Bertha weeping, he awoke. Bertha and Peter married each other by that giant oak tree, and when the fog again disappeared, Bertha and Peter also disappeared.

"Bertha and Peter disappear together," said Laura to herself. "A romantic ending, I suppose. I just need to find the right tree."

Rather than look for a tree, Laura rode the tram into the city, hoping to find release in a quiet corner of a quiet café. She walked through the First District and finally chose Café Hawelka, which she had read offered poets and writers the smoky inspiration which enabled them to finish a tale. "Perhaps," she imagined, "Fritz and Franz and Mister Winkelmnn might be there." After one hour and two small coffees in the rear of Hawelka, Laura thought she saw Fritz and Franz, or perhaps two men resembling the twins, both draped in long green overcoats, get up from a table near the entrance and argue through the door. She quickly rose, hopeful that she might have some words with two of the three people she had met in Vienna.

As she left Hawelka, Laura hesitated, looking left and right into the dense fog, hoping to discover the trail of Fritz and Franz, but she only saw the dense grey wall into which the Wassermanns had apparently vanished. She heard the sound of two voices and heavy footsteps somewhere to her left, and so she decided to follow them, hoping that she might catch the twins and ask for more of their stories, all of which had conclusions. She quickened her pace and came closer to the two figures, who turned to face her as they heard her approach. Even as near as the figures were, Laura was not certain what confronted her–a tall cleric dressed in red robes and holding a staff with a wondrously curved top, St. Nikolaus, it seemed, out days too early with his demonic companion, Krampus, horned like a hairy goat with a huge red tongue descending from his evil eyes and a serpentine tail from beneath a large basket which hung from his back. He carried chains and stiff reeds and only spoke in guttural curses, as he sought out misbehaving children whom he might punish for their evil ways. Laura felt their gaze linger over her body for too long. And then the fog seemed to wrap itself around the figures, who disappeared into the Vienna night.

As Laura tried to decide which grey, narrow street might lead her back to her apartment, she heard the tap-tap-tap of something striking the cobbled street and drawing closer to her. She saw the golden tip of the cane before she recognized Mister Winkelmann emerging magically from the dense fog.

"Mister Winkelmann?" Laura asked. "Is it you?"

"Ah, the woman from Augarten. Good day, wonderful lady. What brings you out on such an evening?"

"I am trying to find my way home," said Laura. "And you, Mister Winkelmann, what errand are you on tonight?"

"My dear, I come to the First District each night to see what magic the city might devise to entertain us all."

"On such a night, I could well use some distraction. Do you have any wisdom which might help me?"

"Wisdom I lack. The machinery of the world is far too complex for a simple man like myself. But perhaps a story from Vienna's past might keep you warm on this foggy evening."

"Yes, please do tell me such a tale."

"My dear, have you heard of the miraculous bagpiper, Lieber Augustin?"

"I have not."

"It is said that during the plague of 1679 in Vienna, the bagpiper der liebe Augustin slumped drunk in the gutter one night. Taken for dead, he was put in the plague pit. He woke and attracted attention by playing his pipes, and he was rescued. Miraculously, they say, he did not catch the plague. For centuries Augustin has been a protector of the city."

"That is," said Laura, "a tale which does give some hope, I

suppose."

"Indeed, it does provide hope and solace, and perhaps some warning against overindulgence. We might also learn that no act is final–perhaps it is true that nothing can occur only once. We might imagine ourselves at the end of time, which it too often appears we are. But perhaps it is also true that everything is counterbalanced by another. Thus, we may anticipate both unforeseen harmonies and endless returns. And now, dear lady, I must be on my way. There is still so much of the City to inspect before I return to my beloved Eighteenth District. Good evening."

"And good evening to you, Mister Winklemann, and my thanks." Laura listened to the sounds of Herr Winkelmann's cane echoing through the inner city's deserted lanes and hoped that Augustin could again fill the Vienna nights with magical music from his bagpipe.

Laura did not know how long she walked, but she finally found herself outside her apartment. She saw herself then as a weary figure who stood outside an apartment building, and that weary figure struggled to fit a key into the building's one entrance and then struggled again to open the apartment door. The fog had sucked the energy from Laura's spirit, and so she sunk into the only chair which the owner had supplied. She had escaped Nikolaus and Krampus, and she had escaped the chilling force of the fog, and, at least for the moment, she felt as if she had some rights to the sanctuary of the apartment and even more the comfort of a warm bed.

But as she slept, Laura could not escape the past, which that night haunted her dreams. Nikolaus appeared, but rather than the aged bishop's smile, she saw an infant's face, with tears in his eyes. Then suddenly Nikolaus was gone, and in his place stood that devil-goat, that hoary monster, who put the infant into his basket and then turned directly to face Laura. It was Jonathan Hopewell, transformed and reaching for Laura's throat. She felt that she was in a dream dreamed by someone else, a dream that she was on the verge of understanding. Just then, she awoke, trembling and hoping to end the nightmare, but knowing that the person she would meet would still be herself. She reached for the light and tried to find a tale of the Wassermann brothers which would enable her to outlast the night.

Heinrich Steier

There are many strange and wonderful creatures in the Pötzleinsdorf Schlosspark. There are flying deer, dancing squirrels, and singing roosters. However, the strangest and most wonderful creature of all is the talking crow. The talking crow has golden wings and a silver beak, and he is the king of the park. Heinrich Steier knew about the talking crow, and he was determined to capture him. And so Heinrich took his net, his rope, his bag, and his magic stones to the park. He covered himself with leaves and pretended he was a tree. The deer flew to his arms; the squirrels danced around him; the roosters sang at his feet. But the talking crow did not come, and so Heinrich remained motionless. Finally the crow came to Heinrich's arm, but Heinrich could not move. 'You are a silly person,' said the crow. 'Now you will always be a tree, and I will always be the king of the park.' And so Heinrich himself became the strangest and most wonderful creature in the Pötzleinsdorf Schlosspark.

Laura was not sure if she was that silly person transformed in the park or the talking crow who was so wise. All her magic stones could not help Jonathan Hopewell, nor could her wisdom keep her son alive. Now she was alone in another country with only the tales of the Wassermann brothers to rock her to sleep. "I'm the ruler of the whole wonderful park," said the crow, "Yes I am. I am."

The voices of Russian crows awakened Laura the next morning. The fog had lifted from the streets and sidewalks, but it still was suspended over the city in a misty haze that made every building seem to stop suddenly at the fifth floor. From her apartment window, she seemed to peer down from the clouds to the shrouded figures trudging on their way to bakeries, shops, or classes. Everyone seemed intent on the next step, and no one looked up to see why Laura gazed on them.

"A day to remain inside," thought Laura, "and to see if the Wassermanns offer any release from this oppressive fog."

Sabine

On Sunday mornings, Sabine Steinbock would always go to Schönbrunn. She loved the flower gardens and always dreamed of living there. Sabine spent many hours walking the gardens, where she would pretend that she was Empress of Schönbrunn. Many other people would be in the gardens, but they never saw Sabine. She was a small, quiet child and people seldom noticed her. On one still and clear October morning, Sabine once again went to the gardens, where she stood before the fountain. She removed her clothes and disappeared into the waters. The next morning, a small rose bush began growing near the fountain. Soon the rose bush was the largest and most beautiful flower in all of Schönbrunn.

"Such a hopeful story," Laura said to the apartment walls.

"I wonder if Fritz wrote this one, or if his tale was translated by Franz. I should return to Augarten to ask them."

As Laura left her apartment, she was confronted, once again, by the dense fog, a deadly embrace which she felt both threatening and irresistible. She turned to her left, but could not remember how many blocks she should walk before turning to her right. The third street seemed to be familiar, but then so many streets had so many apartment buildings, all of which offered the same grey doors and the same closed windows. Laura knew that she could not find her way to Augarten on that day, and she feared that she might never escape the chilled, humid air which was reaching deep into her lungs. After twenty minutes of confused steps and misdirection, she came to a tram stop, one which, she hoped, might take her to Schottentor and the familiar safety of the Inner City.

The fog obscured all those landmarks which might have seemed familiar: even the voice of the tram announcing the next stop seemed reduced to a murky whisper. The only clear message was that the tram had reached Schottentor, the end station at which Laura followed the other passengers to the underground passage to the Inner City. The First District alone seemed immune to the effects of the fog, so that Laura was able to find her way to Café Central, where she could sip coffee, read the papers, and watch other people watching other people, still looking for her story.

Laura, who had slept very little the night before, sat waiting for her mélange and resenting nearly everyone and everything. She again sat at a table near the entrance to Café Central, not reading a newspaper for hours this time, but scribbling and erasing, writing and revising in an attempt to write her own story.

> I have listened too long to the stories of others, and
> so now I must compose myself. My life has been,
> for the most part, a fairly easy one. I had a com-

fortable childhood, a privileged education, and a successful career. If it weren't for my marriage and the death of my son, and Jonathan Hopewell, poor Jonathan....

After two hours at Café Central, Laura slowly walked toward the Ring, trying to see if she was cursed, exhausted, or simply haunted. She could not focus on what she thought were beautiful Italian women, who must have lives of romance and glamor; she could barely watch her feet take the next step. And then, on a kiosk near Schottentor, where all those lines meet, she saw a most curious poster. And, thought Laura, she saw her name next to the announcement:

> An honorary Reward is proposed to any Cabalist who shall demonstrate that the Letter Z contains more occult Virtues than the Letter X.

This, thought Laura, was a puzzling announcement, like an enigma overheard by a mystic, one she had never heard from any of her clients. But on that mid-day in November, Laura simply told the poster: "I'll tend to you tomorrow. What I need now is someone who will listen." And so she went to a café on Stefansplatz, opposite Stock im Eisen, where merchants from Vienna had driven nails into a tree, hoping for good luck. On this day, Laura was hoping to find a way to begin.

But on this dreary November day, she'd grown too tired for any writing–on napkins, on postcards, on any surface at all. To keep up appearances, she looked at the menu–as if she had been up all night writing another version of her story, or sitting at a smoky café all morning. She breathed in and out as she imagined a writer should breathe, and she rubbed her eyes the way writers, all writers, must rub their eyes after hours of work. In fact, Laura had to rub her eyes just to see the menu:

Mélange	25 Ö.S.
Rotwein	35 Ö.S.
Guilt-Memory-Anxiety	Good for nothing but Sin
Weisswein	30 Ö.S.

"Why do I need any more anxiety?" thought Laura, "and what is it doing on the menu? How many orders did they have today? Everyone else at the café is sitting content." Those who had gotten their coffee seemed happy. Or at least quiet.

Directly opposite Laura sat an elderly Austrian, a gentleman who must have disliked Hitler, thought Laura, and so could claim to have fought in the resistance. Or rather, at one time, he was a gentleman, or at least a man with a title, who now wore the same gray suit which he had worn at the funeral procession of one of the last Habsburgs, and the same faded brown shoes which he wore at the proclamation of Perpetual and Disinterested Neutrality. He probably would order a large cup of Sorrow and enjoy sipping it all afternoon.

As the resistance fighter puffed and spat in time into a small brass cup, he turned to face Laura, and he moved his lips, and Laura heard the voice again: "Every person with self-respect enough to become effective has had to account for herself somehow, and to invent a formula of her own for her universe, if the standard formulas failed." Laura had heard these words before; Laura had heard all the words before, but she had no napkins to write on, and she was very, very tired. The old man turned back to his coffee, as if he had not spoken to Laura, but had merely tried to clear his throat in the damp November air.

No one else noticed Laura.

"Don't these people know what I have been doing all year?" Laura dug into her pocket where she found yet another beginning which she had written on napkins from another café in another part of the city:

When I reached the summit, I sat on a summer-hikers' bench and looked over the city, spread out below me, indistinct in the falling snow, but radiant, whole, glorious. On Schafberg, above the complaints of friends and the demands of family and above memory.

The cold moved slowly through my toes and feet, and I realized that if I did not leave soon, I would have difficulty walking down the hillside. I had heard of homeless men found frozen on the streets of Vienna, even in the City, and I knew that few people walked the Vienna Woods this late in the snow. But I also knew that I could not yet let go of the vision of the City below me. And so I stayed–minutes and minutes longer–so that when I came down from the mountain, I could recall my fantasy of Vienna–complete, whole, wondrous, finished.

She stared through the empty wine glass at a world of distorted faces and fantastic shapes. A golden ball emerged from the crowd and moved quickly toward her.

"Tap-tap," she heard, louder and louder, "tap-tap, tap-tap, tap-tap." Laura put down the wine glass, and saw a familiar figure approaching the chair opposite hers.

"You do not mind if I join you?" he asked.

"No. Of course. I am alone."

"Have you been alone since we last met?"

"Yes, although I seem to have descended into greater solitude today."

"I believe Fritz and Franz left their tales with you. Perhaps they provide some companionship."

"They have enabled me to find some companionship, Mister Winkelmann. Yes. The tales are wonderfully useful." Even on that dreary day, Laura could not resist a smile.

"Such fictions often enable us to find solace. They link us to the universal myth of the chain of generations, I believe," said the old man with the golden cane. "And perhaps they make the thought of dying more acceptable and relieve some of the terror that comes of knowing death."

"Do you often think of death, Mister Winkelmann?"

"At my age such thoughts are intimate companions. I am forever engaged in a conversation that takes place between infinity and eternity. I have come to realize that years do not change our essence: I have read that stones want to go on being stones, forever and ever, until they crumble to dust. We learn very little during our lives, except perhaps that happiness holds no mystery because it is its own justification."

"My son died three years ago, and I have been in Vienna for only such a short time. I am not sure I have learned anything."

"Perhaps you must learn how to deal with your own death as well. Such thoughts can provide the beginning of what is beautiful, for only when we contemplate death, does beauty emerge as possibility."

"I don't know, Mister Winkelmann."

"Perhaps you must then release yourself to the tales you did not finish before you came to Vienna," said the old man with the golden cane, as he slowly rose from the table. "Perhaps you must leave the City of Dreams, eh?"

"I believe I must."

Mister Winkelmann tipped his hat and nodded farewell to Laura, the tap-tap-tap of his golden cane on the pavement fading with each step he took.

"Yes. It is time for me to leave Vienna."

Laura sipped her wine and used the pen left by the waiter to write another beginning to another tale on the backside of yet another postcard. But Laura could not finish even the task of a beginning, and the tale soon dissolved into meaningless circles on the edge of the postcard, wordless, interminable.

On the morning of her final day in Vienna, Laura gathered

the tales of the Wassermann brothers, and released them out the window to the treeless courtyard below. A light breeze caught the sheets and scattered them across the narrow streets of Vienna.

On the flight from Vienna to Chicago, Laura first tried to sleep, but in one of the rows in front of her the sound of an argument between two men became louder and louder. The men spoke and then shouted in German, and so Laura could only make out occasional phrases amid their angry insults. After a few minutes, the men became quiet, although one of them seemed to whisper words in English: "oaf," "primitive," "betrayal." As the plane drifted across the English Channel, one of the men rose from his seat and seemed to look directly at Laura and speak her name: "Sabine." A woman in the row in front of Laura turned to the man and smiled. The man simply walked past Laura, who could not find him again.

Laura began doodling, circles within circles and then boxes within boxes. At the bottom of the third page of her intricate scribbling, she hesitated, and then added the names of people she must see again. She did not include her ex-husband. Laura hesitated before adding Mrs. Hopewell, but she then began doodling again, over and over, circling Mrs. Hopewell's name with finely drawn lines. She dropped the pen beneath her seat and finally drifted to sleep. Just before she awoke, she imagined her mother and her father, marching hand in hand behind the bagpipers–the volume turned higher and higher– shaking the windows, waking the dead.

Chapter 5
Culpable Nouns and Mysterious Fog In the City of Dreams
Vienna, 1981-1983

I. Nouns of Delight

Two years before Laura came to Vienna, an academic treasure had been granted to the fairly well known and respected Professor of Semantics and Anglo Languages, Professor Bernhard Wagner, the same Professor Wagner under whom Fritz and Franz Wassermann were studying English when Laura met them.

Funds from the Austrian Ministry had enabled Professor Doctor Bernhard Wagner of the University of Vienna Department of Language and Linguistics to hire three assistants for what he called his Nominification Institute. Although he had many responsibilities and had treated many colleagues as his assistants, he had in fact never conducted interviews or reviewed the credentials of candidates for assistantships. He thus arranged a meeting with Professor Doctor Reinhold Schneider, a distinguished senior colleague who had experience with assistants. After Professor Doctor Wagner explained the significance of the Ministry's trust in his judgment, he asked Professor Doctor Schneider if he had any suggestions.

"Why, I may have several qualified young scholars who may be of assistance."

"Indeed. Excellent. Whom would you recommend?"

"There is one young scholar whom you might consider, although you should not let her physical appearance deceive you."

"Her appearance? What is it about her appearance which might affect her position?"

"Her name is Johanna Stubblemeier, and she has a quite ... pleasant appearance."

"But is she qualified?"

"Indeed. She has a fine record of respectable research. Very attractive research. Very well done."

"Perhaps you could arrange a meeting for me with Magisterin Stubblemeier?"

"I may be able to do so. But you must realize that I have many professional obligations."

"Of course. As we all do."

Professor Doctor Wagner, being a man of action if not focus, devoted considerable thought to the credentials of Johanna Stubblemeier, whom he hired after a brief conversation.

Johanna suggested to Professor Doctor Wagner that the Ministry's funds would support two additional assistants. "Perhaps," Johanna told the Professor, "the Ministry might look favorably on your institute if the staff were a bit larger—and of course we will have more than enough work."

"I have had the same thought, Magisterin Stubblemeier, precisely what I was considering last week. Obviously, I must carefully review any candidates, but then I have many other obligations. Do you know of anyone who might meet the Institute's standards and have the necessary credentials?"

Johanna had anticipated Wagner's crowded schedule and his regard for the Institute's reputation, and so had brought with her the resumes of her good friends, Beata Fuchstberger and Gunter Stadtbad. Both Beata and Gunter had been in Wagner's classes and received the highest grades, and Wagner had written the same response to both their final seminar projects: "fine work, although a bit short of complete annotation." Being a busy man, however, Wagner remembered neither Beata nor Gunter but still approved hiring them as Johanna's assistants.

Johanna often walked through the Pőtzleinsdorfer Schlosspark to escape the academic confines of the University. From the hillside of the Schafberg, high above the Inner City, she could envision a world without the bother of busy men, a world in which she could complete the work too often credited to others. Unknown to Professor Doctor Wagner, she had begun her doctoral dissertation under the direction of another faculty member—Professor Sylvia Mayer, who encouraged Jo-

hanna to write her feminist reading of modern American po-
etry, a topic with which Professor Wagner had no familiarity
but for which he had considerable disdain. Johanna endured
the work at his Institute, but she enjoyed the company of Beata
and Gunter, two close friends from the Department of English
and American Studies.

Beata was a year younger than Johanna and had not yet
finished her degree or her final seminar project on Nathaniel
Hawthorne's critical essays. Beata worked diligently each day
at the Institute, and each weekend she spent camping with
members of the Austrian Medieval Reenactment Society—a
society which gave Beata an alternate identity and access to
costumes from ages past. Gunter likewise spent his weekends
outside Vienna, but he devoted himself to white water rafting
and to revisions of his project on animal characters in carnival
tales from the English Renaissance.

All three of Wagner's assistants agreed to meet each Thursday morning for a walk through the Schlosspark where they
would talk of their plans and avoid all mention of Professor
Wagner, who had begun spending Thursday mornings at Café
Landtmann with his colleague Professor Doctor Schneider.

Two weeks after the three were hired, as Wagner and
Schneider waited for their Thursday morning coffee, a young
man hurried past them, knocking a chair into Schneider's table and excusing himself in what was, to Wagner, very clearly
a Midwestern American accent. The man was in fact, young
Felix Kulpa. Felix left the café without explaining his hurry
to either Professor Doctor Wagner or Professor Doctor Schneider. Reinhold Schneider, a very careful and a very fair man,
was above all a very orderly man. He liked coming to Café
Landtmann each Thursday for coffee with Professor Doctor
Wagner, and he very much disliked disturbances.

"My dear, Professor Wagner, these Americans have no
manners and no sense of decorum. They act like buffaloes,
whether they're on the prairie or in the café."

"Quite so, Professor Schneider, quite so."

"Indeed. They fail to understand the expectations we have for careful scholarship and thorough documentation. I am afraid that at times these New World academics pay far too little attention to documentation."

"I believe it may be possible to describe their behavior in grammatical terms," answered Professor Doctor Wagner, likewise a very careful and a very orderly man. "Yes. A most fitting example of the potency of the noun."

"You must understand, dear colleague," continued Professor Doctor Wagner, "that the verb is never more than the universal expression of attribution, whereas nouns proliferate in endless differentiation, and this taxonomic function is manifested in language by the substantives. At one time, I toyed with the possibility of a language that had no nouns, as dear Borges wrote, 'a language of impersonal verbs or incalculable adjectives.' However, I soon realized my error." (Wagner had never read any Borges, although he had heard Borges' name mentioned by a colleague whose name he did not recall and who frequently quoted this passage.) "Indeed, my colleague, language itself is nothing in itself but an immense rustling of denominations that are overlaying one another, contracting into one another, hiding one another, and yet preserving themselves in existence in order to permit the analysis or the composition of the most complex representations. We must, dear colleague, always keep in mind that there forever remains a dormant nominification–all words, of whatever kind, are dormant nouns."

Professor Doctor Wagner had observed that in English grammar books–proper English grammar books–the discussion of nouns occurs in the first chapters and therefore occupies much of students' attention. "Quite deservedly so," Professor Wagner asserted, then continued, failing to notice that Professor Schneider was politely ignoring his words.

"Indeed, Professor Schneider, of the fifty-six English as a

Second Language grammar texts which I have studied, forty-five devote one of their first three chapters to nouns. In seven of these forty-five, the third chapter includes a discussion of nouns; in sixteen of the forty-five, the description of nouns is found in chapter two. In twenty-two, nouns make their appearance in the first chapter. This is," Professor Doctor Wagner stated, "a rather remarkable statistic, in fact, quite a grammatarian epiphany. My dear colleague, if we place our trust in our profession," Professor Doctor Wagner said–as he had frequently said, and here repeated– "and if we make a practice of the preaching we do, we should follow these occurrences to their quite reasonable results."

"And these results are?" Professor Doctor Schneider interjected, as he rubbed his glasses clean and looked across the café at what appeared to be, without his glasses on, a very attractive female student.

Professor Doctor Wagner would have offered his findings to anyone who would listen to his position on the consequences of a noun-centered curriculum. Professor Doctor Wagner was convinced that the taxonomy he proposed was quite complete, although he was aware that many of the specific class exercises remained to be developed. However, he spoke with confidence: he had developed a thorough system which was adaptable to a variety of educational contexts. And thus when Schneider asked, Wagner was willing to explain.

"The classification provides," he argued, "a pedagogically-sound approach to the systematic study of the English language. To wit," he reported (as much to the surrounding tables as to Schneider), "separate units should be devoted to the following:

1. compound nouns
2. collective nouns
3. proper nouns
4. plural nouns

5. abstract nouns
6. nouns without precedence
7. nouns with stature and nouns without
8. nouns in positions of particular significance
9. power nouns
10. nouns to be used when in doubt
11. nouns without modifiers
12. nouns of desire
13. tentatively modified nouns
14. action nouns
15. nouns constructed from weak verbs
16. nouns constructed from powerful verbs
17. nouns which would prefer to be adjectives
18. adverbial nouns
19. seldom used nouns
20. frequently used nouns
21. new nouns
22. nouns from German
23. nouns from French
24. nouns from Latin
25. nouns with no recognizable origin
26. nouns which properly belong in other languages."

"I see," said Professor Schneider as he replaced his glasses on his very prominent nose. "Yes. Very interesting."

As Professor Doctor Wagner further explained, he had first presented his system to Austrian language instructors at a conference held each November in Niederösterreich. The response was not as enthusiastic as Professor Doctor Wagner had hoped, but he believed that the teachers were not properly trained in classical linguistics, nor were they prepared to accept the consequences of Professor Doctor Wagner's discovery. Nor, it seems, was Professor Doctor Schneider, who continued to glance at the young woman at the other table.

Although Professor Doctor Wagner found that much of his

energy was devoted to locating additional funds for the continuation of his project, he did find time to assign tasks to his
three assistants. Professor Doctor Wagner believed that he was
most fortunate in his choice of his assistants. Each one pos-
sessed skills necessary for the project, but none of the three
seemed, at least to Professor Doctor Wagner, capable of com-
prehending the whole. Thus, Professor Doctor Wagner seemed
assured of maintaining control of the research and power over
his assistants.

However, it seems that Professor Doctor Wagner was mistaken.

Magisterin Stubblemaier first suggested that the assistants
slightly modify Professor Doctor Wagner's list to see if he indeed checked their work. She therefore added the following
subchapters:

    a. nouns we would rather not know or use
    b. nouns which speak of private matters
    c. four- and five-letter nouns
    d. nouns of love and hate
    e. nouns children use to speak of excrement
    f. furniture nouns
    g. genital nouns
    h. nouns we use without understanding their
       meaning
    i. hospital nouns

Professor Doctor Wagner was an extremely busy man: he
had committees to serve on, consultations to render, funds to
secure, and friends like Professor Doctor Reinhold Schneider
to avoid, except on designated Thursdays. And so, Professor Doctor Wagner did not notice his assistants' additions. At
least they seemed busy, and so he complimented himself on
his choice of pliable workers. Yet he was also skeptical of their

ability to function independently without proper supervision, and so he felt it his duty to the Project, to the University, and to his assistants themselves to secure a capable Project Director.

Although Professor Doctor Schneider likewise attempted to avoid Wagner, both professors valued order and routine above personal likes and dislikes, and so Schneider and Wagner agreed to meet again on a chilly Thursday in early October. Schneider arrived ten minutes past the agreed-upon rendezvous time; Wagner came fifteen minutes later, breathing hard and offering an excuse before a greeting. He asked Schneider to order a mélange for him, but then looked at his watch.

"Oh my, dear colleague," said Wagner, "I believe I may be late for a doctoral examination. Excuse me, please, would you mind?..."

"Of course not," Schneider replied, with more than a hint of annoyance. "I will take care of the bill for my coffee."

Wagner hurried away, justifying his haste with his reflection that his time was inevitably taken with cumbersome meetings and the details of his Institute. When he arrived one hour late for the examination, he felt no need to apologize. Professor Doctor Wagner was a responsible person, however, and so he was unwilling to accept the thesis committee's judgment without his own interrogation of the candidate, and he was unwilling to cancel his appointment with the director of the Austrian National Institute for the Preservation of Language, for which, unfortunately, he was already thirty minutes late.

"Professor Doctor Wagner, we have nearly completed the oral examination. Do you have a question or two which you would care to put to the candidate?" No one on the committee remembered the candidate's name, although two of the four had actually read the thesis.

"Yes, yes. I must apologize for my tardiness. I am glad

you proceeded in my absence. I do have a few questions that should require only a bit of time."

"Good. We all hope to complete the examination by 17:00." It was then 16:55.

"Of course. I myself have an extremely important appointment at . . . oh, my. It seems I have lost track of the time. I must excuse myself immediately."

"And your questions, Professor Wagner?"

"Yes. Yes. My questions."

"Perhaps you would be willing to accept our summary of the candidate's previous responses?"

"No. That would be completely irresponsible and unprofessional of me. The oral examination will proceed as scheduled. The candidate need only come with me to my appointment."

"You are not going to continue the examination at a public café, Professor Wagner?"

"Of course, not. I will present my questions and the candidate will present the answers as we walk from the Institute to Café Landtmann. Come: we have no time to lose."

And so Professor Wagner asked the candidate about the persistently innocent character of nineteenth-century American domestic novels at the corner of Liebiggasse and Rathausstrasse, about the comic representation of tragedy in *fin de siecle* drama at the corner of Rathausstrasse and Grillparzerstrasse, about parallels between Anglo-Saxon and central Bohemian great vowel shifts as they crossed Ebendorferstrasse, and, just as the tourist bus from Bratislava crossed in front of them on Reichsratsstrasse, about the significance of nominification in English-language instruction in Upper Austria.

"I see. Yes. Well then. Hrrrmph." Even Professor Doctor Wagner found it difficult to conclude a doctoral oral examination in the middle of the Rathaus Park. "Yes. You will be contacted by the committee, I am quite certain. Good day."

Wagner scurried through the park and across the Ring once

again to Café Landtmann, where he apologized to Professor Doctor Friedrich Friedelhof, the Director of the Austrian National Institute for the Preservation of Language, for his tardiness ("You have no idea–the committee meetings and these doctoral candidates–quite unprepared these days") and shared more than one bottle of French wine. Professor Doctor Wagner was therefore more than willing to accompany Professor Doctor Friedelhof, whom he now believed to be one of his very trusted and beloved colleagues, to Café Hawelka.

Felix Kulpa had arrived at Hawelka only minutes before Wagner and Friedelhof and had found the only remaining empty table. Professor Doctor Wagner and Professor Doctor Friedelhof stumbled through the crowded café toward Kulpa, whom Wagner did not recognize as the same man who had disrupted his morning coffee with Professor Doctor Schneider a few days earlier at Café Landtmann.

Felix looked up from his glass of wine and motioned to Wagner to join him.

"Please," he said, motioning to the empty chairs. "You are most welcome."

"Ah," said Wagner, "you must be American. Am I not correct?"

"I am," said Felix. "And you must be a professor of English studies. Am I also not correct?"

"You are indeed. And I am joined by my esteemed colleague, Professor Doctor Friedelhof."

As Friedelhof and Wagner carefully lowered themselves into their chairs, Felix caught the attention of a waiter and ordered three glasses of peach schnapps.

"You are very considerate, Mister . . .?"

"Kulpa, Felix Kulpa. And I am most honored by your company."

"Come, come, Mister Kulpa, we are pleased to join you. Let us toast international friendship!"

The toast was followed by three more rounds of schnapps.

After his fourth glass, Wagner was confident that Felix would serve quite well as his Project Director at the Nominification Institute, although he was only dimly aware of Felix's qualifications. The evening ended with yet another round and another toast to international relations and to all nouns.

Felix, however, was never told what he would do or, in fact, exactly where the Institute was located. He found that most of his time was being taken up with his attempt to become a strassenbahn driver. Though he left a small payment for Felix on his desk for a couple of weeks, Professor Doctor Wagner soon forgot his "Project Director," remembering him only when the newspaper reported what was called, "An Unlucky Encounter between Truck and Tram." For the next six weeks, work continued at the Institute, despite the death of Felix and the many preoccupations of Professor Doctor Wagner.

As the Christmas holiday break approached, Johanna Stubblemeier noticed Professor Doctor Wagner's disregard for her expansion of his lists, and suggested to Beata and Gunter that they continue their modifications on a global scale. Professor Doctor Wagner had often lectured his assistants on their need to be aware of the international repercussions of his work, and Johanna felt it only appropriate to take him at his word.

Johanna, Beata, and Gunter suggested to Professor Doctor Wagner that his work would achieve greater international renown if it were available to colleagues throughout Europe, a concept Professor Doctor Wagner heartily endorsed if little understood. He agreed to secure funds for the necessary equipment and consultants–for Professor Doctor Wagner felt that his assistants would not on their own be able to develop the sophisticated procedures appropriate to his linguistic system.

And so the Nominification Newsletter was born.

Beata knew all the essential procedures for editing, printing, and distributing a newsletter; Gunter secured all the necessary equipment; Johanna wrote the text, considerably embellishing The Wagnerian System. She also issued a call for contributions and received responses from more than one hundred network linguists in thirty-nine countries:

    j. nouns used in lower-class houses
    k. nouns from the kennel
    l. nouns to be used on the subway
    m. nouns used to disguise death
    n. nouns of pain and illness
    o. nouns of the body
    p. nouns of the heart
    q. nouns of the mind
    r. nouns used in the 1700s but no longer
       understood
    s. nouns from the dictionaries of arcane sciences
    t. nouns no one accepts
    u. nouns of love
    v. nouns for parts of the dog

The plans of the three assistants elicited such a range of responses that all three enjoyed their work more and more each day. At the end of each week, they reported to Professor Doctor Wagner the number, but not the nature, of the contributions.

When the University returned to session after the New Year, Wagner himself was so pleased that he could not resist asking Reinhold Schneider to meet him at Café Landtmann for what Wagner called a "confidential meeting."

"I assume you have a report on your work at the Institute," said Schneider. "Have you made any progress?"

"Given my other obligations, which require, as you are well aware, a great deal of my time, and, of course, require me to entrust the initial groundwork to my assistants, who at times appear a bit unreliable, matters are proceeding."

"And that one assistant, whose name I only faintly recall—is it Stubblemeier"—how does she appear?"

Wagner hesitated for a moment. "She appears to be sufficient, although lacking in initiative, as one might expect."

"I see. And what of that work you call the 'Nominification' project?"

Wagner could not resist the opportunity. "It appears that the project has aroused a considerable amount of interest; in fact, an extraordinary amount of interest from distinguished linguists in many of the continent's leading institutions. But I must ask you, as a trusted colleague, not to mention this interest or the progress I have made to anyone else. It is, as you might suspect, in the early, but very promising, stages. Yes. Very promising. But not a word to anyone."

"Of course—not a word," promised Schneider, who very much resented Wagner's success, but who also knew that Wagner would almost certainly fail. Schneider thus had already made plans to spread news of the responses to what he considered a ridiculous program.

"Yes, of course," Schneider repeated, "not a word."

Schneider, however, reconsidered his intention to publicize Wagner's project. Instead, he in fact would honor his promise, for he believed that once Wagner's system would be made public, he would have no need to speak of it. However, Schneider did believe he needed a few more details about the work, and at the end of January, he requested another meeting with his colleague.

"It has been said that you have now a Project Director, correct?"

Wagner hesitated.

"Ah yes, the most unfortunate American. He has, in most extraordinary circumstances, left this earth, and I have been forced to hire a most competent replacement, a young man highly recommended by one of my assistants." Since hiring Johanna's older brother, however, Wagner had not seen him, nor did he recall why in fact he had given the position to him.

"Yes," he continued, "a young scholar, of some distinction, I believe. He is working independently, using his expertise to develop a formal plan of action."

"Indeed," said Schneider. "A formal plan of action is requisite for such complex projects, is it not?"

"Why of course, but, oh my, my esteemed colleague, I have lost track of the time. My apologies. I have an important meeting with my staff, and it seems as if I may, unfortunately, be a few minutes late."

Wagner had no such meeting, but he realized that he must leave before Schneider asked anything else which might compromise the project.

"Of course, I understand. Good day, Professor Wagner."

"Good afternoon, Professor Schneider."

When Professor Wagner reached his Institute, he turned to his assistants, who had turned to their work, and said to the Institute itself, which alone seemed to merit his attention, "Ah, yes. The work goes on." He scuttled across the room to his office, closed the door, and looked again at the schedule of meetings which he had missed.

Two weeks later, Johanne's brother had still not visited the Institute, nor had he met with Wagner. The three assistants, however, did indeed have plans for the day: each had rented costumes for a parade through the First District. The Viennese Chamber of Commerce had decided to include tourists in the annual ball season. Although some skeptics thought that few visitors would travel to the city in February, the Austrian Minister of Culture and Entertainment supported the plan by providing funds for what they called in their English-language promotion, "A Festival better than Venice! Revelry better than Vegas!" The festivities would conclude with a grand parade throughout the Inner City.

When Beata heard of the plans, she knew that she could call on the Reenactment Society's collection of medieval and renaissance costumes so that Johanna and Gunter could join her in the parade. Johanna suggested that they dress as the Three Witches of Wagram: Gunter and Beata agreed, and Beata found all the necessities for witchcraft.

On this early evening in mid February, the entire Inner City was transformed into a festival, a grand bacchanal in the final week before sacred ashes replaced carnival masks.

And on that night of excess and revelry, Professor Doctor Schneider had made yet another appointment to meet Professor Doctor Wagner at Café Griensteidl, "to discuss some matters of mutual interest," he had assured Wagner. In fact, Schneider was increasingly envious of Wagner's success in funding the Nominification Institute, and he was eager to learn the source of the funds. However, Professor Doctor Wagner had many other meetings that afternoon, meetings for which he was always late and from which he always left early, somehow managing to lose more time than seemed possible in a few hours. "There are so many demands on my time," he confided to Professor Doctor Schneider as he arrived at Café Griensteidl, only thirty-seven minutes late, and so, by Wagner's calculations, remarkably early.

"Tell me, please.... Oh yes. Mélange. And a slice of strudel.... Where was I? Oh yes. Tell me, please, my dear colleague, how have you been in such times?"

Professor Doctor Schneider resented Wagner's solicitude as much as he desired Wagner's confidence, and so he restrained the acrid bile that he yearned to pour on Wagner's head.

"We survive, do we not? We survive."

"My goodness, Professor Schneider! What is that noise?"

With a man in a tiger's costume at its center, the carnival procession had reached St. Michael's plaza, where the crowd swarmed about the famous Roman ruins and began a chant which seemed to originate from the very soul of Vienna's past.

Reinhold Schneider looked out the café window and shook his head in disgust. "Carnival, dear colleague, merely foreigners disrupting our lives once again. Bah!"

"Do they appear dangerous?"

"I am certain you will be quite safe if only you maintain decorum, Professor Wagner. Revulsion, as you must know, is the fundamental virtue, and decorum is the most sincere of all passions."

"Ah yes. Of course."

By this time the crowd surrounding the tiger and surrounded by its tail had grown even larger, joined by masked figures from throughout the city, among them, Professor Doctor Wagner's assistants–Johanna Stubblemeier, Beata Fuchstberger, and Gunter Stadtbad–dressed as the Three Witches of Wagram, who had made Napoleon's victory so costly to the French Empire–and an even stranger figure–a man, if the figure were indeed a man, whose face was concealed beneath a cod's head mask, muzzled like a unruly hound on the U-Bahn–a type of barking fish, it seemed to Johanna.

Inside Café Griensteidl, Professor Doctor Wagner grew more and more uneasy. "The revelers appear to grow a bit too festive, my dear colleague. Don't you agree?"

"Bah! Keep a door shut in their faces, Professor Wagner. A door shut."

"Yes. Yes. Of course."

"A door, my dear colleague, is designed neither for going in or coming out, but for keeping closed, Professor Wagner, for keeping closed."

"Yes. Yes. Of course."

"If I might quote your beloved Borges, 'Everything in the world can be the seed of a possible hell.'" Much like Wagner, Schneider had never read Borges, although he felt that an approximation of what Borges might have intended to write would be enough to convince Wagner. "Our task is to recognize satanic agency and strike before it consumes us."

"Indeed. Yes. Strike first."

"And, of course, this unruly world today is a reckless improvisation by fools lacking imagination. Fools, Professor Wagner, reckless, unruly fools!"

"Oh, dear colleague, I have lost track of the time. Another meeting. It seems we must continue our discussion. Another time, perhaps?"

Professor Doctor Schneider looked politely disgusted, and simply nodded his understanding of the pressures of academic life.

"Of course. I too must be leaving. Please. Allow me."

"No. No. You mustn't. Ah. The time. I must depart. If you could ...."

"Of course. Waiter!"

Professor Schneider attempted to catch the attention of the waiter, while Professor Wagner hurried out of the café, just as the end of the tiger's tail swept past, wrapping Professor Wagner in festive terror.

"What is the meaning? What? What? Please. I must go."

As Professor Wagner was spun round by the tiger's tail, the First Witch of Wagram sped past, asking him for a noun of release. "What? What? What is it?" Wagner turned round and round, past the Second Witch of Wagram, who requested a noun of retribution. "What? What?" Round and round and round, till the Third Witch of Wagram joined the crowd and caught Wagner by the arms. "The ninety-ninth noun of God," she growled. "The final noun of God."

"Oh my! God help me!" Wagner could not resist–a spinning toy in the control of animals, clowns, and witches. He spun toward the center of St. Michael's plaza, his eyes shut against the mad crowd and the tiger's tail. And then, suddenly, the noise ended, and he came to rest amid the plaza's famous Roman ruins, the plaza entirely deserted except for two figures–one, like himself, lying face down in ruins; the second scurrying across the plaza away from him. The only sound came from the tap-tap-tapping of a distant cane on an unseen street.

Professor Doctor Wagner opened his eyes. Once certain that they were indeed gone, he rose as quickly as decorum and his knees would permit, excused himself, and walked down Schauflergasse, intending to file a report with the police.

The incident on St. Michael's plaza only temporarily disturbed Professor Doctor Wagner's equanimity. After he spoke to his assistants about the grossly indecorous behavior of the foreign element, he seemed to regain his assurance that at least his Institute was in order. After reviewing responses to his work, he was confident that his increasing reputation–although a bit misinformed–was certainly long overdue, and he accepted the acclaim with typical public modesty. To Johanna, Beata, and Gunter, however, he continued to be as overbearing as ever–more so, in fact, for he felt that his growing fame demanded an international conference in his honor, and his assistants found that they were to organize such an academic festival on their own.

Johanna was growing weary of the role she had played in constructing the catalog, and so she was determined to end her relationship with Wagner and to reveal him for the self-centered fool she believed him to be. She therefore began adding categories on the Nominification Newsletter, and she added an offer by P. D. Wagner himself to conduct seminars on any of the categories in his universal taxonomy of significant English nominalizations:

    aa. vegetable nouns
    bb. those nouns which define functions
    cc. those nouns which do not
    dd. nouns from the kitchen
    ee. nouns of lust
    ff. nouns of agony
    gg. nouns used to disguise ignorance

 hh. nouns often heard in public bath houses
 ii. symphonic nouns
 jj. post-structuralist nouns
 kk. melodic nouns
 ll. nouns which enable us to buy food in foreign
   lands

Wagner had little time to spare, and so he only glanced over the catalog and was pleased that they had gone so far into the alphabet. He called for a meeting with his assistants, whose names he could only dimly recall. He said nothing of Johanna's brother, whose name he had forgotten but whose absence he did not regret.

"Magisterin Stubblstein, is it not?" Wagner began, "you have used my research to good effect. Although I am pleased with the progress, I do have a few suggestions, which, of course, you should incorporate into the next phase of the project."

"Of course, Professor Doctor Wagner."

"And you—what is your name again?"

"Beata Fuchstber..."

"Fuchstber, unusual name. And you there"

"Gunter Stadt..."

"Stadt. Another curious name."

"Professor Doctor Wagner?" said Beata.

"Yes."

"My name is not Fuchstber."

"Of course. Well done."

"Professor Doctor Wagner," asked Johanna. "What recommendations do you have in mind?"

"Well, first ... oh my. I am sorry, but I have a conference with the Dean, and I am already 10 minutes late. Please do carry on."

"Of course," said Johanna.

Response to the P. D. Wagner newsletter was so enthusiastic that he received twenty-seven requests to speak at international conferences. Professor Doctor Wagner naturally attributed this regard to the strength of his insightful taxonomy, but he was puzzled by the topics on which he himself was asked to speak:

> mm. nouns which appear to be useful but which prove cumbersome
> nn. nouns which are found in university catalogs
> oo. nouns of promise and denial
> pp. nouns used in place of thought
> qq. nouns to discourage unwanted advances on public transportation
> rr. menu nouns
> ss. nouns with unusual suffixes
> tt. nouns invented in response to difficult questions
> uu. nouns of seduction and nouns of denial
> vv. nouns which always seem appropriate and nouns which never do
> ww. nouns used to disguise atrocities
> xx. nouns used to convince a reluctant lover
> yy. nouns of wonder and awe
> zz nouns used by God in the first six days
> aaa. pointer-finger nouns
> bbb. committee nouns
> ccc. nouns capitalized only in conversation with postal workers
> ddd. nouns of glory and wonder

Despite his initial confusion, Professor Doctor Wagner readily agreed to a series of speaking engagements throughout Europe on both linguistics and aesthetic theory. Although he seldom failed to bore audiences in Saarbrucken (a crowd of 23, if the maintenance crew were included), Lyon (15), Klagenfurt (19), and Bruges (12), everyone agreed that he was among the most challenging thinkers to appear in several months. He was, in short, a celebrity.

During the early months of 1983, Professor Doctor Schneider grew more and more incensed at Wagner's fame and his increasing arrogance. Nonetheless, Schneider again agreed to meet Wagner to discuss the vagaries of the European academy.

"When will you present your findings, Professor Wagner?"

"Let me see, Professor Schneider. My conference begins the first week of April, and I believe I am scheduled for the first session on Sunday morning."

"Ah! An excellent time! You will not have to deal with the dilettantes."

"Yes. I do believe ... Yes. Yes. I am scheduled for the 9:00 session on Projective Linguistics and the Rule of Law. Dombowksi and that woman from Heidelberg will be on the same panel, but then ... what is one to do?"

"Of course, Professor Wagner. You must simply state your findings. They are self-evident. Tell me again the title you have chosen."

"I have the paper right here. In my briefcase. Here. It must be right here.... Oh my! I do believe I have left the paper at the Institute. Please excuse me, Professor Schneider. I must return immediately. Please. Excuse...."

Professor Doctor Schneider seldom smiled, and he did not smile at this latest misadventure of his colleague. But the mirror across from his table reflected a slight movement in his lips, a movement tending toward joyful malice.

Professor Doctor Wagner was not smiling, however, as he hurried from the restaurant to the car which he always parked in the same spot, or as he sped to the Eighth District, where he always spent thirty minutes searching for a parking spot, even late on this midweek night. He was not smiling as he left his car, for earlier that same day he had used the final parking permit required of anyone not living in the Eighth District and he knew he must hurry to the Institute and hurry back, or his car might be towed to the outskirts of the city.

And Professor Doctor Wagner was certainly not smiling when he found the door to the Nominification Institute locked from inside. He knocked, looked at his watch, and waited, and then knocked again, and waited, looking again and again at his watch, before he realized that he had nowhere to be and thus could not be late for anyone. Professor Doctor Wagner remained until he was certain that no one could have seen him waiting outside his own Institute. Forgetting where he had parked his car, he was forced to take public transportation to his apartment.

The next morning at 8:45, he called the campus police, who would have the necessary equipment and, even more, the necessary authorization to open the Institute door. Professor Doctor Wagner, however, was taken aback by the officer's request that he present his credentials in person at the office of the Assistant Rector for Security and Safety.

"But, young man, I am Professor Doctor Wagner, Director of the Institute. Come, come, let me speak with your superior."

"The Assistant Rector for Security and Safety is presently not available."

"Well then, what do you suggest I do? Important, quite important papers remain within the Institute. They must be retrieved today, this morning."

"If that is indeed the case, Professor Doctor, it would be good for you to come in person to the office."

Wagner had struck the formidable wall of academic bureaucracy, which he had been accustomed to defend but now must surmount. He hesitated before accepting his fate.

"I see. I will come at 10:00."

"The Office is not accessible at 10:00 today."

"Then I will come at 11:00."

"The Office is accessible today between 9:00 and 9:15 only."

"That is preposterous!"

"Perhaps, but also true."

Wagner would have preferred to consult with the Assistant Rector or the Associate Rector and even the Rector himself about this unreasonable situation, but on this particular day he valued his presentation above his honor—and so he submitted to what he viewed as petty regulations and said he would be at the office before 9:15.

"It would be wise if you came before 9:00," said the Office clerk. "We are somewhat understaffed at present."

Wagner hung up the phone, suddenly recalled that he had left his car at the Institute, and then walked as quickly as a distinguished professor should walk in public to the nearest strassenbahn stop. He arrived at the Office of the Assistant Rector for Security and Safety at 9:05 and haggled for several minutes with the receptionist when he was asked to present his credentials. The receptionist, whose name Professor Doctor Wagner did not ask for, told him that an officer had noticed the lights of the Institute still on earlier that morning and so, relying on his authority and using a universal key had released the locked door.

"Do you mean that the Institute has been accessible to me since early this morning?"

"That does appear to be the situation, Professor Doctor."

"Harumph!" declared Wagner as he stomped out of the office and "Harumph!" again, several times, as he walked the three blocks to his Institute. He unlocked the door, turned on the lights, looked quickly around the rooms, and then left, forgetting to turn off the lights and forgetting his presentation for the conference on Projective Linguistics. Professor Doctor Wagner returned to the spot where he had parked his car, where he found a policeman waving to the tow truck which carried his car to the outskirts of Vienna. For several minutes, Wagner stood still, silently looking at the parking space where his car should have been.

"How could this have happened?" he thought, "and how could I explain this to Schneider? He will certainly hear of the affair from his relationship with the Rector." Wagner knew that he would have to devise some explanation of the last two days so that he could retain Schneider's high regard for him, of which Wagner was, unfortunately and mistakenly, assured. As he walked to Café Landtmann for his regular Thursday morning rendezvous, Wagner felt he had created a narrative which would absolve himself of all responsibility.

"Greetings, Professor Wagner," Schneider called out from the table so frequently reserved for them on Thursday mornings. "How goes it for you this morning?"

"Not so well, Professor Schneider, not well indeed."

"I am sorry to hear that. Please explain your distress."

"You must know, Professor Schneider, how significant the work of my Institute remains and how carefully I must protect its findings."

"Of course, Professor Wagner, of course."

"And you must also know how the work has been hindered by the lack of qualified assistants."

"You have mentioned this issue before. As I recall, it was the reason you hired that unfortunate young American, and then that other young man–to supervise the work."

"Indeed, that was the case. That is, until last night."

"What happened last night?"

"My daily inspection of the Institute was delayed several hours yesterday by another meeting of one of those confounded committees."

"And such work remains a curse on all of us."

"Indeed it does. But to return to my situation. I approached the Institute but found the door locked from the inside. 'What is the meaning of this?,' I said in a rather stern voice. 'Hello in there, it is Professor Doctor Wagner. What is the meaning of this?'"

"I heard what I thought might be the rustling of leaves–could it be?–or perhaps newspapers. I also heard what might have been a human voice, grumbling, a voice in motion toward the door. I struck my umbrella against the door, but immediately regretted, for I only then thought of the possibilities.

"'Thieves! They may be searching for Institute funds, or data!' I thought. 'The police. I must notify the police. Hallo! Anyone! Hallo! Police! Police!'

"No one in the building appeared to respond, and so I drew my umbrella back over my head to assault whoever might be removing the chain from the Institute door. The door swung open, and I stood ready to strike. Just then I heard a voice: 'Please wait a moment.'

"'Young man, is that you?' I said. "'Young man ... I thought thieves.... Whatever are you doing here at this hour? What exactly is the meaning of all this?'"

"And who was this young man?" Professor Schneider asked.

"It seems that this was that brother or cousin of one of my assistants, Otto or Michael or whatever is his name. 'I work here' he said, 'and, if work goes late, I sleep here.' In fact, it appears that this young man had been sleeping at the office whenever he had stayed out too late to return to his apartment.

"'This cannot be,' I told him. 'It must be done differently. You may not ... this is an Institute, not a refuge. No. No. This cannot be. You must go. You must go. It cannot be done this way.'"

"What did this young man say?"

"He said nothing. He simply returned to gather his clothes and papers and left. As he left the Institute, I firmly dismissed him. 'No. No. This cannot be.' I insisted. 'I cannot allow such things. It simply cannot be done this way.' I have washed my hands of this man. He is not to return, nor do I wish to see him again."

"You have acted quite appropriately," Schneider said. "Quite appropriately." Schneider nodded his approval while silently rejoicing in Wagner's humiliation. "Now let's see," he thought, "how that ridiculous conference of his turns out." Schneider rejoiced, and Wagner slowly walked out of Café Landtmann, trying to delay any meeting or thought which might intrude on his outrage.

As he walked out, he remembered how he had grfadually entrusted the simpler tasks of organizing the conference to his assistants. "Because of the demands placed upon me," he said to himself, "others failed to realize that I had to spend much of my time answering queries for which answers are never as simple as they expect." (In fact, he had had no answers and therefore had felt compelled to respond in considerable detail.) So he had provided his assistants with golden opportunities to do the less important work: selecting papers, responding to practical queries, constructing the program, choosing restaurants, refreshments, brothels, hotels, making travel arrangements, booking scenic tours, approving menus, flattering sponsors, and contracting with publishers of the conference proceedings. Yes. He had treated them well, his assistants.

The International Conference on Nominalization

What he did not understand was that Johanna, Beata, and Gunter had grown weary of this work and were finding employment elsewhere. He did not know that as a parting gift, Johanna had issued a challenge in his name. In the February, 1983, issue of the Nominafication Newsletter–had he read it– Professor Dr. Wagner might have seen this:

> P. D. WAGNER WILL SPEAK EXTEMPORANEOUSLY
> ON ANY CATEGORY OF ENGLISH NOMINALIZA-
> TION PROPOSED BY CONFERENCE PARTICIPANTS.
> IF ANY PARTICIPANT SUGGESTS A TOPIC ON
> WHICH P. D. WAGNER CANNOT SPEAK TO THE
> SATISFACTION OF THE ENTIRE CONFERENCE,
> HE WILL RECANT HIS LINGUISTIC SYSTEM AND
> LICK THE BOOTS OF EVERY CONFERENCE PAR-
> TICIPANT.

Although bootlicking was a fairly common occurrence at many academic conferences, this was, in fact, the first time that such an open challenge had appeared on such a global scale. The response, not unexpectedly, was overwhelming. Hundreds of academics had sought to register for The P. D. Wagner International Symposium. Professor Wagner believed that his carefully developed system of nominal instruction was responsible for this gratifying response; Johanna knew otherwise, but she said nothing to disturb Professor Doctor Wagner's academic serenity.

At the opening of the International Conference on Significant Nominalization, Professor Doctor Wagner began the keynote address. Although Wagner himself understood little of what he said and none of its implications, he was pleased that no one asked any questions–to him a sign of the sophistication of his approach.

He was, however, a bit puzzled when someone in a Bavarian hunter's hat and absurdly overgrown mustache challenged him to comment upon "nouns used to describe sexual acts not yet fully perfected." Such a category does not exist, Professor Doctor Wagner insisted, much to the dismay of his admirers–of whom there were a few–and much to the delight of the rest of the audience.

He was about to announce the first of several refreshment breaks–although he himself did not know where the refreshments would be served or what they would be–when another person dressed in a black and orange sweater asked him to discuss "English nouns interjected into requests for directions in French." "Preposterous," Professor Doctor Wagner stated. "Perhaps," the man in a hunting cap interjected, "but what about nouns Freud rejected? Or nouns seen on urinal walls in southern Germany?"

"Yes," shouted a voice from the rear of the auditorium, "please inform us about nouns of ecstasy and delight, and nouns which identify flowers carried by hopeful lovers."

As occasionally happens at conferences, delight began to overcome decorum, as the spirit of comic excess infected more and more of the audience.

"Indeed," a tweeded academic added, "what do you have to say about insufficient nouns, nouns which stand on their own, and nouns which do not?"

"Come, Professor Wagner," demanded the professor from Romania, "you must have something to say about nouns I would like to use correctly and my favorite nouns."

Wagner was distraught. He found that he could not control his conference and that he could no longer be responsible for his linguistic system. It had taken on a life of its own, he was convinced, and at least for that he was pleased. However, he was taken aback by the persistent calls from the audience to lick their boots.

Wagner looked desperately for his assistants, but, as they had found alternative positions, they were nowhere to be found.

There were few words–and no nouns–to describe his plight.

Johanna took little comfort in Professor Wagner's distress, but neither she nor Beata nor Gunter offered any assistance. Johanna would soon begin work on her dissertation with another faculty member; Beata was appointed the head of the Reenactment Society of Eastern Austria, and Gunter left Vienna to pursue his own dream as a professional white-water kayaker. As Professor Wagner's session ended, they met once more to congratulate themselves on the success of the conference.

"Wagner was finally at a loss for nouns—or any other words," said Johanna.

"Yes," agreed Beata, "but I feel a bit sorry for him."

"Don't," Gunter said. "He still has his position at the University and his friends at the Ministry."

"I think he will still be a busy man," added Johanna. "A man with many obligations but few qualities."

"Let's drink," said Gunter, "to nouns, qualities, and each other"

The three assistants toasted their allegiance to each other and to integrity, put their keys to the Institute in an envelope addressed to Professor Doctor Wagner, and closed the Institute door for the last time. It seemed to them that the Nominification Project would quietly fade away just as spring arrived in Vienna.

Comes the April Fog

When the glorious skies of April dispel memories of March, however, Viennese know to be wary: events emerge from chance and whimsy as often as they result from intention. Laughter skitters the edge of fatality; anger and tears lurk in the pews of every wedding. Even on sunny days, it seems prudent to keep your umbrella nearby. Women with grey hair and halting steps emerge to walk to the tobacconist, and they may ask a stranger for the time of day. If someone answers and gives the hour which the women expect, the day may turn out well for both. The stranger may think nothing of the gesture, but he may also feel justified for the time he has taken.

Thousands of miles to the west, Anthony Ignazio welcomed the arrival of spring but also regretted his misfortune in missing the Venice carnival two months earlier. For years he had wanted to escape the tedium of his work as a photocopy repairman based in Burlington, Iowa but routinely sent downriver to Missouri. For years, he had imagined himself on a Venetian gondola basking in the excess of the city's carnival. Unfortunately, Anthony had had too little money for a vacation in Venice and too much work to leave Iowa in February. He had thus resigned himself to a two-week holiday in April, but he had mistakenly registered for a cathedral tour of central Europe, not Venice, led by Father Terence Murphy, not by "Doctor Truelove." Yet Anthony was determined to make the most of his holiday, even if it meant substituting a spiritual pilgrimage for romantic excess.

The renowned linguist Professor Doctor Wagner was likewise determined, but his determination arose from the infamy of the conference and the shame it brought upon the Nominification Institute. Professor Doctor Wagner therefore quickly planned another gathering of the leaders of the New Linguistic Movement of central Europe. Unfortunately, however, his assistants could not be found, and so plans were–even more unfortunately–entirely dependent upon Professor Doctor Wagner. He believed that the post-conference meeting could be held at the Institute, but where, thought Professor Doctor Wagner, could his colleagues be entertained? The April Incident, as his conference session would come to be known, demanded that status be reclaimed, that reputation be no longer tarnished, that, as Professor Doctor Wagner confided to Professor Doctor Schneider, errors and misimpressions be quickly corrected.

"Of course, my dear colleague, of course you must act with determination and speed," said Schneider, with just an undertone of self-righteous delight.

So Professor Wagner planned a dinner, the first dinner he had planned, but what could be difficult in such arrangements? What indeed could go wrong?

Professor Doctor Wagner did not want to commit the entire remaining budget of the Institute to the dinner. He had promised the Language Ministry that their funds would support publication of the conference proceedings, which, he had been forced to admit, would be delayed. And yet he knew that his own reputation, to say nothing of the Institute and, perhaps, the Ministry itself, depended upon the success of the dinner. Professor Doctor Wagner therefore worked with limited funds appropriated from the Ministry, with grand visions of reclaimed academic glory, and with almost complete incompetence.

"It is possible to hire carriages to carry us to the restaurant," he told Professor Doctor Schneider, who looked past Professor Doctor Wagner to the waitress bending over to pick up the umbrella she had knocked from the back of the chair of a family from east-central Bavaria. "You see, Professor Schneider, the horses must return to their barns above Pötzleinsdorf and so the rates are quite decent. Yes. I do believe it is possible that we may be carried to the restaurant by carriages. Quite reasonable, don't you agree?"

"Yes. Yes. Naturally," muttered Professor Schneider, who had paid no attention to Wagner's comments. "Yes. It could be done." The smoke from Professor Schneider's pipe rose higher and higher as he watched the waitress bend once more at the next table, from which a child's spoon had fallen.

"I do believe carriages will be appropriate. Yes, I do believe quite an impression will be made. Would you agree, Professor Schneider?"

The smoke rose higher and still higher as Professor Schneider puffed harder and yet harder, and even higher as he dropped first his fork and then his knife and then Professor Wagner's knife.

"Would you not agree, Professor Schneider?"

"Of course. Of course. It must be done."

Professor Doctor Wagner had, in fact, already hired six carriages to meet his guests outside the Burgtheater at seven o'clock on the night of the post-conference conference. They were to carry them to what he believed was an authentic local tavern, but which was, in fact, a Chinese restaurant of questionable authenticity. Professor Wagner, however, would not ride in a carriage: he had reclaimed his car from the police impoundment lot on the city's outskirts, and so, he reasoned, he should await his guests at the restaurant.

"I must, unfortunately, my esteemed colleague, depart. Obligations, you must realize...."

"Of course," puffed Professor Schneider. "Of course."

Outside the Burgtheater, however, members of the New Linguistic Movement stumbled over curbs and bumped into shoppers from Bratislava, in a vain search for Professor Wagner's carriages. Of the six carriages Professor Doctor Wagner had hired, only four emerged from a dense fog to the rendezvous in front of the theater. Two of the four were immediately taken by a group of American Catholics on a tour of great European cathedrals. They had arrived in Vienna that morning, had visited St. Stephan's cathedral, guided by a knowledgeable priest from St. Louis, and had spent the afternoon shopping on Kärtnerstrasse. They were tired, and so, despite the thickening fog, were willing to pay for a circuit of the Ring, for at least they could finally sit down.

"The train for Prague doesn't leave until 10:00, does it, Father Murphy" asked Anthony Ignazio."

"No. But we must be at the train station by 9:15 at the very latest. At the very latest."

"Excuse me, please," said a voice from somewhere to the group's left. "But I believe these carriages have been reserved by Professor Wagner for the New Linguistic Movement."

"Hurry. Come now. We must hurry."

"Excuse me. I do believe arrangements have been made. These carriages are committed."

"Hurry. Where is Mr. Ignazio?"

"Excuse me."

"Hurry."

Seven people crowded into the two remaining carriages, but only six of them were members of the New Linguistic Movement. In his rush to secure a seat, Eugen Radetzky, professor of comparative language systems at the Free University of Tirana, had joined the cathedral tour for the ride around the Ring. In his place sat Anthony Ignazio, who assumed that all carriages took the same route.

As the crowded carriage hired by Professor Wagner clip-clapped away from the Inner City toward Pötzleinsdorf, none of the New Linguists spoke, although a few could be heard mumbling, cursing, perhaps. The fog grew thicker and thicker as the carriage reached the Gürtel.

... Clip-clap ... apparitions of headlights threatened each window ... clip-clap, clip-clap ... the bells of strassenbahn ... clip-clap, clip-clap ... "damn fog" ... clip-clap, clip-clap ... into the Eighteenth District ... clip-clap, clip-clap.... "Wherever is Professor Wagner?" ... clip-clap, clip-clap ... "Did you attend the meeting? I do not recall your name. Please, excuse me." ... clip-clap, clip-clap ... "I'm with the tour." ... clip-clap, clip-clap ... "The tour? What tour?" ... clip-clap ... "Father Terence's tour. Where is Father Terence? I have a train I must meet. Where are we?" ... clip-clap ... "Damn that Wagner. How far is this restaurant?" ... clip-clap ... "Goodness. That tram nearly clipped us." ... "We should have known. After the April Incident." ... "When will we join the others?" ... clip-clap ... "It is a bit chilly." "Could you please move your umbrella. It is protruding into my side." "Have we passed the Opera house? I read about it. Father Terence said ..." "Damn him. I am cold and hungry." "Where is Professor Wagner?" "Where are we?" "I can't see a thing. Is that the Hofburg?" ... clip-clap, clip-clap ... clip-clap, clip-clap, clip-clap....

Several have sought to explain the magically dense fog of that April evening. Fog, the Viennese quite rightly insist, does not cover the city in April. In November, yes, yes, of course in

November, but never in April. The temperatures are not right; the skies remain distant in April. Yet on this April evening, the fog did appear, and explanations followed.

Some have said that workers mistakenly tapped into the sewers beneath St. Stephan's and released gasses entombed in the catacombs. Others insist that a thermal inversion resulted in the imposition of November onto April. A number of credible witnesses claim, however, that on that very evening the fog emerged from Café Landtmann and, in particular, from the table which Professor Doctor Wagner had vacated, even more specifically from the pipe of Professor Schneider who remained in the embrace of malign happiness at Professor Wagner's humiliation. It seems, according to these witnesses, that as Professor Schneider puffed harder and faster, the passionate smoke from his pipe met the cool air of café decorum and so created a dense fog, even inside the café. These stories are insufficient, however, to explain the extent and the vigor of the fog. Other pipes in other cafés undoubtedly joined with Professor Schneider's and so created a fog of incredible dimension and strength, even by Vienna's standards. Whether the fog emerged from thwarted desire or whether it arose from sewers or descended from the hills, it is clear that on this dreamy evening the fog engulfed the leaders of The New Linguistic Movement as they themselves converged, somewhere near Vienna's Ring.

The carriages hired by Professor Wagner finally reached Pötzleinsdorf in the hills above the city, and six members of the New Linguistic Movement and one member of the Tour of Central Europe's Great Cathedrals painfully emerged into a fog even thicker, even more aggressive than that of the Inner City.

"Where is this restaurant? I am quite tired and hungry," complained Professor Bilosz from Lübeck.

"Yes. Where is Professor Wagner?" asked Professor Dinetzky from Prague.

"Are we near the train station?" Anthony Ignazio inquired of everyone and no one.

"I believe the restaurant is to be found a bit further up this street, Pötzleinsdorferstrasse, I believe," stated Professor Rambauer of the Eisenstadt Institute of Language.

"No, it would be more likely located up the hill, that street," said Professor Türinger from the University of Bamberg. "Yes. It would more likely be higher, for I recall Professor Wagner speaking quite glowingly of the view of the city."

"Wherever it is, I must find it soon and eat. It has been a long, long day." Professor Bilosz suffered from a condition, a condition which appeared to afflict him several times a day, a condition which demanded attention, just as, some colleagues whispered, Professor Bilosz himself demanded attention.

"I should return to the group. Father Terence may be worried. We have a train to catch."

"Come, Helmut," said Professor Ohrnitz to her colleague from the Berlin Academy of Linguistics and Translation Studies, "on such a night, we might have unusual adventures. Do you not agree?"

"Perhaps you are correct, Ingrid," answered Professor Köhler, "perhaps you are correct."

"Come. Let us find this infernal restaurant."

"Yes. This way. I am quite certain."

"No. I believe Professor Wagner left explicit directions."

"No, I don't believe he did," said a voice from somewhere off to the left.

And so it was that Professor Bilosz stormed up Pötzleinsdorferstrasse, followed by Professor Rambauer. Helmut and Ingrid decided that direction offered possibility, but of quite another sort. As the group of four disappeared into the fog to their right, Professor Dinetzky and Professor Türinger trudged up the steep incline of Schafberggasse to the left, in search of a restaurant with a view. Anthony Ignazio remained beneath the end station clock, which was quickly disappearing into the gray chillness of that April evening.

"I wonder how I will find Father Terence?" he asked himself, and, of course, the fog.

As he walked past the restaurant hidden by the fog's damp blanket, Professor Bilosz could not see Professor Wagner, sitting alone and confounded by the choices which the Chinese menu offered, and Professor Wagner could not see Professor Bilosz, more and more in need of food and more and more angrily cursing the night, the city, and the Movement. Professor Rambauer as well did not see the restaurant and he could no longer see Professor Bilosz. But he did see the entrance to Greymüllergasse, which he assumed was a continuation of Pötzleinsdorferstrasse. Helmut and Ingrid followed Professor Rambauer, but they turned from Greymüllergasse into the entrance to the Schlosspark.

At the same time, Professor Dinetzky and Professor Türinger were still walking up Schafberggasse. Halfway up the hill, Professor Türinger stopped to rest, but Professor Dinetzky continued and soon disappeared into the mist, for he knew that the restaurant must be somewhere higher, somewhere with a fine view of the entire city. As he struggled to catch his breath, Professor Türinger noticed the open gate to the Schlosspark just to his right. Perhaps, thought Professor Türinger, the restaurant is located within the park grounds. Yes, he thought, I believe I recall Professor Wagner mentioning a park. And so Professor Türinger entered the park, far above Ingrid and Helmut.

Anthony again checked the time on his watch and on the quickly-disappearing end station clock. He knew that he must find Father Terence and the group soon, but no one remained from whom he could ask directions, for it seemed at that moment that no one in fact lived in Pötzleinsdorf.

"Well. I suppose I must walk to the train station," he thought. "I think it should be somewhere to the left. I suppose."

Anthony followed Professor Türinger and Professor Dinetzky up Schafberggasse, in search of a train station.

By this time, whatever time that could have been, Professor Bilosz had continued cursing and continued walking up Pötzleinsdorferstrasse into the Michaelerwald, farther and farther from the restaurant, and farther and farther into his condition. Professor Rambauer stumbled up the uneven pavement of Greymüllergasse, walking past the palace, which he could not see, and walking back down Pötzleinsdorferstrasse, which returned him to the end station from which he had started. Professor Rambauer decided he might have better luck finding a restaurant, any restaurant, in the city, and so he boarded the last strassenbahn of the night headed back to the First District. As they walked through the park past unseen armless statues and curious deer, Helmut and Ingrid met Professor Türinger, who joined them in another circuit of the grounds. Professor Dinetzky remained confident that he was within a few hundred meters of the restaurant with a view, and so he ascended the pathway along the upper edge of the park. As Anthony continued his search for a train station, a woman in a bright orange scarf emerged from the fog to his left and walked a few steps ahead of him, up and up Schafberggasse and then onto the level ground of Utopiaweg. Anthony would have liked to ask her for assistance, but he was content to follow someone, and so he simply kept pace until the woman disappeared. Once again disappointed, he then slowly retraced his steps to what he hoped was the end station.

When the sun rose the following morning, most of the linguists had managed to return to their hotels in the First District. Only Professor Bilosz remained unaccounted for. Anthony Ignazio spent the night on a bench at the entrance to the schlosspark, unsure what he should do next, but also quite sure he had missed the train to Prague. When the sun finally arose, an elderly man with a golden-tipped cane emerged from the park and sat on the park bench.

"Young man," said the man with the golden-tipped cane, "you seem to have had a difficult night."

"Yes. I am afraid that I am lost and that I have missed my train."

"Perhaps I might help you. Come: first you must take the strassenbahn to the Inner City."

The man with the golden-tipped cane led Anthony down Schafbergstrasse to the end station, where Anthony boarded the early morning tram back to the City Center, retrieved his luggage from the hotel, and waited for directions to a train station, for he believed Vienna had only one train station. Professor Wagner had remained in his chair at the Chinese restaurant, unable to make a decision. He had one glass of red wine and then ventured into the night searching for colleagues in the April fog and hoping that the sun would soon return.

Chapter 6
Klaus Weber
Vienna,1983

1

Klaus Weber, a veteran of the war now fallen on hard times, lived in the Eighteenth District, not far from the park where Bernhard Wagner stumbled through the morning, searching for lost colleagues. Klaus Weber, however, had never studied languages, had never been inside the Schlosspark, and had no friends. For the last eight years, he spoke only with the tobacconist from whom he bought the morning newspaper and cigarettes, the owner of the neighborhood bakery from whom he bought bread every day and one pastry every third day, the bartender at a small restaurant near his house, and the priest who heard his confession each Saturday. Two years ago, the tobacconist had died, and the owner of the bakery had retired. Klaus now spoke only with the bartender and a priest whose face he never saw and to whom each Saturday he confessed to sins from the past.

2

Each morning at 6:00, Klaus left his apartment and slowly walked the fifty steps to the bakery, where, each morning, he bought two Semmel bread rolls, bread crumbs for the pigeons of the Volksgarten, and one coffee. Each morning, he then caught the strassenbahn 41 at Erndtgasse, and each morning he rode to Schottentor. He spent the summer mornings at the Volksgarten, feeding the crumbs from the stale Semmel to the pigeons, who seemed to live forever on yesterday's bread. He then spent long hours in St. Stephan's, praying amid the security of its gray walls and vacant saints. No one noticed Klaus: only the pigeons looked forward to his daily visits, and when the crumbs were finished, they moved on to other people serving other crumbs.

In the fall, he attended 10:00 Mass at St. Stephan's, praying that the shells would never again destroy his cathedral. In the winter, he stayed for the 12:00 Mass, and prayed that spring would come quickly and that the days would grow longer. When he emerged from the cathedral, Klaus walked once more through the Volksgarten, He scattered the last bits of stale bread across the snow and slipped on the frozen walkway and fell to the ground amid the greedy pigeons. An elderly man stopped, put down his cane, and tried to help Klaus Weber to his feet. He quietly but firmly refused any assistance, as if the touch of a stranger might shatter his frozen limbs.

3

Klaus Weber walked carefully to Schottentor, and waited for the strassenbahn which would safely take him home. As he looked out on the women of the night on the Gürtel, Klaus Weber saw in their faces only hungry young women from decades past walking beside the rubble of the city, arm in arm, and the man with crutches and one leg, the other lost to the war, who slowly trailed them–ambivalent hope and desire.

As he did each night before he went to his home, Klaus Weber stopped at the Café Volksoper for schnapps and perhaps a silent game of kegelbahn with the sons and grandsons of his schoolmates. He had only one drink, never spoke to anyone, and never stayed later than 10:00. On this night, however, he ordered one final round for all, for he did not want to return to his home. But when the grandsons of his schoolmates showed him the photos of their daughters, he saw only the beautiful face of the lovely blonde girl, dying of consumption in the Children's Hospital, after the war.

4

On his walk home, just after his peach schnapps, Klaus Weber trudged slowly along the deserted streets of the Eighteenth

District. He paused briefly to look up to the one light shining from the second floor of an apartment building a block from his home. "Nightmares for someone else," he thought, as a woman closed the blinds of the window above him.

"So," he thought, "she had forgotten to turn off the lamp before she settles into sleep." Two hours later, Klaus imagined, the stranger would dream of clots of earth falling onto her naked body as onlookers cheered each of her desperate cries. The person would awaken suddenly, Klaus knew, not sure where she was or how she had gotten to bed. As she turned to the table and the shining lamp, the woman would realize that she was in Vienna. She would turn off the light and look toward the street below where an elderly man hesitated before each step.

5

A week later, by the time Klaus Weber reached Schottentor, a light rain was falling; by the time his strassenbahn reached the stop at Spitalgasse and Nußdorferstrasse, an elderly woman with the red arm band was soaked. And by the time he reached the Gürtel, the ambulances had arrived and orange-coated workers were sweeping the glass and metal into neat piles opposite the corner where the accident had occurred.

Klaus Weber did not stop to look at the car, which had been pushed into the rear of the Volksoper, interrupting a rendezvous between the head usher and a member of the chorus of last year's production of *The Magic Flute*. Miraculously, none of the occupants of the dressing room were harmed. Klaus Weber did notice, but only briefly, the condition of the strassenbahn, which stood intact on the rails, only its front window shattered by the body of the driver, who had been thrown through the window and into a third passing car, which had run headlong into the one tree remaining on the small plot of land outside the Währingerstrasse Station of U-6. Klaus Weber also briefly noted how slowly the emergency technicians worked on that car, as if they knew already that there was no need for haste. Klaus Weber got off the tram at his stop and walked on in the rain toward his café, and the emergency workers slowly separated steel and plastic from the arms and legs of the car's occupants. They worked carefully, for they knew that even though they might not save a life, perhaps they might preserve the memory of a life. They had nearly finished, when someone opened the car's trunk and saw first the face, that wonderful face, and then the entire body, driven through the car and into the trunk by some terrible force.

6

And that evening, as he did every evening, Klaus Weber once again stopped for his schnapps before he closed himself behind the absolute security of doors, dead bolt locks, chains, and steel bars, extra strong steel ... and he drank his evening cup of tea with the lingering taste of safety, and he said his prayers, thinking again of the women of Mauthausen, asking for forgiveness, and praying for death.

Klaus Weber finally lay in bed, trying to sleep but afraid of sleep. He knew that in his sleep he would dream once again, and they would return–the women of Mauthausen, thin beyond belief, as if their skin were a temporary cover for their bones, in which their real identities lay; the women of Mauthausen, in striped gowns, their arms outstretched on the electric fence, their arms in flight as they plunge down the cliff, their eyes knowing all secrets of human evil, refusing to be seen or to look into the eyes of others; gaunt, inhuman, emblems of orderly terror.

Even in his dreams, Klaus Weber prayed that his nightly world of monotonous barbarity would somehow collapse and release him. Perhaps, Klaus thought, this demonic world would end when the number of possible tortures was exhausted. He prayed to a God who had abandoned him or should have abandoned him. If God would not abandon him, then such a God was without memory, conscience, or virtue.

When Klaus Weber opened his eyes after his nightly prayers, the women were waiting for him, surrounding his bed, the women of Mauthausen. They wrapped their arms around Klaus Weber, led him to the window of his apartment, and forced him to jump toward the street, four stories below.

And they were waiting for Klaus Weber when he struck the pavement. The women in striped prison clothes, their heads shaved, and their mouths open just before a scream, took Klaus Weber to a stone walkway on the outside of his apartment and forced him to walk up the uneven stairs leading far above the open window of his apartment. When he reached the top of the stairs, more women were waiting for him, and they pushed him over the edge toward the street, now farther and farther below him.

He struck the pavement, and again the women forced him to climb and to fall, to struggle again and to fall again, and again, and again.

When Klaus Weber finally lay in bed, trying to sleep but afraid of sleep, he knew that in his sleep he would dream once again, and they would return. He tried to will himself to death and dream no more, but on this night, Klaus lay awake, once again alone.

Chapter 7
An Apple Falls from Heaven
Vienna,1981-1983

Klaus Weber did rise from his bed the next morning, but only to face another day of sorrow and regret. If he had friends or funds or if he had known what the government offered, he might have found some relief. But he remained alone, isolated in the past and unaware that Katharina Schmidt lived within a ten-minute walk of his apartment.

At one time, Katharina Schmidt worked at a psychiatric institute affiliated with the University of Vienna and had been asked to serve on a University-wide committee investigating work-load distributions according to gender. Professor Doctor Reinhold Schneider also served on this committee: he found Dr. Schmidt to be a very attractive young therapist, as did many other men on the committee. Dr. Schmidt, who had only recently completed her training in medical school and graduate programs in psychiatry, initially appreciated the attention, but she mistakenly believed such attention resulted from her analysis of data related to gender discrimination. When Professor Schneider complimented her on what he called her professional figure, Dr. Schmidt resigned from the committee.

Dr. Schmidt then began her private practice as a therapist and quickly established a reputation as a careful listener, a calm presence even in difficult situations, and an accurate analyst of her patients' problems. She smiled whenever appropriate, did not hesitate to offer critiques, and had tissues ready for the tears which some patients shed. Almost everyone left their sessions with Dr. Schmidt with a better sense of themselves and their lives. Her nineteenth-century home in Pőtzlelinsdorf was built by her great-grandfather and had remained in the family for nearly a century. The house included one suite of rooms which Dr. Schmidt at times rented to visiting professionals. She had not seen Professor Doctor Schneider for several years, and she did not regret his absence.

According to several of his male colleagues, Professor Doctor Schneider was not, by most accounts, an evil person and certainly not a demonic presence, by any means. However, other than the careful reconstruction of the eighteenth century, Reinhold Schneider enjoyed few pleasures. He would attend the State Opera House four times each season–*La Bohéme* and, of course, *Don Giovanni*, but not *Madama Butterfly* or *Tosca*–and he would only occasionally sleep through more than one scene. He was not an unattractive man, for a sixty-year-old scholar who shunned physical exercise, although his rather prominent nose struck many students as more than would be needed for natural breathing. On four mornings each week, he would work at home until 9:00, when he would read the day's newspaper. He met Professor Doctor Wagner for coffee on Thursday mornings, although he had never enjoyed these sessions, Unless he had a lecture to present, he would spend Thursday evenings with a prostitute from a gentlemen's club near the Gürtel; the other evenings, he would devote to correspondence with colleagues throughout Europe.

Reinhold Schneider could only sleep well if he had written a letter for one of the many professional organizations to which he belonged or if he had completed another paragraph for his study of the social structure of the eighteenth century. He had long admired the orderly life of the Habsburg court, and he sought to retain what he thought to be the principles and values of true Austrian tradition.

Chapter Three: Sin and Depravity

In the court of Maria Theresa, it was believed that luxury entered society through women, its natural victims; greed and corruption soon followed, or so they thought, and then violence. During the same period in London, women were felt to have a perpetual envy of the vices of men. Women were thought to be less often victims than men were, not by choice, but because men restricted them. According to one popular opinion, women belonged to the order of fashion and gentility, and the virtue of women was of more consequence to men than their own.

Pleased with his ability to capture the essence of eighteenth-century attitudes, Reinhold Schneider poured himself a modest glass of brandy and then retired for the night. At 7:30 the next morning, Professor Schneider returned to his scholarly duties. Schneider had made the eighteenth century his own, and he felt as comfortable in the courts of Habsburg Europe as he did on the streets of the Eighteenth District. He felt confident, therefore, that his most recent addition to his volume on modern history was both extremely accurate and quite concisely written:

> It was commonly believed by European natural philosophers that certain African tribal customs revealed the extent to which the civilized nations of Europe had progressed. For example, the eminent court physician Doctor Ignaz Seipel reported that among the Hottentots, for a youth to be received into the company of men, he should prove his manhood by beating his mother.

Of course, Professor Schneider had never beaten his mother, nor did he uncover any evidence of such conduct among the nobility of the Habsburg court. At times, he would recall his father with a touch of disdain but then, he reasoned, his father deserved far more.

Twice each week from September to June at precisely 10:00, Professor Doctor Reinhold Schneider left his home on a shaded street near Türkenschanzpark and walked to the strassenbahn stop at Gersthoferstrasse. He would leave at this time on these two mornings because he disliked the schoolchildren and workers who pressed against him if he left any earlier. He used the ride to Schottentor to organize his notes for the mid-morning class. Reinhold Schneider was a very careful and a very fair man, and he felt that his students deserved a well-prepared lecture. By the time he reached Schottentor, Reinhold Schneider would be prepared for yet another lecture, and he would be prepared to ignore the students gathered in front of the new lecture hall, protesting a reduction in their benefits.

Sometimes after his afternoon classes, Professor Doctor Reinhold Schneider visited Professor Doctor Bernhard Wagner. Professor Doctor Schneider told Wagner that he wanted to maintain contact: he also hoped to impress himself on Wagner's assistant, Johanna Stubblemeier, whom Schneider had recommended to Wagner as an attractive graduate student. Schneider had in fact impressed Johanna, so much so that after ten visits in the first three weeks of October she had assured him that he reminded her of her grandfather, who had recently died.

The week after Johanna's comment, Professor Schneider was forced to awaken early for a university committee meeting which he had hoped to avoid. At 6:45 on a foggy November day, a very unusually early hour from Professor Schneider, he sipped one cup of coffee before leaving to catch strassenbahn #41. He had walked halfway to the strassenbahn stop when he realized that he had left his umbrella at home. Decorum and prudence meant that Professor Doctor Schneider must return and retrieve the umbrella, which he carried to add to his stature and to ward off unwelcome advances. Muttering both ways, on his way back to the tram stop, he walked too quickly for an eighteenth-century scholar and stumbled off the sidewalk into the path of the outgoing 41.

"Here. Quickly," said the woman who lifted Reinhold Schneider from the gutter.

"What! What is it! Oh my."

Katharina Schmidt pulled Reinhold Schneider back to the sidewalk, as the strassenbahn sped by on its way to the Pötzleinsdorf end station. Katharina recognized Schneider, but he was too upset by the insult afforded him by the tram to note her presence or remember her name.

Once he regained his professorial dignity, Reinhold Schneider was irate: "Those drivers have absolutely no sense of responsibility. They are a curse upon the streets of Vienna!"

"Perhaps," said Katharina. "But then we all depend upon their service, do we not?"

"Bah! Rabble! Scoundrels!"

"Good day. I trust you will not be needing your umbrella."

Professor Doctor Reinhold Schneider's umbrella lay broken and twisted on the strassenbahn tracks, a fluttering black, spindly robe, no longer able to ward off the rain or bad fortune.

"Bah!"

Later that day Reinhold Schneider purchased another umbrella and wrote another paragraph on the orderly life of women in the eighteenth century. Despite his distress at the interruption of his morning routine, he was determined to maintain decorum and order as an antidote to the chaos of public affairs. He was therefore again resolved to leave for his office the same time each day, to continue writing his history of the eighteenth century, and to enjoy his regular erotic routine, which he did throughout December, a month whose holiday distractions he found particularly offensive. Armed with his winter coat, military gloves, and elite new umbrella, he had no regard for the weather: January merely replaced the chilly fogs of November and December with winter's cold, safely isolated outside the windows of his office.

Schneider likewise had no regard for the Viennese ball season in February. He felt that dancing was a distraction from his scholarly work and an entirely unnecessary prelude to occasional sexual adventures timed to accommodate his weekly routine. On the day of the year's Opera Ball, however, Schneider was forced to drive to the university in order to attend a meeting of the university academic calendar committee which was considering beginning the next winter semester one day later than the current schedule. The committee's deliberations began at noon and continued through the lunch hour, through the afternoon, and past Professor Schneider's regular dinner time. He was, therefore, considerably distressed.

The meeting finally concluded without a decision after hours of tedious debate, prolonged by academic momentum and professional obligation. Professor Schneider grumbled at his colleagues, snapped at the evening maintenance crew, and snarled at the doorman who held back the door (and his contempt for Schneider). He walked as quickly as a discontented senior faculty member should walk in public so that he could return to his home and write at least the draft of one more chapter on the insolence of women at the Habsburg court.

Katharina Schmidt did not attend the Opera Ball, but she did drive to the First District that day so that she could assist one of her colleagues whose daughter was to promenade with other members of Vienna's elite. Dr. Schmidt assured her friend that the ball was not only a remnant of Vienna's imperial past but in fact a ritual worth attending and left her reconciled to her daughter's participation. She helped the young girl with all the preparations a debutante needed, told her to enjoy her momentary status, and told her colleague not to wait up for her daughter.

Once outside, Katharina hurried to the parking garage where she had left her car, that same garage where Professor Doctor Schneider had parked his BMW, in fact on the same level and the same row. As he backed his car out, he heard the sound of a stick being snapped in two, or perhaps it was the arm of a drunken reveler. Professor Schneider was anxious to leave the First District and return to his home near

Türkenschanz Park, and so he paid no attention to the sound. Katharina, however, noticed Professor Schneider's mangled umbrella, which she carefully picked up and waved to the retreating car.

"Bah!" cursed Professor Schneider, as he first rubbed the steamy windshield and then shook his hand from side to side, as if to strike away the scent of any perfume that might yet linger in the air from any Opera Ball participant who had parked nearby. He paid no attention to Katharina, whose efforts he did not wish to understand.

Within two weeks of the Opera Ball, Professor Doctor Schneider was able to return to his morning coffee, professional correspondence, regular evening erotica, and scholarly investigation of the disorderly effect of women in the eighteenth century. Hoping to avoid any future disruptions to his scholarship and, perhaps, to his lectures, he filed a petition with the University Grievance Committee's subcommittee on Internal Affairs to have the deliberations of the University Calendar Committee declared at an impasse. After three weeks, he had received no response and so assumed that he could ignore any responsibility for changes in the next semester's calendar.

Professor Doctor Schneider, however, genuinely believed that Professor Doctor Wagner's upcoming linguistics conference was a violation of academic standards and a misuse of Ministry funds. His chagrin was increased by Wagner's not inviting him to speak. Or, though he didn't know it, by Johanna, Beata, and Gunter's not inviting him.

Shortly before the conference opened, Schneider ran into Wagner who mumbled something like an apology: "I'd meant to find you a spot on the schedule. Sorry. Assistants, you know, make mistakes. Sorry. Must rush off." Finding in this belated excuse one more proof of Wagner's incompetence, Schneider convinced himself that he certainly would have found a way to turn down the invitation, had it materialized.

In fact, he carried the venom of Wagner's oversight just as he carried his newest umbrella. He disguised this subtle mix of professional jealousy and personal vendetta during the day and then each evening he unleashed these forces in his treatise on 18th-century Vienna.

> Virtue in Maria Theresa's Vienna was to be bought at the market and sold at the court. Such casual morality extended beyond the enticing women of the street to the halls of the University. It was a common practice, particularly in the study of languages, for faculty to purchase tenure and promotion by organizing what in the eighteenth century were called "assemblages" and today are known as conferences. Participation in the assemblages was determined by the amount given to the organizers, who often promised to donate the funds to the Catholic Church for the care of Vienna streetwalkers. Such academic prostitution has continued and indeed flourished, much as the better maintained bordellos have prospered, until the present day.

"That," thought Schneider, "is a good place to stop for tonight. Yes. I am pleased with this analysis."

At 10:05 the next morning, Professor Schneider marched through the Schottentor underpass on his way to deliver his lecture on gender bias in the Habsburg Empire. His progress was interrupted when he overheard a conversation between two women about the State Opera House production of *Don Giovanni*. Katharina Schmidt was discussing the performance with Monica Hansicker, a friend from Germany who was in Vienna to audition with the opera. Katharina and Monica had thoroughly enjoyed Mozart's music and the quality of the lead singers; they also cheered the final demise of Don Giovanni. As Schneider approached Katharina and Monica, he failed to retract his umbrella, and so Professor Doctor Wagner, hurrying to a meeting at the Law School, naturally tripped over that umbrella and tumbled to the floor. Schneider did not turn to see who had fallen, but he resented the delay in accosting Katharina and Monica.

"Pardon me," called out Schneider, six feet away from Katharina, "but I believe you have seriously misinterpreted *Don Giovanni*, as so many others have also done."

"Misinterpreted?" said Monica. "What is it you are saying, and who are you?"

"I am Professor Doctor Reinhold Schneider, of the University of Vienna and an expert in the cultural nuances of the eighteenth century. I simply want to correct your statements."

Monica was neither impressed by Schneider's credentials nor pleased by his intrusion. From ten feet away, Professor Wagner likewise was not pleased by his colleague's actions. He looked at his watch, gathered his papers and his brief case and slinked away to his meeting. But Monica was not one to slink away from any confrontation.

"What is your interpretation of *Giovanni*, distinguished professor?"

"Giovanni is a heroic figure, one who revealed the immorality of European women. Mozart offered an historically inaccurate depiction."

"That's ridiculous," replied Katharina, who again recognized Schneider although he had no idea why she looked familiar.

"And who might you be," objected Schneider as he turned to face Katharina. "Ah, of course," said Schneider, "that woman from the committee." Schneider in fact had no particular committee in mind, but he knew that women and committees were in league against him.

Katharina did not find it necessary to raise her voice, but she shook her head in objection to Schneider. Monica, however, found Schneider's argument without any justification, and Monica had performed in *Don Giovanni* in Germany and Italy. She was well aware that in Mozart's opera Don Giovanni was finally and thoroughly punished for his philandering and cruelty to women. She strode over to Schneider and asked how he could propose such a statement.

"My dear young lady," said Schneider. "My comments are based on my extensive research and scholarly publications. What right do you have to object?"

"Your publications?" countered Monica. "Tell me who has actually read your publication."

"Bah!," said Schneider. "Another amateur. Please know that Don Giovanni was considered an heroic figure by many eighteenth-century intellectuals, most of whom rejected Mozart's opera." Schneider had not yet found any such intellectuals, but he was convinced that he merely needed another month or two of research to support his contention.

The argument in the Schottentor underpass about *Giovanni* had attracted several others to join in the dispute. Many Viennese, it seems, take opera and Mozart very seriously. Schneider found a few advocates, but most in the crowd took the side of Katharina and Monica. One young man, in fact, came within inches of Schneider's nose to protest Schneider's views. Schneider appealed to the rational members of the by-now quite large crowd, but only one man walked forward to assist Schneider. He had to shout his approval above the din of the chaotic assembly.

"Professor," the man yelled into Schneider's ear, "you make a strong case, a very compelling case."

The man, however, also sent alcoholic gusts into Schneider's face, and so the Professor could only turn away and reach for his umbrella as a shield from both the man's hangover and the crowd's anger. Schneider forced his way through those he felt to be his inferiors, only turning once to throw his final spear at Monica and Katharina: "Read my book!"

Katharina and Monica could not hear Schneider's words as

they walked away to the cheers of the crowd.

After the completion of the spring term at the University, Professor Doctor Schneider was able to return to the scholarly routine which he so deeply cherished. No longer must he take strassenbahn #41 to the University; no longer must he tolerate committee meetings; no longer must he risk contamination with the garlic-infused guest workers. At last, he could devote himself to his scholarship—that is, until the unfortunate accident which resulted in considerable damage to Professor Schneider's rather massive nose.

There are several explanations of the damage done to Professor Doctor Schneider's nose. There are those who claim that Professor Schneider became entangled in a violent argument with a State Opera House usher regarding a misplaced umbrella. Others suggest that he slipped on the steps of the strassenbahn, or perhaps he was tripped. The version that seems to have the most credibility, however, concerns a walk he took one summer afternoon in the Pötzleinsdorf Park, when the sky fell upon his face. To understand how such an unlikely event is possible, it seems we must again look to Katharina Schmidt and her garden party with two cousins and Johanna Stubblemeier.

Some claim that it was Katharina's cousin who threw the first of those hard, green apples skyward, as high as he could, some maintain; no, even higher, says another source. There are also those who say it was Katharina herself who snatched the apple which her cousins were tossing back and forth and then threw it at the insistent flock of crows. Most versions, however, state that Johanna was the first to throw an apple straight above her, showing that she could release her artistic impulse while harming no one but herself.

It seems unlikely that we shall ever learn the truth, but it is certain that we know the unfortunate effect. The small, hard green apple was carried by the crows, or perhaps it was the magical wind on those days before the solstice, past the street outside Katharina's home and past Herr Winkelmannn lightly tapping his golden cane to the rhythm of children skipping rope on the park's sunny playground. When the perhaps-magical apple fell, it fell onto the paths of the Schlosspark, where Reinhold Schneider walked alone, enjoying the sunset and planning his book's final chapter as the apple dropped steadily towards his nose.

This unfortunate incident, however, did not diminish Professor Doctor Reinhold Schneider's plans for the summer. Soon after the accident, Professor Schneider was again spending his usual six evenings in his cottage on the hillside of the Schafberg, tending his garden and speaking of the weather. From within the carefully-fenced enclosure, he and his neighbors could share the quiet breezes and look down on the hazy inner districts of Vienna. And as was his custom, late on the Thursday afternoon following his injury, Reinhold Schneider remained in the city, where he visited a prostitute from near the Gürtel. Professor Doctor Reinhold Schneider gently rubbed his bruised and still-swollen nose as he emerged from the whorehouse after one hour, sweating slightly and exchanging words with the proprietor.

"Ah dear Professor, I trust you have enjoyed your visit."

"Indeed, my friend, I have. You continue to provide the orderly context for pleasure."

"And your injury, dear Professor?"

"An accident prior to my visit. An accident, nothing more."

Chapter 8
Wish Fulfillment
Budapest, Rome, St. Louis
1982-1991

It may be possible that breeze from this magical apple created a ripple of desire which traveled across western Europe, the Atlantic Ocean, and one-third of the United States. It may also be possible that this global wave increased rather than diminished as it moved so carefully but ever westward for the next six years. Whether or not such rumors are accurate, it is certain that particular effects occurred in the dreams and nightmares experienced on Sherwood Circle in June of 1990. Whatever the later effects, the wind first blew poor Anthony Ignazio out of Vienna in pursuit of Father Terence.

Budapest, Rome, and St. Louis, 1983

The most immediate effect of these waves occurred in Budapest and then in Rome, in the late spring of 1983. Anthony Ignazio, that unfortunate photocopy repairman who had been stranded in the Vienna fog, tried to reunite with Father Terence and his tour of the grand cathedrals of Europe. He first took the train from Vienna to Budapest, where he learned that Father Terence and his devout tour had made a last-minute cancellation of their reservations at the Budapest Hilton.

"Do you know where they went?" a distraught Anthony asked the hotel concierge.

"Unfortunately, I do not. I am most apologetic," he was told.

Luckily for Anthony, a high school band leader from Indiana was at the very moment checking out of the Budapest Hilton. "Excuse me, sir, but I could not help but overhear your conversation. I may have some information that will help you."

Anthony had relied on divine intervention for most of his life, and so he was relieved but not surprised at the man's words.

"Yes, yes. Please let me know anything you might have heard,"

"Well, I was in the hotel lobby two days ago when the manager took a call right here at the reception desk. He just listened for a few minutes, only saying that he understood, it was a shame, and that he would issue a refund."

"Did he say anything else?"

"He turned to one of the desk clerks and said that the group of Americans from Missouri had decided to go directly to Rome, and so they would not need any of the eight rooms they had booked. He then noticed that I was able to hear his conversation and simply told the clerks to do what was required. That's all I heard. I hope it helps you."

"Yes," Anthony said. "That's very helpful. Thank you very much."

Anthony turned to the concierge and asked when the next train to Rome left the station.

"I must make a few inquiries. Could you please wait at one of the welcome tables here in the lobby?"

"Of course. I'll wait right here at this table close by."

The concierge motioned for Anthony to take a seat while he made his phone calls. However, a very distressed middle-aged man in a rumpled black suit approached the concierge and interrupted that first call. Anthony tapped his foot on the lobby's tiled floor while the concierge tried to console the man. "I'm sure we'll find the dog," Anthony could hear. "Please, just be patient." The concierge briefly looked back at Anthony as if to tell him that his questions would soon be answered.

The concierge returned to the phone; Anthony returned to tapping his right foot, joined by his left-hand fingers on the marble-topped round table. But again the call was interrupted: one of the hotel's room staff walked past with a wooden broom, a breach of hotel decorum. Anthony did not understand what the concierge was saying, but the young woman seemed to accept her scolding as she very quickly turned to the hotel's back staircase.

Anthony no longer tapped fingers or feet: he got up and began circling the table and clapping his hands every other step. Finally, the concierge completed the call and called to Anthony from behind the reception desk.

"Sir, I have acquired some helpful information."

"Yes, yes. When can I leave for Rome?"

"It appears as if there is no longer direct train service from Budapest to Rome: the authorities have suspended such train lines effective earlier this morning. It may be restored this coming weekend."

"Earlier this morning? When?"

"Apparently at approximately ten o'clock this morning."

"Ten o'clock? Five minutes ago?"

"It appears so, yes."

"But I must get to Rome. I need to catch Father Terence, but I have very little money left. I gave most of it to Father Terence."

"I may yet be of some help to you. We have several schedules of international bus lines."

"A bus?"

"Several buses, I believe."

"Several? How many?"

"Let me check the schedules." The concierge opened a drawer and placed five brochures on the reception desk table.

"It seems you must begin at the Budapest main bus terminal and take the afternoon bus to Vienna."

"Vienna? I've just come from Vienna."

"You need not go all the way to Vienna. You exit the bus at Semmelweis and look for the express bus to Klagenfurt. Unfortunately, it appears as if there is not an express bus, and you must take several buses with stops in Neunkirchen, Mürzzuschlag, and ... several other Austrian towns and villages. At Klagenfurt, only seven hours after your departure, you switch buses and travel through Venice to Bologna and then, merely ten hours later, you arrive in Rome."

"Ten hours? I'll never catch Father Terence."

"It seems as if you have few other options. Here are the schedules. Good luck in your travels, and I hope to see you again here at the Budapest Hilton." The concierge shook hands with Anthony and then turned to other business. The German couple on the fourth floor needed tickets to the symphony; a woman on the seventh floor required a taxi to the city's best hair salon, and there was that missing dog.

Anthony stood for several minutes, not sure what to do next. "Almost twenty hours on buses," he thought. "Could I endure twenty hours on a bus?" But Anthony also knew that he did not have enough money for a plane and that train service would not be ready for at least two days. Even more, Anthony still believed in Father Terence and the prospect of a private audience with the pope, which Father Terence had promised him.

And so Anthony boarded the bus to Semmelweis, and the six local buses to Klagenfurt, and the buses to Venice and Bologna and, at last, to Rome. He needed a bed, a shower, and food, but he had no time to waste on himself: he still hoped that Father Terence and the tour would still be in Rome, and he still hoped to sit down with the pope. "I must go now, right now," he mumbled to himself, "right now to the Vatican, to Father Terence, to the pope." After eighteen hours on seven different buses, Anthony walked as if a surrounded by a thick haze which made each step slower and slower. But he did walk on, walk on, like some woeful knight of rueful figure, first to an information booth at the bus terminal, where he knew he could ask in English for directions to Vatican City.

"Walk to the Vatican?" the information clerk asked. "Yes, it is possible, but it is a long walk, more than four and a half kilometers."

"Four and a half kilometers? How far is that in miles?"

Vincent asked.

"Let me see. Four and half kilometers . . . It is two point nine miles. A long walk. Here is a guided map with several important sites you may wish to visit on your walk."

"I have no choice. Thank you."

Despite his fatigue and despite the uncertainty of finding Father Terence, Anthony now had a mission, a goal which only seemed to require resolve and Catholic determination. He walked out of the bus terminal, slowly but steadily toward the Vatican. He had no time to stop, no time to look any-where but at the pavement ahead, and four hours later ("only four hours," he thought, "the buses took so much longer"), he stepped inside St. Peter's Square, where thousands of pilgrims had gathered to catch a glimpse of the pope. "Could Father Terence be here?" he asked, first himself and then a young man in a red, yellow, and blue Harlequin suit with his hands folded in front of him.

"Father Terence?" the man said.

"Yes, Father Terence, an American priest with a tour group."

"There are many Americans here, sir, and even more priests."

"But Father Terence promised a private audience with the pope."

The young man smiled as if he had heard this many times before, and yet must still act as if it were the first time anyone had spoken of a private audience.

"Sir, I am afraid that a private audience with the pope is very, very difficult to arrange. Very few people have such a privilege. Perhaps you should speak with your Father Ter-ence."

"He's not my father. That is, he is the tour leader, a priest, an American priest."

"I understand, and I am sorry, but I must answer questions from these other people."

Anthony no longer felt as if he had a mission; he only knew that he must sit down, somewhere, anywhere, but there were no chairs in St. Peter's Square and no way for a private audience. In fact, Father Terence had not promised a private audience: he had only promised the opportunity to see the pope from his balcony above the square. Only the most devout, Father Terence had told the group at the informational meeting months ago, the most influential Catholics have private audiences; we will be blessed if only we have the chance to see the Holy Father from his private balcony. Anthony felt that he was among the most devout, even if he had little influence other than on photocopy machines, and so he interpreted Father Terence's words to mean that he might have a private audience. But as he sat at a small café outside Vatican City and sipped a glass of red wine ("any red wine," he told the waiter), Anthony grew more and more disillusioned. He now just wanted to get home and return to his work.

Anthony did have with him his ticket for a return flight: Vienna to London to New York City to St. Louis. He again resigned himself to bus rides, many bus rides, from Rome back to Vienna. When he finally got to Vienna, he went directly to the airport. "I've seen enough of Europe," he thought. "I just want to get back."

And he did get back, with perhaps some assistance from the wonderful, magical breeze, and with no adventures, no delays, and no sight of Father Terence. When he did again see Father Terence, it was at a ten o'clock Sunday Mass at Holy Innocents parish in St. Louis, three weeks after his return. When Father Terence turned to the congregation to invite their personal petitions, Anthony stood up and spoke loudly and directly to the priest: "Pray that you won't go anywhere with that priest up there," said Anthony. Father Terence, and the entire congregation, were more than a little taken aback by Anthony's words, but Father Terence only hesitated a few seconds before he responded, "Let us pray," and moved on to the next petition.

On the Monday after Anthony's petition, his manager asked that he go to the parish hall at Holy Innocents where their copy machine was not printing correctly. "I prefer not to go there," Anthony told the manager. "In fact, I prefer not to go to any Catholic churches, anywhere." The manager was a very considerate man, and he valued Anthony's expertise and his years of faithful service to the company. "Such a request is very unusual," he told Anthony, "but you have earned some privileges not given to others. Alright, I won't ask you to visit any Catholic churches or schools or parish halls. Let's call it an executive dispensation. Just don't mention it to anyone else."

A cosmic phenomenon much like that which carried Anthony from Vienna to Budapest to Rome and, finally, back to St. Louis also carried Laura Stone across the Atlantic a year later. The wind from the east swept Laura away from her troubled months in Vienna, toward her family home, and free of her dreams, or so she hoped. As she rose from her seat in row 32 and reached for her carry-on bag in the compartment above, she smiled at the man across from her as he too tried to retrieve his large grey suitcase wedged into the storage compartment. Laura smiled because she still heard the bagpipes and imagined her parents once again marching through their house. "I'm home again," she thought. "I'm ready. No more nightmares."

Or so she thought.

Laura used the momentum of return after a long flight to accept the wait for her luggage, to carry her suitcases from the carousel, and then to wait again for her final flight from Chicago to St. Louis. She fell asleep on the plane and dreamed that the man with the golden cane was telling her to wake up. Once the plane landed, she again had to fetch her suitcase and find a cab for the drive to her late parents' home. She tried to keep her eyes open as the driver chatted about the weather, the traffic, and the lack of good coffee at the airport, but she felt herself slipping in and out of dreamless sleep. When the cab stopped outside her parents' house, Laura roused herself from sleep, thanked the driver, and pulled her suitcase along the sidewalk. She tried three keys before she found the right one to open the door to rooms which seemed at once too familiar and too quiet. On the plane she had resolved to stay awake at least until sunset, but inside the house she found herself so tired that she could only open one suitcase and search for the Austrian chocolates she had bought in Vienna. "Just some tea and a bit of chocolates," she thought, "and I'll do the rest tomorrow morning."

Laura hoped that she had left her dreams and nightmares in Vienna, but on that first night she dreamed again—of waltzing with a man who held her too tightly and for too long. She ran from the dance hall but she was too late to catch her son before he floated away. Laura woke up at 2:00 a.m., not certain if she could sleep again but too tired to rise and put her socks in the sock drawer, the dresses hung in the right closet, and the sweaters in the sweater drawer. She tried to sleep on her right hip and then on her left hip, and finally on her back. "It must be the jet lag," she thought. "I just need to get past this first night." An hour later, Laura rose, went to the bathroom, where the face which greeted her seemed too tired to be awake. "What time is it in Vienna?" she thought. "It must be time for coffee. Oh, I wish I could have a mélange delivered this morning. I should call Fritz or Franz and ask them to join me." But Fritz and Franz were thousands of miles to the east and were too occupied with arguing over their latest story to join Laura.

Laura spent the first week trying to find a permanent office for her practice in St. Louis, calling friends of her parents, looking for ways to attract clients, and, when she had too many spare moments, organizing paper clips by size and color. She ate by herself and tried to sleep by herself, but too often her dreams were crowded by strangers who chased her into burning houses. One night she dreamed that her former husband was lying next to her: just as he leaned over to kiss her, his teeth fell out and she began laughing. The next night she held her baby son in her arms, but when she moved the blanket to look at his face, she saw the face of Jonathan Hopewell, grinning at her until she tossed him aside and waited for her punishment. All her dreams seemed to remind Laura that the dead do not lie quietly nor do they obey our commands.

"I need to see someone," she admitted to herself. "I need to find someone to listen to me and to help me. I just wish I could sleep peacefully again." But Laura also knew that there were some other wishes she would not like to confess to others and probably some, she knew, which she did not care to admit to herself. "I need someone like Winkelmann, someone who would say only what little needed to be said and nothing more."

Herr Winkelmann and his golden cane, however, remained in Vienna, just as Fritz and Franz remained there. Laura's only hope, she realized, was to write to Winkelmann, whose address she did not know. Her first letter, which she knew would never be sent, began as an apology for not writing sooner. It was a short letter, merely telling him that she had arrived safely and was now living in her late parents' house. "I will begin seeing clients soon," she wrote to him, "and I promise to keep in touch with you. My best to Fritz and Franz." She folded the one-page letter, put it into an envelope, which she sealed and addressed to Herr Winkelmann, Vienna, Austria, and put the letter into the drawer of a desk next to her bed.

A week later, she wrote again, a longer letter this time, one in which she told Winkelmann that she had begun to see a few clients and was becoming more familiar with the house and the city in which she had grown up. "Oh, and I went to the cemetery, to visit the grave of Jonathan Hopewell, whom I told you about, the poor young man who committed suicide.

I bought some flowers to place on his grave, but as I went closer I saw his mother holding a rosary as she stood over the grave. I felt out of place there, as if I were eavesdropping on her silence, and I wasn't sure what to do. And so I left. Do you think that was the right thing to do? Please do write when you have time." She folded the two pages, placed them in a large envelope, sealed the envelope, and put it alongside her first letter.

Laura wrote to Mister Winkelmann once a week, on each Sunday morning for two months, and then once a month, and finally, after a year, only on the day her baby son had died or on those days when she wished she were in Vienna. The drawer could no longer contain all her letters, but she could not throw any of them away. They found a home in one of her parents' old grey metal milk boxes, stored safely in the attic.

St. Louis: 1989

Too soon, however, that magical wind which had driven both Anthony and Laura homeward died down over the Midwest, becoming no more than a whisper of its Viennese glory. Perhaps natural forces such as the wind, especially a dying wind, have little influence on matters ecclesiastic. Some energy outside of mere human reason, however, had enabled Father Terence Murphy to succeed Father Bischoff as pastor of Holy Innocents Church in 1982. Father Bischoff had been elevated to the rank of Monsignor and appointed adjutant bishop of the archdiocese in 1983; three years later, Monsignor Bischoff became Bishop Bischoff and head of the diocese in Butte, Montana. In 1989, few parishioners at Holy Innocents recalled Bishop Bischoff with fondness, although most thought he was a very devout man, well versed in scripture, and strict in his religious practices.

Father Terence, however, had recently created more than a few doubts among his parishioners when he announced that he would give a slide show presentation of his 1983 tour of European cathedrals. Unfortunately for him, Anthony Ignazio's tirade about the pilgrimage was still remembered by several of those parishioners, including Sarah Taylor, Irene Trilling, and Gertie and Felix Kulpa, Sr.

"Well," Sarah Taylor had said to Irene Trilling as they left Mass the morning he announced his plan, "do you recall that outburst about Father Murphy by that angry, disturbed young man? He certainly had an odd petition back in ... wasn't it 1982? I wonder why he resented Father Murphy so much. But then, perhaps Father Murphy..." Sarah hesitated, to give Irene time to offer some possibility. Irene, however, only said that she couldn't imagine what the priest might have done. "What do you think, Gloria?" Sarah then asked her daughter, who resented her mother on most days—even more when she drew attention to herself.

"Nothing, Mother. I don't know."

"Well, all I can say," Sarah said as she turned her back to Irene, "is that Father Murphy is certainly full of energy, isn't he?"

"Yes, Mother," Gloria responded. "He's full of life."

Sarah turned once again to face Irene, hoping for a more receptive audience.

"But, Irene, don't you think he should devote more of that energy to Holy Innocents? I mean, that pilgrimage was certainly a grand idea when he proposed it, but he was away from the parish and especially the school and our young boys and girls. I don't think he should start pushing to do it again. Don't you agree?"

"I suppose so, Sarah. But that tour was long ago."

Disappointed with Irene's lack of support, Sarah looked among the crowd outside the church for anyone else nearby who would listen to her. She saw Felix and Gertie Kulpa speaking with Mae Terwillinger and heard Felix say very loudly that no one should have interrupted the memorial mass they had paid for in memory of their son. "I don't give a damn what happened to that jackass in Europe," Felix shouted to Mae. "We gave money to the church for Felix's soul. That damn jackass has no right to...."

"Felix, please, stop it," Gertie whispered, as she wiped tears away from her cheek. "It was a long time ago. It's not worth it. Just forget about it. Let's get home."

Mae held Gertie's hand and simply nodded that she understood. As Felix and Gertie moved away, Sarah Taylor took her place. "It's a shame, isn't it, Mae?"

"Mother, please, let's go home," Gloria pleaded.

"What's that?" said Mae. "Oh it's you Sarah. Yes a shame. Young Felix had so much talent. But, well, he just tried to live in the starry time, didn't he?"

"Oh, yes, Felix," Sarah replied. "But I was talking about Father Terence."

"What about Father Murphy? Is he that young priest up there today?"

"Why yes, Mae, don't you know Father Terence Murphy? He's been at the parish now for seven years."

"He has? Well, he doesn't look like it. But I have to go now. Felix and Gertie are giving me a ride. Goodbye Sarah."

Sarah watched Mae slowly trudge to the Kulpas' car, and then turned to catch someone else in whom she could confide her suspicions, but, unfortunately, she found herself alone on the church steps. "Well," she said to closing doors of the Church of the Holy Innocents. "Well now ..." she said to Gloria, "we should just go home." Disappointed but still convinced that Father Murphy should spend his time in the parish, Sarah pointed to her car and led Gloria away from the church.

On her ride home, Mae asked Gertie who that woman was outside the church, the one who talked to her about Felix.

"Why Mae, that's Sarah Taylor, you know her. She lives on your street."

"Taylor? Yes. That's right. Sarah Taylor. I never really

like her much. She always looked at Gus."

"Mae, Gus has been gone so long."

"Yes. He's been gone. Well, thank you for the ride. Bye now, Gertie, Felix."

"Goodbye Aunt Mae. Take care of yourself."

"I always try."

Years ago, before Gus died, Mae had always seemed to know a person's character better than the person herself knew, but she never spoke badly about anyone. Gertie always trusted Mae's judgement, until she began to ask Gertie about the names of people they both had known for years. Gertie now recalled that time, years ago, when Mae first looked out her window and asked who Sarah Taylor was. Only later had Gertie learned that every time Mae looked out her front windows and saw Sarah Taylor outside, she said her name out loud. "There's that Taylor woman, something Taylor. Sarah. Yes. Sarah Taylor." At about that time, on her rides to and from church with the Kulpas, Mae had begun naming to herself all the buildings on the north side of the street: Village Paints, Monroe Hardware, Harold's Delicatessen, Creamy Delights, Thomas Food Mart, The Burger Den. On the way home, she would name all the buildings on the south side: Townhouse Apartments, Johnson Lock and Key, Canterbury Gardens, the Norris family home, the Garrisons, the Thompsons. She'd told Gertie more than once that she thought it was a shame that the Smith house had been torn down to make way for the lock and key shop.

"Doesn't seem right, does it Gertie?" she'd ask.

"What's that Mae? What doesn't seem right?" Gertie would respond.

"That shop there, the one where the Smith house used to be."

"Well, John and Karen just couldn't keep it up and there was no way anybody could save it."

"Still it was a shame," said Mae.

Gertie had accepted the pattern, the repetitions. As Mae rode past the old Smith house, she would try to make herself remember all the names on the street. Early on, she only had trouble recalling who owned the Garrison house. A few years later, she rarely paid attention to the stores on the street or the names of the people who now lived in the houses. On the way to church and on the way home, she would tell Gertie the names of people who lived on the street when Gus was still alive. By 1988, though, she spoke mostly of Gus, hoping she might raise him from the dead. By December, 1989, she very rarely went to church. On most Sundays, IvaLou, one of the nursing home assistants, would help her out of bed to watch mass on television. Gertie was surprised, and grateful, that Mae had been willing to come with her to Holy Innocents that morning.

By the first week of January, 1990, IvaLou was wheeling Mae out from her room to sit by a window at 10:00 each morning. IvaLou would carefully lift her out of the wheelchair and onto a rocking chair; IvaLou would then slip a belt behind the rocking chair and around Mae so that she would not fall. "Here you are, Miss Mae," she'd say. "Safe and sound. Just look at that January sun." Most mornings, Mae said nothing: she slowly rocked–back and forth, back and forth, back and forth, back and forth, back and forth—looking out the window and waiting. She said nothing to the man sitting nearby who looked down toward the floor and tried to untie his shoes. She did not hear the woman in her blue robe as she walked to the nurses' station and cursed them for being alive. Mae just looked out the window, whispering to herself: "Gus, Gus ... Gus, where are you? Why are you hiding? Gus ... Gus."

A week after Valentine's Day. Mae looked up from her bed to the ceiling and saw Gus floating up toward infinity.

Everyone on Sherwood Circle went to her funeral.

St. Louis, 1990-1991

Victor Trilling was there, in the fourth pew with his mother, Irene, and his father, John. It was the first time Victor had been inside Holy Innocents since grade school. The summer after he finished grade school, Victor had only left his house to mow the front grass; he only left his room to eat his meals. His parents were at first puzzled and then desperate. They sent Victor to a boarding school run by the School Sisters of Notre Dame, where he did acceptable work, good enough to be admitted to the state university, where, again, he did acceptable work. He'd returned to St. Louis a month after his graduation, telling his parents that he "just needed a little time to sort things out."

A few days after Mae's funeral, Irene woke with a severe headache. "I'm not feeling so good," she told John. "I just want to sit down." Her headache grew worse, and she told John that she felt tingling in her cheeks, and then she lost control of her right arm: "John, I can't see you clearly. John, something's wrong." She tried to stand but quickly fell to her knees and then to the floor. "John, Victor, what's happening?" She lost consciousness, and never awoke. The ambulance came in ten minutes, and for the next thirty minutes, the paramedics tried electric shock and IV drugs. "Cerebral hemorrhage," one of the medics said. "Get her stable and then let's move out." John and Victor looked on without speaking, but there was no need to move out.

Felicia Hopewell stood in the row behind Alice, James, and Grace Preston at the cemetery, which she knew quite well. Seven years ago, she had buried her son at the same cemetery. For the first four years, she knelt by his grave each Sunday morning—and in the next year, one Sunday a month and she always placed roses on his tombstone for his birthday. When she drove past his grave on the way to the service for Irene Trilling, she saw someone who looked like Laura Stone. But she couldn't be certain.

This was the second trip to the cemetery in a week for Felicia, and for Alice, James, and Grace Preston. Alice and James tried to comfort John Trilling with a silent embrace. As a senior in high school, Grace wasn't sure what she should say or do, but she also knew enough to stand nearby and wait for her parents. Once or twice at the church she had looked at Victor, whom she had heard about from her parents but whom she only knew as a troubled young man. "He only looks sad," she thought. "I wonder how I would look if my mother had just died." Grace also looked for Gloria Taylor and her mother: "Where is Gloria?" Grace thought. "She should be here." Grace and Gloria had never been friends. Gloria was a few years older than Grace, who always felt that Gloria looked down on her. But Mrs. Taylor had promised that Gloria would help Grace prepare for college.

Father Terence also should have been at the cemetery: in fact, he should have been at the church and he should have been at the funeral home to offer comfort to the Trilling family. The day of Mae's funeral, however, Father Terence was too occupied with his own affairs to console others. He had to pack what few clothes he owned, put his three cassocks and two collars in the rectory storage bin, and leave a note, at least a note, explaining his departure. He also had to call Gloria Taylor again to make sure she was ready.

For the last two weeks, Gloria had had stomach problems every morning: "I must have eaten something bad," she told her mother. "Go to the doctor, then," her mother told her. "I'm tired of your complaining."

She called Terence Murphy, and together they went for her pregnancy test. "If it's positive, it could still be wrong, couldn't it?" she asked the nurse.

"No, my dear: a positive is a positive. Is that your father in the waiting room? He should know."

"Yes, that's my father. I mean.... "

"I understand dear. Just be sure you get a doctor's appointment as soon as possible."

Gloria did get an appointment, but only after she and Terence Murphy had left St. Louis and found a motel in southern Illinois. Grace didn't believe the story she heard whispered in the pews of Holy Innocents church the following Sunday. At first her mother said nothing, but on the car ride from church, Alice turned to Grace and just said: "Well now, that's quite something." Grace sat still, not yet certain what to say. "Gloria, how did this happen?" she thought. "You're pregnant? What will you do? ... I'm glad I'm not."

Two days later, Grace was not yet ready to talk about Gloria and Terence Murphy, but her mother knew that Grace would soon have to reconsider her plans for college. "Gloria was going to help Grace when she moved to campus, James. You remember that, don't you?"

"Of course. She'll have to make some new arrangements. Do you know how?"

"I'm not sure, but I know she'll find somebody. She's grown up so much these last three years."

"Yes," Grace's father said, "she'll find somebody."

News of the elopement of Gloria and Terence reached the Butte, Montana diocese offices two weeks later. The adjutant read the notice in the Catholic Messenger, a weekly report sent each diocesan center, and hurried into Bishop Bischoff's office, where the bishop was trimming his fingernails.

"Is this Terence Murphy the same priest who came after you in St. Louis?"

"Murphy? That is a name I do not wish to remember."

After his mother's death, Victor remained at his parents' home to help his father cope with life without Irene. John tried to wake up each day when he always woke up, and he tried to have the same breakfast of eggs and toast which he always had. He tried to walk into his office as he always walked, and he tried to get home at the same time he always got home.

But nights were no longer the same: he hoped for angels soaring through his soul to carry him into a peaceful sleep, but he always woke up in a lonely bed.

Victor tried to help his father with talk of the good times they had shared with his mother, but Victor also could not sleep. He shared loss with his father and owned nightmares of his own. At the end of the summer, John believed that sending Victor away would be best for his son. John also was reluctant to admit that he did not want anyone to intrude on his grief.

"Victor, we need to talk," John said one July morning.

"Of course, Father, of course."

"I've been thinking, very carefully, lately."

Whatever John said next, Victor was afraid to hear what his father had been thinking.

"Very carefully, Victor, very carefully."

"Yes?"

"Victor, I think it would be best for you, maybe for both of us, if you went away for a while—some time away, a sort of vacation."

"I'm not sure that's best, father, after what's happened, I mean...."

"Don't worry about me, Victor. I'll be ok."

"But I do worry. What will you do?"

"I'll take care of myself ... the house and ... things."

"Where would I go? What would I do?"

"You should go elsewhere. St. Louis hasn't been so kind to you. Get away and maybe then you'll feel better about..."

"About what?"

"Everything."

Victor never knew what his father had learned about Monsignor Bischoff, and his father had never mentioned anything about the priest. But Victor was tired of being in the house and being near the church.

"Well, perhaps it would be good if I were gone for a little while."

"Yes. And your mother left some money for you just in case you needed it."

"Mother left money for me? Won't you need it?"

"Not now. Maybe some time in the future you could pay me back. But right now, you have the money to take a trip, a long trip if you like. Go to Europe: lots of young people are going to Europe after college. Get away...for yourself."

Victor accepted the money and the suggestion. After months at home and especially after his mother's death, Victor finally awakened to the possibility that he had been living in a dream world, often a nightmare world. He thought that he might find relief, or at least distance from the past. Two weeks later, he left St. Louis and flew to London.

The magical wind nearly lost all its energy as it crossed the Rockies and slid toward the Pacific Ocean. In fact, most people in California took no notice of what remained of its force. One elderly man out for a walk on the Santa Monica pier felt a slight tingle on his right cheek, but he dismissed it as the effect of the nearby rollercoaster, which he now resented as a noisy intrusion. But he was wrong: no natural dynamic ever wholly disappears, and many natural forces, such as our Vienna wind, eventually regain their force as they travel across the globe. What had once been a force strong enough to carry apples through the air and move Anthony from Vienna to Budapest and Rome and Laura from Vienna to St. Louis, quietly subsided as it moved across North America. The wind, however, regained energy as it left Santa Monica and churned relentlessly across the Pacific. It swirled sand throughout Mongolia, lingered over Kazakhstan and Ukraine, caught its breath again in eastern Slovakia, and then quickly skipped over Bratislava so that it could, finally, return home to Vienna in November 1991.

Much had changed since that June afternoon in 1983 when

the wind began its life. Fritz Wassermann had completed his study but had not written any more tales. Franz was expelled from the University after he attacked Professor Wagner with Wagner's own umbrella for refusing to pass Franz's examination. Professor Wagner remained an important member of various University committees whose meetings he seldom attended, and remained a scholar who had never learned to think.

Since that unfortunate incident of the falling apple, Professor Doctor Schneider had spent more and more of his time away from the classroom and isolated in his study, where he worked tirelessly on finishing his study of the Habsburg court of Maria Theresa—"Maria Theresa: Restoring the Noble Tradition." In October, 1985, he sent the completed manuscript to what he considered the most rigorous and most esteemed academic press in Europe. "They will recognize the errors of contemporary historians," he said to the associate deputy secretary of the Austrian Education Ministry. "I am certain this press, above all others, understands the true nature of scholarly endeavor." Professor Schneider waited patiently for two years for a response to his submission; on November 29, 1987, he received the following reply:

Dear Professor Doctor Schneider:

It was with great pleasure that your scholarly and carefully annotated study of Maria Theresa and the court of the eighteenth-century Habsburgs was received and thoroughly evaluated by our editorial and historical committees, whose work has been, as you noted in your letter, for years known for its adherence to the strictest standards of scholarship and accuracy. Your manuscript was praised by the review committee for its attempt to do what you name as the "restoration of academic rigor to the study of the Habsburg court and the Archduchess of Austria" and for, as you state in your lengthy introduction, "its inclusion of the specifics of that court's domestic and foreign entanglements."

As is rightly pointed out, Maria Theresa has been cited as a monarch who attempted to instill discipline and order on the Habsburg legal, economic, agricultural, and political systems of the time and to establish a strict morality on the at times rather loose sexual mores of the late eighteenth century. It is also to be commended that Maria Theresa's antisemitism and censorship are referred to in your study.

However, the study is also weakened by its failure to recognize the monarch's position as the only woman of her times to assume such a powerful position for the decades of her reign. The reference to "a woman unable to move beyond the duties of a mother and wife" seems to overlook her abilities to deal with the responsibilities of her family duties while at the same time negotiating complex international relationships and a succession of military and diplomatic challenges. The committee felt that notwithstanding the several strengths of your study, the neglect of the monarch's reform of educational, legal, and medical institutions as well as the disregard of her humane and indeed often humble persona (e.g., the manuscript nowhere mentions her use of the Viennese German dialect used by many of the commoners of the city) appear as flaws in the manuscript. As many of her contemporaries and indeed most current historians have noted, Maria Theresa was and continues to be known for her determination, practicality, and perceptive mind as well as her personal warmth and care.

It is therefore decided that at this time we cannot accept your manuscript for publication. If you wish to review the committee's lengthy and very specific evaluations and to revise your manuscript accordingly, the press would be willing to reconsider its decision.

Professor Doctor Schneider read the letter, put it aside for a day, read the letter once more and then dropped it in the trash bin next to his desk. Two days later, he emptied the bin into a brown paper sack, which he took to his hillside retreat and set on fire. He left the ashes for any passing wind to remove. Six months after receiving the letter, Professor Schneider suffered a heart attack during what was described by a key witness as "vigorous sexual activity." It left him unable to continue his research. Schneider retired from his position at the University and, like so many lonely old men, spent his days feeding the pigeons in the Volksgarten. He died in 1988.

Three years later, Johanna Stubblemeier was a full professor of American Studies. Her colleague, Beata Fuchstberger, was elected president of the Austrian Association of Medievalism three times. Gunter Stadtbad, after several years as a professional white-water kayaker, unfortunately drowned while training in Switzerland. Katharina Schmidt became one of Vienna's most highly respected psychiatrists and lived quite well in a family home in the Eighteenth District large enough for her to rent several rooms to visiting scholars.

Yet in fact little had changed in Vienna. The Ring still encircled the inner city; tears and applause, and dying love still haunted the State Opera House; St. Stephan's still ruled imperious at the center, and the strassenbahn still roamed throughout the city. Perhaps more importantly, Herr Winkelmann continued to look after Fritz and Franz, and the sound of his golden cane tapping still echoed through the streets. As the wind brought with it the early winter fog, much would seem familiar, but death, desire, and infinite dreams would bring about magical change.

Chapter 9
Requiem
Vienna, 1991

The wind felt at home in Vienna and had no reason to surge westward. Victor, then, encountered no head winds on his flight from Chicago to London, nor indeed did he meet any resistance as he traveled to the east on the continent. And east he must go, for he knew that he must follow his cousin Felix and go to Vienna, where Felix had died some ten years earlier. "Perhaps," Victor thought, "Felix found something or someone in Vienna, or perhaps he found relief or redemption." Regardless, Victor knew that he must visit the City of Dreams. After aimless days spent walking the streets of London, and two days in Paris avoiding Notre Dame, and a weekend in Rome ignoring the Vatican, he was taken by train to Vienna. He wrote to his father that he had managed to secure a grant from what he called an important agency in Vienna: "I'll be doing research on the role of the priest in Austrian parishes. And besides, I'll be able to find out more about Felix." Victor believed everyone in St. Louis would accept such a rationale for his time, and, through this imaginary grant from an anonymous institution, he could justify to himself nearly anything he would do. Victor did not know, however, that he would be in the city for the 200th anniversary of Mozart's death.

In Vienna, he soon was surrounded by a city of classical music and its tradition of gala funerals. Each day posters announced in German and in English the grand music, religious pageantry, international recognition, and public festivities which would celebrate the anniversary of Mozart's death, if not his funeral. Mozart's Requiem would be performed in St. Stephan's cathedral, the posters declared, the religious and historical center of the City of Dreams. Sir Georg Solti would conduct, the Vienna Philharmonic would perform with the State Opera chorus, soprano Arleen Auger, alto Cecilia Bartoli, tenor Uwe Heilman, bass René Pape would be featured, and warm red wine would be available in stalls outside the cathedral, with the Requiem displayed on a huge screen mounted on the church exterior. It would be an event befitting the death of a great composer, a composer whom Victor knew at least by name.

Among the thousands of other people who had yawned through November and yearned for December in Vienna were two young Americans: Ernest Stanton, a young writer studying contemporary Austrian fiction and hoping to write his own stories in Vienna (He had a title, *Tales of the Eighteenth District*, but no stories.) and Robert Foxworth, awarded a grant to study the history of Esperanto at the Austrian Institute of Linguistics. Victor had not yet met Robert, but he knew Ernest from a lecture both had attended on the Austrian writers' response to sexual abuse. Since they met, Ernest had not made any progress on his collection of stories, but he had met Professor Johanna Stubblemeier at a wine and cheese reception at the University of Vienna and, through Professor Stubblemeier, Beata Fuchstberger, the president of the Austrian Association of Medievalism. Ernest was also determined to make the most of the Mozart celebration.

Ernest called Victor to urge him to join a group he was organizing to attend the concert. "I have to admit," he told Victor, "I'm enchanted by the possibility of aesthetic inspiration on such a gathering, particularly one available at no cost other than for the wine we'll need on a chilly December evening."

Victor was not so enthusiastic. "Ernest, I'm not here looking for inspiration."

"Well then, why are you in Vienna?"

Victor had come to Vienna after what he called his "personal research" in England, France, and Italy. "I have difficulty staying anywhere for more than a few weeks," he said.

"Ok. You're wandering around Europe, but why Vienna?"

Rather than answer, Victor simply agreed to meet Ernest outside the Aida pastry shop near St. Stephan's an hour before the Requiem would begin. He had grown accustomed to crowds with their faces of anonymous concern, but he was not looking forward to the mass of people congregating on

Stefansplatz outside the cathedral.

Ernest next spoke with Katharina Schmidt, the Austrian psychiatrist and Ernest's landlady, who he hoped would join them. When Ernest asked Robert to join the group, Robert appeared to be reluctant to spend too long in the cold: "Last December I buried my father," Robert explained to Ernest. "I got so cold at the cemetery that it took me two weeks to move my fingers." He did not tell Ernest that for him death was to be forgotten, not celebrated; instead, he agreed to join the group outside St. Stephan's.

A week later, crowds gathered at Stefansplatz to celebrate another death. Victor had been the first to arrive, twenty minutes before Ernest walked down the Graben, looking around the crowd to see how he might create a story. Johanna and Beata arrived next, not certain whom they were to meet. Katharina came at 7:40; Robert was last to arrive. Someone had bumped his arm, spilling his glass of glühwein on an old man who limped through the crowd. Robert apologized, and the man walked on slowly.

After Robert joined the group, they all listened carefully as they sipped their warm red wine, and they all spoke during the Kyrie, but neither God nor Mozart punished them at that time.

"It must have been like this the night he died," thought Victor. "Cold, Vienna cold, and the snow. Perhaps Mozart was impatient for death that night."

"Tell me, Robert (That is your name, isn't it?)" asked Katharina, "how do you enjoy the Requiem?"

At first, Robert did not reply. "I'm sorry, what was it you said?"

"The Requiem," said Katharina. "I asked if you enjoy the Requiem."

"Oh, yes," said Robert, "Yes. Of course."

Next to Robert, Ernest seemed enchanted in a world of his own. "What an occasion!" he thought. "Friends, music, and wine, to celebrate the occasion," he said.

Johanna thought Ernest was a bit too American, but she also thought he brought some needed cheer on such a cold night. As Ernest spoke, she looked at Beata, who seemed to share her opinion.

Robert turned to Victor, who seemed to have retreated inside his overcoat. "Victor, Ernest told me that you're doing research on the priesthood."

Victor pretended that he was focusing on the music from inside the cathedral and that he had not heard Robert, who then ignored Victor's silence.

Ernest, however, felt inspired by the wine, if not the music, and he wanted everyone to share his enthusiasm. "The cathedral is so . . . immense, so historical, isn't it Katharina?"

"Yes, Ernest," Katharina said with a slight grin. "St.Stephan's is indeed historical. Victor, have you been inside, perhaps to attend a mass?"

"No. I seldom attend a mass."

"But you're studying ..." said Ernest,

Robert could not resist interrupting. "St. Stephan's has no soul, no magic, no forgiveness," he said.

"Yes. I believe you are right, Robert," said Katharina. "There is nothing to hide behind in St. Stephan's. Its secrets are in the detail of colors hidden by a grayness throughout, as if the walls had themselves absorbed the December fog and made it tangible, permanent, decorative. There is no refuge in St. Stephan's, only crowds and space in which you might be lost but never hidden."

"But Doctor Schmidt, such sound, such music!" said Ernest, who seldom listened to symphonies, operas, or requiems, but who was inspired by his second glass of wine. "Please. Just listen. Please!"

"There are so many altars," Katharina said to Robert. "But there are no recesses; there is always space remaining to be filled. The music is always inadequate; no matter how full, how complete, space remains. The only hiding places are remote, inaccessible. The walls and statues allow our eyes to hide in surprising detail, but inside St. Stephan's, finally, there is no sanctuary."

Victor knew that too many churches offer hiding places, but he kept silent.

"You may be right, Katharina" said Beata. "But it seems tonight that we must grant Mozart his due."

"I think those two must drink more and talk less," Johanna told Ernest. "We have heard this all before...."

"Really?"

"Several times..."

"But," said Ernest, "if you would just ..."

"We won't," Robert insisted.

"Share your wine ..."

"Or go for more," said Johanna.

"Yes. Someone must go for more," added Beata, "before the stands close."

"Yes," said Katharina. "Please go. Victor, would you please ..."

Victor had turned away from the group, looking upward to the screen on the cathedral wall.

No one went for more wine. If they sought release through the wine, they would only grow colder. If they sought sanctuary on this December night, on the night Mozart died, they also knew, although no one spoke of it, that they would not find it inside St. Stephan's, packed tightly with well-paid musicians who drew on their talents to honor genius. Nor would they find it outside, where the crowds had gathered to watch the screen hung on the cathedral's wall.

Robert had brought his pocket recorder to tape the Requiem on that night. He taped their jokes, their talk, their hidden fears, hoping that he might find some absolution for sins of his youth and some relief from his sense of loss.

"Whenever I will feel the chill of the fog," thought Robert,

"I will play the tape, and I will recall a group of people who came together on this night and who are sharing–at least–these hours, these moments when death seems centuries remote and only the music and the wine are close at hand."

But they could not imagine the night that Mozart died. None of those who gathered at Stefansplatz had danced with angels; none of them had died. Robert and Victor, however, had lived with the dying and the dead, and so they could not celebrate on the night of the bicentennial. Ernest's father remained only a melancholy memory which he seldom invoked; Katharina knew the sorrows of others and, at times, her own sorrow. Johanna and Beata had lost parents and friends. But all thought they could look to the screen on St. Stephann's and listen to the Requiem and drink their wine and make any comment they chose. God did not keep Mozart alive, and God would not strike them dead for anything they said, as they watched, and sometimes laughed, and heard the wonderful music from inside St. Stephan's.

"Someone" Beata repeated, "must go for more wine."

"I will," said Robert, "but wait ... after the Sanctus...."

"But inside St. Stephan's," Katharina would continue, but even Ernest was moved by Mozart's mass.

"Listen," Ernest said, as he listened to music he had never heard before,

They stayed together on Stefansplatz on the night when Mozart died and when Vienna and the world celebrated his Requiem. A few joked, and they drank, but more than all they listened.

When the Requiem was complete, when the chorus had disbanded and the orchestra retired and the soloists gone their own ways to approval, certainly, and to love, perhaps, they went in search of a warm cellar and smoky cheer, a café where none of them would have to be alone. Despite their jokes and their laughter, they all knew that they did not want to be alone on that night, the night that Mozart died.

They did not know each other very well, but they all knew that none of them could laugh as easily alone as they all could laugh together. And so they went in search of a refuge on this cold December night.

Although Katharina, Johanna, and Beata had lived in Vienna for most of their lives, they did not know the Inner City very well; Ernest and Robert knew only those cafés which they said did not offend them or which they could afford. As the crowd at Stefansplatz went their different ways, they tried to agree on a bar, a café, a direction. It took too long, they all agreed, but at least they could use the remains of the wine and punch to stay in good cheer and to ward off the chill of the fog.

When they finally straggled to Café Myloo, just off Augustinerstrasse, not far from the State Opera House, they found a table in the rear, a table with room for them all in a safe corner, in a space where they could hide, if they needed to hide. Café Myloo provided the sanctuary they all needed, and it provided the beer, and the wine, and the food they all could use to keep the music alive.

"Even if you would promise me Mozart's Requiem," said Robert, "I could not seek out death the way lovers seek ecstasy–but I would have you all for my pallbearers!"

Of course, all the others agreed. A Requiem would be worth dying for–of course.

"And if I could die the way they die at the State Opera House," said Johanna, "I would die happily, gloriously, finally!"

But they could not agree on the aria.

"Mimi," said Beata, "Consumed by love!"

"And," added Johanna, "her infected lungs."

"Who is Mimi?" asked Ernest, who only listened to opera if it was featured on the sound track of a cartoon.

"No," objected Katharina. "Much better Tosca. If I only had such a chance. To leap into hell, cursing every Scarpia I have ever known."

"Have you known many?" asked Victor.

"Why not Senta" asked Johanna. "She leaps–if she's not too heavy–for love–and to redeem that irresistible Dutchman."

"Who is Senta?" Ernest again asked, "and what is a Dutchman?"

"Male fantasy, perhaps?" said Victor.

Katharina hesitated between puffs of her cigarette, looked at Ernest and stated that "All opera is male fantasy."

"Carmen! my favorite," added Beata. "At least she doesn't give in to the tenor."

"Whose fantasy?" asked Ernest.

"Perhaps."

Robert objected to Carmen: "She just rolls cigarettes and her eyes."

"But how she rolls them!" added Beata.

"No," said Katharina. "Not Carmen or Senta or even Mimi."

Ernest tried to join the chorus, but he could only ask about women he had never met: "Who then?"

"Yes," said Victor, "Who else dies?"

"Butterfly," said Katharina, "Madama Butterfly."

"But again," objected Robert, "male fantasy."

"No," said Katharina. "Not this one. Not Cho-Cho San. Not Butterfly."

"Even worse," said Johanna, "A western fantasy of Japan!"

"Japan?" asked Ernest, "Butterflies in Japan?"

"Perhaps," said Victor. " Perhaps ..."

"Listen to her," Katharina insisted. "Look at her. From the opening she lives under her father's death-blade ..."

"And then," said Johanna, "she must put up with that American tenor ..."

"Yes," Robert agreed, "The insufferable Pinkerton factor!"

"But when she dies," said Katharina, "she dies for us all; she dies so that we may hear and that we may remember her voice. I hear her voice; I hear her dreams and her regrets. Butterfly expresses desire and longing. Her death itself is less important than her longing."

"Too many women" added Beata, "die at the State Opera."

"Too many women" said Victor, "die in Vienna."

"Yes," Katharina agreed. "Too many women die."

"Too many die," said Robert.

Some argued on for Senta or Mimi or Carmen or so many others. But finally they could only agree that it is good to die at the State Opera House and to rise again with the curtain. They talked, and they drank, for hours. They spoke of death as they spoke of books they had read, or plays they had seen. They laughed in the face of imaginative death, and they needed and consoled each other.

Even as they talked, however, they knew that some of them would die in pain or in refuge from pain. Robert had held his grandmother's hand as she quietly receded further and further away. A year later he had sat with his father, as he slipped away from suffering to silent release. Not long afterwards, Victor had watched as they carried his mother away, never saying goodbye. Even Ernest, who to others seemed so distant from grief, even Ernest thought once more of his father and those others left behind. Katharina quietly smoked another cigarette; Johanna and Beata could only imagine what funerals they might soon have to arrange.

Still, that night at Myloo, they could talk happily about dying at the State Opera House and about toasting Mozart's Requiem. And they could talk happily, and they could drink to Mozart, and the night, and each other, and they could try to forget the faces of death which had driven them to Vienna.

When they left the café, the winter fog had returned on the night Mozart died and had cast everything and everyone within a grey and chilly spell. And then, they came suddenly upon the cathedral. The wine and their desire, and the tales of romance they had been inventing for hours after the Requiem, carried them through the narrow streets of the Inner City, but they were not prepared for the vision of St. Stephan's arising out of the fog and insisting that they be silent.

They encountered St. Stephan's suddenly, magically. The fog had transformed the night, and the cathedral's spires floated above the plaza. It seemed to each of them as if any moment it might disappear into the fog and ascend to heaven, leaving only a memory or perhaps a space quickly swept and put to good use.

Against the locked door of the cathedral, the frozen body of a street beggar lay quietly. Her eyes gazed beyond them all, perhaps toward the life she once knew before the fog settled on Vienna, perhaps toward an opera house in another city, in another time. Her mouth seemed frozen in agony and regret, and they could not turn away and they could not help her. They could not look at her face, and they could not avoid her eyes. She tore into their souls, and she accused them of neglect.

Finally, Victor spoke.

"This afternoon, before I came to the Requiem, I saw another body, another frozen body, from the windows of the bus, #1a–just before the Graben, in the First District, not far from St. Stephan's. Three police held a black plastic sheet across the sidewalk on the left side of the corpse, three more held another sheet on the right side, as if they could shield those who walked by from the person's contorted face. I could only look from the window of #1A over the red and white police line, toward someone checking the pulse, or looking for identification, or, perhaps, certifying death. I could only see the crossed, stiff legs, and those black plastic sheets, as if the police had torn lawn waste bags into strips, bags we used each November to collect the fallen leaves from our maple trees. I could not see the face, only the face of death–official, cold, helpful, relentless."

As Victor thought of the frozen man near the Graben and

the frozen street beggar, the voice of the fog seemed to call to them all, and they put aside their selves, and they listened together.

"They have all died," the fog whispered, "and so too will you. And I will remain, to hide your sins and your weakness and to give you sanctuary. But you will die, and few will remember you and no one will gather at Stefansplatz to drink warm red wine and hot punch on the anniversary of your death. And I will return, always, every December, always."

They listened to the fog, and they had no answer.

Those who remained could only walk away from St. Stephan's and the frozen street beggar, with hunger and regret frozen in her hands, in her soul. The police van broke through the fog, its blue light burning their hearts as they turned away. And they walked toward Stefansplatz, looking away, looking for someone to tell, looking to report death....

Thought Robert	and Victor	and Ernest
"She looks so cold,	my mother gone	and they played
could never have	tried to hold my	hand to heaven and
moved, just as my	own ... and	I will walk with you
father seemed	too cold, too cold	and I will talk with
so light, so solid yet	to have held me and	you, and we sang
father was gone	to sing with me	in paradisum,
would not return	and if only	may angels lead you
and would never sing	we would never die	in paradise, we
would never sing	and would never	sing, still...."

Still, they walked just beyond St. Stephan's, into the plaza surrounding the church where they had listened to the Requiem and where they had seen the face of death and heard the voice of the fog.

And suddenly, perhaps magically, they came upon the streetcleaners, who had come to sweep away the trash from the crowd at the Requiem and who did not intend to perform or to console.

But they did. They worked slowly, gracefully, or so it seemed. And they persisted in the face of the cold, and the loneliness of their early morning tasks, sweeping away the excess of people who only pretended to be in danger.

The fog and the floodlights from the cathedral made their orange suits appear even brighter than they would be in daylight. They moved slowly, carefully, their brooms gathering in whatever remained. At times they moved in pairs; at times, they were alone, sweeping, ever carefully sweeping, and they covered the entire plaza, moving slowly, carefully, choreographed by necessity, without a sound save the swish-swish-swish-swish of their brooms.

And from some balcony in some apartment in the heart of Vienna, the mourners heard the music, and they knew they were not alone that night, the night that Mozart died. It was Puccini: it was the interlude from *Butterfly*, the humming chorus, when we know that he is a scoundrel and that she will die. But while she waits, motionless, the delicate strings and chorus, at least for a moment, suggest graceful, eternal love without regret.

And so the orange-coated streetcleaners moved to the sounds of the interlude, as they cleaned the debris from the Requiem and unknowingly comforted those who remained in Stefansplatz. The fog hung suspended just above the cathedral, and a light snow fell on Stefansplatz. Amid the entire sleeping city, only a very few were alive to hear the music of the streetcleaners.

"I will not forget this night," thought Victor. "I will recall the voice of the dead and the face of death and, more than anything, the dance of the streetcleaners. Perhaps some day I will be able to face death and myself and say: 'Come. I have friends. I have memories. I am not alone.'"

On that night when Mozart died, those who remained seemed to have found consolation, hope, perhaps, outside the cathedral and they thought they could again share love and desire in the face of death.

They lingered on the fringe of Stefansplatz for a moment, and then each left to catch the final strassenbahn of the night. The streetcleaners finished their work, and they too departed– perhaps themselves to seek refuge from the cold and the fog; perhaps to sweep another plaza in another part of the city. An elderly man crossed the empty square, and the tap-tap-tap of his golden cane resounded through the vacant city.

Chapter 10
The Woman in Orange and Blue
Vienna, 1992

Victor had not seen Ernest since the night of Mozart's Requiem; for weeks Victor also had put aside what he called his research on Austrian priests. "I'm taking a few days off," he wrote his father, "so that I can have a little distance in my research. I think I'm still unsettled. You know what I mean." Victor's father did not quite understand Victor, but he was very familiar with Victor's delays, his impatience, his weeks of silence when he went away for high school and again when he was in college. He tried to accept Victor's months of traveling throughout Europe, but he could not understand exactly what he was doing in Vienna. "Perhaps," his father thought, "he'll find out something about Felix."

"Victor is doing some advanced study in Vienna," his told Alice Preston. "He's very interested in the church ... in the priests."

"Well, at least he's in Vienna," Alice said. "James and I have always wanted to go there ... to hear the music."

"Vienna is a beautiful city, at least from what Victor has written."

"He's so lucky. I know Grace would love to be there with him."

But Victor was not feeling lucky as January's cold spread throughout the city. Even on sunny days, he spent most of his time inside his apartment, taking notes on his plans for the next week, and for the week after. When the phone rang on the afternoon of the last day of the month, Victor at first was startled: no one had called in days, and his first reaction was that something terrible had happened to his father.

"Yes, yes, what is it? Who's there?"

"Victor, it's me, Ernest Stanton. How are you?"

"Oh, Ernest, it's you. Yes, I'm fine. How have you been?"

"Well, I've made some progress on my stories. Just finished one about an American guy named Felix Kulpa, who caused a wreck on the trams. It's based on an actual event . . . happened a few years ago."

"Oh, yes. I know that man. He was my cousin. I'd like to learn more."

"Really? Your cousin? Here's what I found out in the archives of one Vienna newspaper—*Die Presse.*"

"*Deepresse*? Not a happy title, at least in English."

"Maybe not, but according to an article from ten years ago, this Kulpa person ..."

"My cousin, Felix."

"Yes, yes, your cousin Felix, took over strassenbahn #41 at the Pőtzleinsdorf end station, near the top of Schafberg mountain, and drove it down toward the City Center."

"Did he make it all the way down?"

"He didn't—seems as if he ran into a garbage truck, or maybe it was the other way around, and died in the crash. That's all the story said about it. Did you ever hear anything else from your family?"

"No. No one really talked much about Felix. I'll let the family know what you told me."

"I'll see if I can find out anything else. We should get together and talk about that. But I just called to see how you're doing and see if you want to meet for coffee."

"I'm not sure. I've got a lot of work to do ..."

"Come on, Victor. You're not a monk in some Austrian monastery."

"No, I'm not. It's just that..."

"No excuses! Let's meet at Café Eiles on Tuesday, 10:00. I've had an interesting experience I want to share. Might become the basis for a new story."

"Ok. Tuesday, 10:00 at Eiles."

"Excellent. Don't be late."

Victor arrived at 9:45 and found a table in the rear, away from the morning crowds. Ernest was only a few minutes late, but he came in rush and began with an apology.

"Sorry Victor, but I let the earlier trams go without me. I waited for twenty minutes, just to see if she would return."

"If who would return?"

"Oh, yes. The woman in orange and blue. Let me tell you about her. Last Monday, I did as I always do every Monday: I took strassenbahn #41 from my apartment, but I forgot my pass and so I had to get a daily ticket and, on this particular day, take a detour on #5. The tram had almost reached the Albertgasse endstation when a young woman dressed entirely in blue and orange boarded at the Florianagasse stop and sat opposite me. She wore a bright orange scarf above a light blue tunic; one pant leg was blue, the other orange. The shoe on her blue pant leg was orange; the other shoe was blue. She struck me as someone whom I should watch carefully, particularly after she began to search under each seat on the tram car, and so I could not help but follow her as she moved from the front to the back of the car. Fortunately, I got up from my seat before she reached me, and so I could then quickly get off and find the closest Vienna Transport Office to buy an annual pass."

"Were you really so concerned about that annual pass?"

"Well, it's cheaper to buy one of those than to pay every day. And it's much easier. But let me get back to that woman in orange and blue."

"Yes, get back to her. Did you see her again?"

"Listen to what happened on the next day, a Tuesday. I left my apartment at my usual hour and walked my one hundred steps to the strassenbahn stop with my annual pass in hand."

"You've counted the steps?"

"Well, I needed something to do when I first got to Vienna, and that way it looked as if I had something important on my mind. But forget about the one hundred steps. I was just getting to the tram, when I hesitated before taking my usual seat ..."

"You have a usual seat?"

"It seemed to me that everyone had a personal seat, a seat somehow reserved for them. But don't interrupt."

"Go on, please."

"I wanted to be on that tram to see if the woman in orange and blue was on board. She wasn't yet anywhere to be seen, but at the next stop, she very confidently boarded the same car. She didn't say anything to me—in fact, no one on the tram spoke to me or to anyone else. But the woman in orange and blue did smile brightly as I pretended to look past her at the passing buildings. I got off at Floriangasse, just behind the woman, who walked down toward the City Hall and the Ring, a few steps ahead of me."

"Ernest, don't tell me that you followed her."

"Just listen. I did feel a little awkward following her, and so I slowed down and stayed on the opposite side of the street. She turned once and simply nodded what I thought might be encouragement, or at least acceptance. She walked steadily ahead, so steadily that I had to speed up after one street light turned against me."

"You're lucky she didn't call the police."

"I didn't think of that at the time. I was just doing some research for my stories."

"You were just being a perverted American man."

"Victor, stop it. Just listen to what happened next."

"Alright. Go ahead."

"I had arranged a meeting with an Austrian writer that day at Café Landtmann. It might have been merely a coincidence, but the woman in orange and blue had entered the café about five minutes before my appointment, that's what Ingeborg told me. When I got to Landtmann, I saw Ingeborg Häupl ..."

"She's the writer."

"Yes, the writer. Well, I saw her at a table next to the table of the woman dressed in orange and blue. Ingeborg waved from across the café and motioned for me to join her. As far as I could tell, the woman in orange and blue had not spoken to Ingeborg. I joined Ingeborg, and tried to hide my interest in the other woman, but she was difficult to ignore. On that day she wore orange shoes and bright orange pants. She had a white pullover, with blue and orange trim, three blue rings and a blue bracelet–bright blue streaks in her black hair, and an orange backpack, which seemed to be empty. She also seemed very concerned, very intent, very worried. Very sad. She soon left."

"Did you say anything to Häupl, that writer?"

"Not immediately. We talked about some of her novels and about my stories. She's quite good, very well known. I think she could help me."

"And what about the woman in orange and blue?"

"I just asked Ingeborg if she had noticed her."

"Had she?"

"She said something about her clothes, thought they were ... distinctive, I think that's the word she used."

"That's all?"

"We got back to my stories, but I did want to tell her a bit about the woman and see if she thought she might be a good character in a story."

"What did she think?"

"I told her that I had not met her; I didn't know her name, and didn't know if she rode the strassenbahn at the same time every day."

"Did you tell her that you were stalking her?"

"I wasn't stalking her. I just told Ingeborg that I thought the woman in orange and blue was quite lovely and that she probably was Turkish. That struck Ingeborg as an odd thing to say.

"'Why do you think she's Turkish?' Ingeborg asked. 'You really don't know anything about her.'

"I felt silly, ignorant, too American," Ernest admitted.

"You were," Victor told him.

"Ingeborg told me that such a person would not fit into many stories. 'She would just draw too much attention to herself, too much a distraction,' she told me, 'unless you have a compelling story about her, about her background, her motivation. Without that,' Ingeborg said, 'you have a caricature, not a story ... or perhaps a personal obsession?'"

"'No, I'm not obsessed,' I told her, 'just interested. I'll let her go her way and get back to my story about the American and the strassenbahn.'"

"Cousin Felix," said Victor.

"Right, your cousin. But let me get back to the woman in orange and blue and Ingeborg's advice."

"What did she tell you?"

"'Good,' she told me as she got up to leave. 'Keep on that one, and forget this strange woman.'"

"Ernest, I think Ingeborg has given you good advice. Now, I need to finish my coffee and get back to my own work."

"How goes your research on priests and bishops?"

"It goes."

"That's all?"

"Yes ... for now. Sorry, but I must leave."

"Of course. Stay in touch. Let's meet again soon. Take care, Victor."

"And you as well."

Victor did not, however, return to his work or to his apartment. Instead, he thought he could devise a better plan for the next week if he walked through the Inner City and perhaps if he had another coffee. When he left Café Eiles and as he crossed the Ring, a man in black, entirely in black—hat, coat, pants, shoes–but no collar and not a priest, bumped into him from behind, said nothing, and continued on his way. Victor was at first annoyed and wanted to follow the man and ask why he had knocked his arm. "But then I'm just acting like Ernest and that woman in orange and blue," he thought. "And I'm not a writer."

And yet, Victor seemed unable to release this man in black from his watch. To escape the loneliness of his apartment and the tedium of what he called his work, Victor followed the man across Heroes Plaza, past the Hofburg palace to St. Michael's plaza where the man entered St. Michael's church, opposite Café Griensteidl. Victor sat at the café but had not yet ordered when he saw the man leave the church and walk along Augustinerstrasse to the Augustine church. Victor hesitated for a minute, then followed the man inside. Victor stood at the back of the church as he saw the man kneel quietly inside the simple grace of the church, seemingly unaware of or perhaps uninterested in the 500 years of Hapsburgs who had worshipped there. Victor did not pray with the man of the churches, but he followed him through the early morning crowds on Kohlmarkt and the Graben to St. Peter's church. The man seemed just as intent here as he had been earlier. But Victor saw that the man of the churches stayed only long enough for a few beads on the rosary he carried with him—he seemed to be tireless and perhaps driven by terrible sins.

After making the sign of the cross, which Victor did not do, the man of the churches walked at a slow but steady pace to kneel outside two small and ancient churches–Maria am Gestade, and then St. Ruprechts. He lingered on the steps of each church, as if centuries of guilt and absolution might bring him peace. Then he continued his penitential walk to the Jesuit church, and then the Franciscan church, where he completed all the beads on his rosary. Victor felt the man's simple ritual didn't match the elaborate faith decorating the walls and ceilings of the churches, a faith which Victor had long since abandoned. Finally, the man of the churches crossed the Ringstrasse and went inside Karlskirche, where he lost himself in the mid-day crowd of worshippers and tourists. Victor hoped that he might at last have received forgiveness. Again standing at the rear of church, Victor attempted to pray for the man, and for the souls of the departed, but the tourists from Germany were themselves too intent on gazing on the past. Victor could only recite a simple prayer for the dead which he had learned from his mother and catch the #41 back to the apartment. He tried to recall all the churches, but he could only list the names, the many, many names. There were too many churches, too many frescoes, too many sins, and too many confessions. He only recalled that the man of the churches never entered during a mass or when any priest might likely be nearby.

That night, Victor slept the uneasy sleep of uneasy souls. He woke twice during the night: the first time, he got out bed and looked out his apartment window to the hills of the Vienna Woods. No one else seemed to be awake, at least no one walked on the sidewalk beneath his window. He tried again to sleep, and perhaps he did, but he also dreamed— of a figure in orange and blue who floated above him in his dream and whom he reached upwards to bring toward him, and then of another figure entirely in black who grabbed hold of Victor's arm, his shirt, his legs to drag him away from the woman in orange and blue. Victor awoke, left his bed, and did not get back to sleep.

The next morning Victor called Ernest, the only person he knew in Vienna who would listen to his story of the man of the churches.

"I encountered a most unusual man yesterday," Victor told Ernest. "Most unusual."

"You did? In what way was he unusual?"

"He seemed to be on some sort of pilgrimage, or perhaps an obsession."

"I think most pilgrimages are a version of obsession—but tell me more."

"This odd fellow was dressed entirely in black—hat, over-coat, pants, shoes ..."

"You looked at his shoes?"

"I had some time to myself yesterday, Ernest, and so I could engage in a type of surveillance."

"Go on then, what else did you see."

"This man went from church to church in the First District,

almost all afternoon...."

"How do you know this? Did you follow him?"

"As I said, by coincidence, I had a few free hours that afternoon."

"Was he a priest or prelate of some kind?"

"I don't believe he was, but I can't be certain. Now, isn't that a strange event?"

"Yes, very odd. Perhaps as odd as that woman in orange and blue."

"Ah, the woman in orange and blue. Have you seen her again?"

"No, but I did try to write a story about her. It didn't come to much."

"That seems to be for the best. Alright now, Ernest, I must go. At least I have to pretend to be working on my research."

"As I pretend to be writing. Good bye, then. We'll have to meet again soon."

Outside his apartment, fog had silently surrounded the building and erased all sense of distance and location, for Victor, an irresistible force which drew him from his rooms to the street. He found brief refuge in the tram ride from Pötzleinsdorf to the city center, and then again in the Schottentor endstation beneath the Vienna streets. But the fog called to him, and he rode the escalator to the Ringstrasse. The city seemed to be crowded with ghosts wrapped in overcoats and moving quickly out of the mist, only to be replaced by other ghosts who never looked up.

Victor caught only a glimpse of what might have been an orange scarf, a trail of expectation leading through the narrow, cobbled streets of the heart of the Inner City. Gray figures emerged from uncertain doors and floated past him, their disconnected steps echoing across the stones above the Roman ruins. The fog seemed to multiply and confuse the streets, creating imaginary alleys and intersections which made his progress almost impossible. Across the square, a woman's shape moved through the halo cast by the iron lamp and then disappeared down Judengasse. Following as quickly as the uncertain light would allow, Victor pushed through the mist and turned onto the narrow passages of Seitenstettengasse, steps shattering the quiet opposite the Synagogue. Unseen hands seemed to pump the insistent fog deeper and deeper into his lungs, forcing him to pause, desire no longer outpacing breath. A tap-tap-tap-tap of footsteps seemingly repeating a familiar route sounded behind him, on the slight incline leading to St. Ruprecht's Church. Turning quickly and glimpsing only the shadow of an echo, colorless and vague, he walked back toward the church, hoping for any sign of the woman in orange and blue, a vision of loveliness that might dispel the chilly gloom of February.

Fog made each step tentative, and so Victor stumbled down the stairs beyond St. Ruprecht's and stumbled across the vacant plaza toward Franz-Josefs-Kai, where occasional headlights flashed across the sidewalk. As he walked along the canal, the fog grew even thicker, a graying blanket covering feet, legs, trunks, moving steadily toward throats, constricting, deadening. Victor seemed to be sliding toward the water, unable to breathe and unable to resist.

He did not find the man of the churches that day. For the next week, he followed the same disjointed regimen in his futile search. The man of the churches seemed to have disappeared. Or perhaps he had died.

Victor, however, did not forget him. Victor was intrigued by what he thought was the man's obsession, and he wanted to uncover his motivation. The man of the churches might have been a man of immense guilt; Victor believed that he might also have suffered immense pain, much as Victor had. Victor felt it important to follow his steps, regardless of the effort that demanded. Victor did not complete the task that day, so in the next week he abandoned his putative research on Vienna's priests and instead looked for the man of the churches–at the church of the Minorites, the Dominican church, the Church of the Nine Choirs of Angels, the Chapel of Maria Magdalene, and finally, St. Stephan's, the cathedral at the center of the city and of the Austrian Catholic church. He saw penitents who looked as if they had lived too long and tourists who looked as if they had never believed. But he saw no one who looked like the man of the churches.

When Lent began Victor made a resolution to continue seeking the man of the churches. The cold did not now bother him, but he thought that perhaps the man of the churches had retreated to warmth in some corner of the city, a corner which Victor had not yet found but which he hoped was not in the basement of some parish church.

Victor had not seen Ernest for three weeks, and when Ernest called, Victor was glad to hear his voice.

"Hello again, Ernest. It has been too long since we last met."

"It has been too long. How have you been? How is your work going?"

Victor hesitated. He had not met with any of the Vienna clergy and had not done any research in the liturgical archives. He realized that soon he would have to write his family about some sort of progress in this imaginary project, but he no idea what he should report. He also had found out nothing more about his cousin Felix.

"I am doing what's possible," he finally told Ernest. "Progress is quite slow."

"As is mine," Ernest replied. "I can't seem to do much with that story of your cousin and the tram accident."

"And the woman in orange and blue? Have you seen her again?"

Ernest chuckled. "Oh no. I haven't looked for her, haven't seen her, and I've abandoned her as inspiration for a story. She is not, unfortunately, my Viennese muse."

"That's probably best. You would only get into trouble."

"And you? What of that man of the churches?"

"I've lost him. He was probably just a religious tourist, or maybe someone from the countryside where they seem to have stronger faith than anyone in the city."

"Perhaps you're right. But let's meet in person to talk about such matters—and just to get together. How about this Sunday at the Pötzleinsdorf Schlosspark. You must know it—it's in your district, on the outskirts of the city near the Vienna Woods. We've both been too long secure inside our apartments. Let's defy the short winter days by a walk through the park."

"Yes. I have been inside too long. What time?"

"Early afternoon? 1:00?"

"Good. I'll see you on Sunday. Let's meet at the bench inside the entrance off Hockegasse."

On that Sunday afternoon, Victor sat at the bench and looked on as children played at the Schlosspark. They slid on their backs down the icy hill on sleds, on cardboard boxes split to form toboggans. The younger children used their feet as brakes, sometimes even from the top of the hill. The older ones went faster and faster, coming as close as possible to the iron gates of the playground, trying to put themselves in danger but never in pain. When Ernest joined him, Victor shook his hand, sighed and decried the long winter gloom,

"The days are still so short," he told Ernest, "and the cold wind always seems to find ways into my soul."

"Well Victor, perhaps you're being punished for your sins," Ernest said with a grin.

"If so, I'll soon be out of Purgatory."

"When you get to heaven, then, please put in a good word for me."

"I will, but you'll have to write a story about me first—not about that woman."

"Oh, I think I told you that I've given up on her, but I'm thinking of a new story, or at least the basis for a story."

"Please tell me more."

"I don't like to talk about any of my writing until I've gotten a good bit done, but this is just thinking about a way I'll look at Vienna, a different sort of point of view."

"Well, tell me what you can."

"Here's what happened. One afternoon near the University, as I was walking toward Schottentor a shabbily clad woman asked in English for two schillings–milk for her children, from Bosnia, she said, hungry, sick, dying. I saw the woman ask someone else, and heard what that man said, what I knew I must say–'I have no money; no, I have no money'– that's all he could say. But I knew that the woman did not believe him, and she followed. She told him again and again of her pain, of her sadness, of her children. But he had a sentence which absolved him."

"Did she approach you? Did you give her any money?"

"Well actually in truth I didn't have any coins, and I wasn't about to give away my bills—and so I walked away, thinking about a story...."

"About the woman?"

"No, not about the woman, but about the man who said he had no money."

"And about yourself, perhaps?"

"Perhaps."

"What did you do next, before you went home?"

"I hate to say it, but I moved quickly, as if time were important and the next strassenbahn could not be missed, and so I sought refuge in the line of people waiting for the tram. But opposite the stop, I saw someone else who looked as if he might be a beggar. Like the woman from Bosnia, the man seemed to be asking for money," Ernest told Victor, "although he might have been asking for directions. It seemed fortunate at the time," Ernest said, "to notice the man in time to turn away from him as well. It was not the money: I had hundreds of schillings with me. It was the difficulty of it all, the need to speak and the need to be seen. And the need to understand the man's pain."

"There are so many beggars in the city, too many."

On the hillside across the park from their bench, the children went faster and faster down the hill. Even the younger ones had pulled in their feet and had no fear.

"Once I got home, I began a new story, from my viewpoint as an innocent observer."

"An innocent...." Victor said. "You've never been innocent."

"Don't make light of the matter, Victor. I am not usually so affected by other people."

"But you're a writer. Don't you need to understand people, have sympathy for them?"

"Only for the characters I create. But now I might try something else, just to see how it turns out."

"What will you do?"

"Here's what I'm going to try. I'll tour the city, and I'll go to the end stations of every line. I'll ride from one end station to the opposite end station. You see, Victor, Vienna has no beginning stations, only two end stations for each line. The strassenbahn seem to have no beginning: at each end they simply turn and face the opposite end. Perhaps," he told Victor, "the strassenbahn correspond to the sadness–a torment without clear beginning and forever reaching a momentary end. I think that could give me a fine story."

"It might, but who needs such a sad story?" ("Why doesn't he talk to people," Victor thought. "Why did he give up the woman in orange and blue?")

"The story might be sad," Ernest responded. "I don't know yet, but here is what I'll do. I'll ride the strassenbahn so that I can watch the people who travel with me. I'll try to catch the eyes of the riders," he continued. "I'll try to guess what tribulations they have faced, but I'll never speak. I'll seek out the sadness and turn it into fiction, like most people turn it into nightmares."

Children slid down the hill, screaming in delight, kicking snow as they tried to stop.

"So, what about your research—and that man of the churches you followed?"

"I'm just taking notes, not much more—and I think I told you that I haven't seen the man since January. I should be going to more churches myself, at least to listen to the sermons. But I've only visited Steinhof..."

"I've heard of that," Ernest interrupted. "Some sort of art deco palace, isn't it?"

"No, not really. It's a small church which sits atop a hill overlooking the city. It has a golden dome above the altar and a stained-glass window, with angels above the apostles, who shimmer in the afternoon sun. I haven't seen a church like it in the city," explained Victor. "But on the hillside below the church lies an asylum, home for those who could no longer bear their lives. It just seems like such a terrible contrast...."

"I should go there," Ernest said.

"Yes, you should, but not to write about."

"You're right. I should look somewhere else, somewhere which would be a little brighter." The cries of the children on their sleds caught his attention. "Look there, Victor, those children over there on the hill. There's a scene of pure delight. I remember when I was their age: I wanted to go faster and faster and stay out longer than anyone else. How about you? Were you a fearless sledder?"

"For a while, I was. But it got dangerous; everything got dangerous. I wish those kids would go home before they get hurt."

"Victor, you're being too cautious. Come on, let's go the city and get some coffee."

On the hillside of the park, children rode faster and faster, with sounds of steel blades icing down the slope and the joyful cries of crashes avoided.

As they left the park to catch the #41 at the Pötzleinsdorf end station, Ernest looked back at the children and smiled; Victor turned away, trying to avoid slipping on the icy sidewalk. They took the tram to the other end station, at Schottentor, where they stopped to decide on a café on that second Sunday of Lent, the season of sin and guilt. Ernest suggested Havelka, where he could pretend to be a novelist. "It might be a bit crowded, and it's usually smoky, but the atmosphere just seems authentic," he told Victor. Victor preferred Café Landtmann, where he felt secure. "Wasn't that Freud's favorite?" Ernest asked Victor, who did not respond. They settled on Café Griensteidl as a good location for watching other people.

As they sat at Café Griensteidl waiting for their coffee, Ernest pointed outside to Ernesterplatz, where a tall figure in a grey cassock stood in the middle of the circle of Roman ruins, holding a large crucifix in one hand and pointing heavenward with the other. He seemed to be shouting to those who passed by, but no one seemed to be paying any attention to him. "Look there, Victor, is that the man of the churches? He seems too tall. What do you think?"

Victor knew that the man of the churches was indeed much shorter and always wore black, but he could not admit to Ernest that he had followed the man of the churches so closely.

"I don't believe he's the same man, Ernest, but I'm not sure."

"Come, let's go see what he's saying." Ernest got up quickly, without waiting for his coffee. Victor was annoyed by Ernest's impatience, but he left enough money to pay for their drinks and a small tip.

A small crowd of Italian tourists had gathered around the grey figure, and as Ernest joined them, a woman dressed entirely in orange and blue emerged from the Hofburg and walked directly through the crowd, acknowledging neither sin nor passion. Victor saw Ernest carried by the crowd close, closer to her as she tried to work her way across the plaza, and he tried to push his way through the dozen people who surrounded the grey figure. But Ernest only reached out to grasp her hand. It was the closest they had been in months. But the grey figure had seen Ernest's approach, and he thrust the crucifix between Ernest and the woman in orange and blue and grabbed hold of Ernest's arm.

"Do not be waylaid by the man collecting shadows," the man shouted at Ernest, "the man of shadows, made entirely of muck."

Ernest struggled to be released, watching the woman in orange and blue disappear into the shadows of Herrengasse, Victor grabbed the crucifix, tossed it aside, and took Ernest by the arm and led him back towards the café.

As Victor and Ernest walked away, Ernest laughed and asked Victor. "Where did she go?"

"Who? Who was it? Are you hurt?"

"No, Victor. I am all right. But she was here, here, in the crowd."

"Who was here? Everyone was here."

"The woman in orange and blue. The woman from the strassenbahn. Where did she go?"

"I didn't see her," Victor lied. "But come. Let's find somewhere warm away from this charlatan."

"Victor, you're just spoiling my fun," Ernest smiled as he dusted off his pants and tucked in his shirt. "She got away again. What a shame."

"Let's go back to Café Griensteidl, if we haven't lost our table."

"I'd like to, Victor, but I need to go home and write up this incident. Could become a good scene in a comic story."

"Go ahead, Ernest. Do what you must."

"I will. Take care," he said as he walked quickly away. "And stay in touch."

Ernest and Victor did not meet again until April, when only the foolish leave their homes without umbrellas and overcoats. They met across from the University, at Café Maximilian. Ernest had not yet completed his tours on the strassenbahn, and he was concerned that it had taken so long and, even more, that he hadn't yet written about it.

"I have seen so many people. But I have not seen her again for so long."

"Seen whom? Oh ... that woman, that woman in orange and blue? Give up. She's a phantom."

"Oh, I've given her up, again," chuckled Ernest. "I think you're right: she's a phantom, or at least a clever trickster."

"Perhaps. Or perhaps she just is a lonely person who like to dress in orange and blue."

"Well that just makes her a dull little woman, not fit as a good character, no different from your man of the churches. What about him? Has he also disappeared?"

"I've not seen him," Victor told Ernest, "but then I haven't been looking for him."

They spent nearly an hour talking about the late Vienna spring, their unfinished projects, and, again, about that elusive woman in orange and blue, who had become a part of their shared Vienna. When they left, both knew they had very little else in common.

Two weeks later, however, Victor himself met the woman in orange and blue, or what would have to pass for a meeting just outside the Volksoper at Währingerstrasse and the Gürtel. As Victor rode past the Volksoper on strassenbahn #41, a small child brushed against his arm and awakened him from his self-absorption.

"Oh, Yes. I see," Victor said to no one, as the child was drawn into her mother's lap on the seat opposite.

Through the window, past the smiling child and her mother, on the sidewalk outside the Volksoper, there was a woman in orange and blue, offering roses to the men and women who waited in line to buy tickets for the final performance of Mozart's magical flute later that evening. Victor hurried to the door and pressed the button for the door to open at the stop under the U-Bahn, just across the Gürtel from the opera house. "This time, I'll talk with her. I hope she knows English," he thought. "I've got to find out about her."

As Victor walked toward the line of men and women outside the front entrance, it seemed as if the people knew why he was there. They seemed to part as the sea once parted, so Victor could walk directly to the woman in orange and blue. As he approached her, not knowing what to say, she offered him a rose, which he accepted, paying twice what even a desperate lover would have paid after too many glasses of wine at too many cafés. The woman in orange and blue said nothing: she simply put the bills Victor had given her into that blue wallet hanging from her wonderfully orange belt, nodded at him, and walked back into the crowd.

The next morning, he called Ernest and told him of what he called his wonderful meeting.

"I saw her, Ernest, I saw her and she gave me a rose."

"Is that you Victor? Do you know what time it is?"

"Yes. I'm sorry, but I did see her."

"Who did you see?"

"The woman in orange and blue, Ernest, I actually met her. She was selling roses outside the Volksoper."

"Did you talk with her? What did you say?"

"Well, I didn't really say much. She was busy, don't you see, she's a rose peddler. That's what she has been doing all this time."

"Victor, how do you know that and why didn't you say anything? Are you making up a story now, or were you just daydreaming?"

"I don't really know. But you must not put her into one of your stories."

"Oh, don't worry. I've long since forgotten about her."

"Good. Just don't break this promise."

"I won't. Now, you should stay home yourself and get something done about those priests."

Victor did not want to tell Ernest that he had abandoned the project, as he hoped Ernest would abandon the woman in orange and blue. "Yes. I must finish soon," he assured Ernest.

"Just don't work too hard now. Write for an hour or so and then go take a walk."

"That's good advice, Ernest. Thank you. Take care now."

"I will. Call when you want to meet for coffee."

Victor left the apartment and walked toward the porcelain palace at Augarten. He crossed the Danube canal at Friedens-brücke and saw a woman's form rise toward the water's surface and simply disappear. A tall man dressed in black pointed to the spot and called out for help, Victor looked again, into the dark, cluttered water, and the figure rose once more, a vision of distress, and what seemed to be a bright blue dress set off by a flaming orange cape. He clumsily stepped atop the wall lining the bridge, removed his shoes and overcoat, and, for just those few seconds, stood, wavering, as if awaiting directions or certainty. And then he jumped into the canal, not knowing what else could be done.

The canal swallowed Victor, and he sank quickly into its cold and brown waters, and tried to escape the forces that first pulled everything down, down, and then forward, toward the spot where the woman in orange and blue had appeared. Victor knew, however, that to find and save her, he must resist the water, or a demon beneath, which held fast to his pants and shirt, trying to rip off his clothes. "No, no," thought Victor, but his body shed the useless clothing as he fought to regain the surface. He seemed to look down on his struggles from above, not from the bridge and not from heaven, but from a fixed point always out of the water but always aware of its irresistible force. Then he burst through the water into the cool night air of that April evening. The current drove him away from the bridge and toward the spot where the woman in orange and blue might be waiting, but he realized that the canal's force was both irresistible and ceaseless, and that it would drive her away as well, and it would not release anyone.

But he did not sink this time. He was carried forward, ever forward, with closed eyes, imagining a ride on that magical comet at the Prater amusement park, that ride that sucks your breath as it pulls you backward into secure, chaotic thrill. And again, he felt himself to be outside the canal, outside reason, gazing on ecstasy from somewhere above the water's surface. He could not open either eye, yet he saw the woman in orange and blue come closer and closer, even as he began to be driven down to the canal's bottom, where any point in that terrible mud might be a center, but every center was bottomless. He tried to call out and gather what energy remained. He thrust upward, and again broke through, shedding his last remaining clothes, both arms extended into the air and mouth open and free, eyes fixed on the skies above the city. But the demon would not release him, and he was pulled back into the awful brown waters, disappearing once more, water within water.

Victor felt a gentle pressure on the soles of both feet; his toes merged with the canal's aged mud and his body sank into release, content with oblivion, floating slowly, slowly, ever closer. His body turned gently, spinning its final pirouette. He opened one eye, as if to see not what was left but what was relinquished, and there appeared a vision of a woman's figure, appearing in a mist and on the verge of fading away, shrouded in hospital sheets of orange and blue. Together they danced slowly through the murky water, until he released her hand, and she was borne away in the irresistible pageantry of death. And then, somewhere above him, a lightless fire reached down. He pushed away from death through the annihilating water toward the light that grew stronger and stronger, rising through memory and regret.

When Victor reached the surface, he first saw the golden

tip of a cane reaching toward him, and then he heard the voice of an elderly man giving directions to the other figures in the small wooden boat.

"Fritz, please, stroke carefully; Franz, a bit stronger.... There, there we almost have the body. Hold steady, you are no longer young boys, you must hold steady."

Victor extended his arm through the chilling waters and felt his three fingers close around the golden tip of that magical cane. He was being pulled into the boat, and then the water rushed from his lungs, and the cold night air embraced his naked body.

"Fritz, Franz, quickly now. Toward shore."

The two men pulled as if they were united into one force of redemption, and the boat moved directly to the edge of the canal. Above the canal, a crew of streetcleaners stopped their work and gathered to cheer as the man with the golden cane directed the boat toward shore. Fritz and Franz lifted Victor out of the boat and placed him gently on the grass lining the canal's walkway; one of the street cleaners took off his orange overalls and tossed them down toward him. "Please return them as soon as possible to the Sanitation Office," he called to Victor.

"Many thanks, sir streetcleaner," the man with the golden cane called out. "Yes, of course. We will see to it.... Many thanks."

The streetcleaner nodded and waved as if in salute and returned to his work. Fritz and Franz rubbed Victor's arms and legs, and he slowly awoke, first to wonder and then gratitude.

"It was so dark, so cool.... You saved me."

"Of course," said Herr Winkelman. "It was fortunate that we were on the canal. Truly fortunate."

"Yes. Fortunate. So very fortunate. Did you see her?"

"Fritz, Franz, come. We must help this person; we must cover him quickly, or we will have saved someone from the water only to die of the air."

"Did you see her?" Victor asked again.

Fritz and Franz helped him sit up, and then they helped him into the orange overalls which the streetcleaner had left.

"Should we call the authorities?" asked Franz. "Perhaps we should call for assistance."

"No, no. Please," Victor told them. "I will be fine in just a few minutes. I only need ... but tell me, did you see anyone, anyone in the canal? A woman in orange and blue and a man in black, he might have been a priest."

"We saw no one else. Were you with someone, a woman, perhaps?"

"No. I just thought that I saw her once again. I must have been mistaken. Yes. I was mistaken. I am fine now, quite fine. Thank you. Thank you."

The man with the golden cane nodded to Fritz and Franz and pointed his cane toward their boat.

"We shall then return to the canal. Sir, you should find hot tea and a warm bed and consider the possibility that the universe can tolerate disorder which we should take care to avoid. Come: Fritz, Franz. We have obligations, as you know. Good night. I hope sir you will be able to avoid such early morning exercise in the future."

"Of course. Thank you again."

The two younger men lowered the boat into the canal once again, and the man with the golden cane sat silently in the prow, looking past Victor. Now, however, Fritz struggled against Franz, erratic stroke against uneven pull, so that the boat veered first toward the opposite shore and then back again toward Victor, only slightly upstream.

"Fritz," Victor heard Franz exclaim, "you are a weak and clumsy boatman."

"Franz, you row like an alpine oaf, an ignorant provincial."

The man with the golden cane smiled slightly as the boat recrossed the brown waters, and he tipped his hat, a final courtesy to Victor. Victor stood up, waved farewell, and, in the first light of another April morning, slowly walked toward his home, still wearing the orange overalls. "I must look a bit silly," he thought, "but they do keep me warm." He crossed over the canal on the Friedenbrucke and kept heading to the north, into the Eighteenth District through the Ninth District and onto Währingstrasse, more than an hour of slow, measured steps as he tried to forget the dark waters of the canal. When he reached the Gerstoff stop for the tram, he saw a young woman, perhaps a girl of seventeen, he thought, dressed in what seemed to be a second-hand grey coat. As he passed the figure, he caught just a glance of her face, turned down as she waited for the tram.

"She looks so young," thought Victor. "and familiar, in a way.... That Preston girl, what is her name? Gloria? Sarah? No ... Grace, yes she looks like Grace. I wonder what she is doing this morning?"

He walked on, still in the orange overalls of the streetcleaner, toward Pötzleinsdorfstrasse and the end station near the Schlosspark, where Felix Kulpa had begun his fatal tram ride. "I'll go up to Schafberg," he thought, "Yes. I'm feeling better. I'll go up to Schafberg."

Chapter 11
Anna, Amalia, and
the Mother of Austria
Vienna, 1992

As Victor walked slowly past the Gerstofstrasse stop, the young woman, wrapped in a worker's tunic, turned to look at this strange figure wearing the orange coveralls of a street worker, but not carrying a shovel or broom. She was named Anna, and as she stood waiting for the 6:37 a.m tram, once again she was thinking of lovely women. Anna knew Vienna as a city of insistently beautiful women, and she knew she was not among them. In brief encounters on the strassenbahn, she would note the young women who seemed to know themselves and their world, those beautiful women who seemed to have known no other contact save that of angels' wings. They were always thin, very thin, and they always seemed to be alone, even when their hands were held by beautiful young men. Anna was not very thin, but she was often alone.

Until she was 18, Anna lived in Mariahilferdorf, a small village in Burgenland, almost 100 miles to the south of Vienna and just over three hours by bus. Local legend says that the village was named in honor of Maria Theresa, Queen of Hungary and Archduchess of Austria. To celebrate that heritage, the village fathers had in January 1889 dedicated a small memorial sign at the entrance to the town: "Mariahilferdorf The Mother of Austria Lives on in Our Hearts." According to the official proclamation, Maria Theresa represented the best qualities of the Habsburg dynasty: Catholicism, Chastity, and Order. Unfortunately, the mayor of the village when the plaque was dedicated was known to visit a Vienna bordello each weekend and to beat his wife when she refused his advances. No one in Mariahilferdorf, however, ever mentioned these lapses.

Anna's mother tended to Anna and her father, who, before each meal, led the family in prayers to the Blessed Virgin Mary, Mother of God. Each Saturday evening after the family dinner, Anna's mother cleared the table, washed the dishes, and sat by the window telling Anna of the glories of Vienna.

"I was a few years older than you are now," Anna's mother told her, "and I remember the wonderful city—the Ringstrasse, the Heldenplatz, and, more than anything else, the opera house. We went to an art museum, but it looked like a palace to me—such a staircase, marble statues, and carpeted stairs leading upwards toward heaven, I thought. Outside the museum, Maria Theresa sat like a queen over her lands. But the opera—oh the opera; you must go to the opera. My parents could only afford two tickets in the upper balcony, but we listened to *Tosca* and, in the intermission, we walked through the promenade, seeing the beautiful women sipping champagne brought by the beautiful men in their finery...."

"Bah," Anna's father always interrupted, "the city is cursed. You are not to go to Vienna, you are not to go to the opera, and you must not be tempted by those prostitutes and their gentlemen in their city clothes."

But there was little money for Anna's family, and there were no jobs in Mariahilferdorf for Anna. "I'll find work in Vienna," she told her parents, who reluctantly agreed. Her mother packed Anna's few clothes and hoped that she might someday go to the opera. Her father said little, only again warning her of the dangers of the city. Anna left her village with her one overnight bag of clothes, an almost unlimited goodness, and a strong desire to please.

Anna spent her first day in Vienna looking for inexpensive housing; she finally found a one-room apartment in the Eighteenth District with a common bathroom and invisible neighbors. Her room had only a single bed, a night table, two mismatched chairs, a bookcase without books, a bowl and pitcher, a soap dish, a crucifix above the bed, and yellowed wallpaper. The next day, she went in search of a job with the only skills she could offer: washing dishes and obeying instructions. Café Griensteidl in the First District needed women with these credentials, and so Anna found her position.

For her work in the café kitchen, Anna wore a long flannel blouse and skirt and a heavy apron to protect her from the hot water and soap. At night, Anna thought of her family in Mariahilferdorf: there were times at night when she would look in the mirror, run her hands across her body, and imagine that a handsome young man was soon to return with a glass of champagne. But those were only dreams which ended each morning.

As she rode each day from Gersthof to the Gürtel and then to Schottentor, she would see the emblems of beauty lining the gray streets of the gray city. Palmers' underwear ladies, their scarlet bras struggling to contain their scarlet breasts, looked without concern from billboards lining the streets: the legs of the women from the Big Apple Disco, armored thighs and tight butts, seemed inviting and invincible; the bride in McDonalds' billboards, her long black hair and pure white gown against a bright red background with hamburgers, saying—"*Ja, ich will.*"

As she glanced out the window to a passing tram, she would briefly catch sight of the face of beauty, but never did her eyes linger. Inside the tram, at times she met the eyes of the beautiful young women, but in passing she did not learn the secrets of their beauty. On a few occasions, a beautiful woman would sit next to her, and the young woman would brush her leg against Anna but Anna only felt her own coat pressed against her own leg.

Anna worked in the Inner City, and she knew it well, for each day she walked the streets trying to snatch glimpses of the beautiful women. She followed the same route every day, a circular path which enabled her to walk freely and ignore others who also walked their same routes, until she had to retreat to her work inside the café. From St. Michael's plaza, she walked through the Hofburg to the Heldenplatz, and then to the Ring and the State Opera House. From there she would take Kärtnerstrasse to Stefansplatz and then the Graben to Kohlmarkt back to St. Michael's plaza and Café Griensteidl, where she worked in the kitchen, out of sight. At night when she finished work, she walked the same route in the opposite direction, but she only occasionally glanced at the face of beauty.

She needed to be at the Opera each night at 8:30, so that she could look through the windows on the intermission promenade, and, if she worked late, at 10:00, so that she could see the beautiful women as they left and wonder why she was not among them. During the intermissions, she would catch sight of the slender faces of young Austrian women as they smoked their thin cigarettes and listened to admiring young men—an atmosphere of song which seemed to sing itself but which Anna had never learned.

Anna began her work at Café Griensteidl at 7:30 on that April morning, as she did every day. She first hung her tunic on the hooks provided for the kitchen workers and then put on the same apron she wore every working hour of every day. The breakfast dishes had not yet arrived, but when the first cups, saucers, plates, knives, forks, spoons, and glasses arrived, the same routine she had followed for what seemed like endless days began once again. Carefully place the glasses in one sink; the cups, saucers, and plates in another; the knives, forks, spoons in a third, whether they had been used or not. Rinse the glasses first and then move them to the washing tray, which ran them through the conveyor belt, showering them with soap and hot water and then drying away any hint of human contact. The glasses once again were virginal emblems of the beauty and order which the café treasured. And then she must repeat the same procedures with the cups, saucers, and plates, and then again with the knives, forks, and spoons.

"Take pride in your work, young lady, and do not shirk your duties," the supervisor reminded Anna each morning. "You are engaged in work which benefits those beautiful people who come to us for the comfort which Café Griensteidl provides. Take pride, take pride in your work."

Anna was not allowed to enter or leave the café from the front door, and so she could only imagine the people who would sip their coffee or munch on their strudel from dishes she had washed so carefully. She took enough pride in her work to enable her to return each morning.

That evening, Anna left Café Griensteidl after another day of washing dishes. As she began her walk to the opera house, she felt the spring chill taking hold of her fingers and her arms, and she grew weary of the necessities of her solitude. Black satin dresses and cashmere gloves in Kärtnerstrasse shop windows looked past her to woolen scarves draped across woolen coats on plastic bodies forever young and immune to the touch of desire.

A woman's face appeared in the glass next to Anna, a pale face with bright red lipstick and a worn black scarf wrapped tightly around her head.

"They are beautiful, aren't they?" the woman's voice said.

"Yes."

"It is very cold tonight, isn't it?"

"Yes. It is very cold for a spring evening." Anna turned to face the woman, who smiled brightly into Anna's eyes.

"I seldom look in these windows. Everything is so expensive, but it is beautiful."

"Yes. I walk past every night, after my work is finished."

"Do you work nearby?"

"At Café Griensteidl. In the kitchen."

"Ah. Are you a ...?"

"I only wash dishes. Every day, every night."

"Your hands must be tired of such work."

"Yes. But at least through the winter they remain warm. Oh, pardon me, but I should be leaving."

"Of course. It is too cold to stand outside. I am going to a café nearby. Would you like to join me? Just for a few minutes."

"Oh. I don't know. I must catch the strassenbahn at Schottentor. I cannot miss the last tram."

"We have more than two hours. Please. It's too chilly."

"Perhaps. For a few minutes."

"My name is Amalia," the woman said, again smiling deeply.

"I am Anna."

"Come then, Anna. We must stay warm tonight."

Amalia took Anna's left hand, and together they walked through the April streets of the Inner City toward a café, where they could linger away from the cold, if only for a few minutes.

"And you, Amalia, what do you do in Vienna?"

"I am a rug maker. I braid rugs and sell them each Saturday at the Naschmarkt. Ah, you see my arm: I have always learned to make adjustments, accommodations."

Anna looked deeply in the woman's eyes: she might have been twenty or perhaps twenty-five. But her eyes reached into eternity.

As they crossed the Ring, their arms slipped together as if their coats had been closeted for years on adjacent hangers. Anna neither followed nor led, nor did Anna say another word until they reached the café in the Eighth District.

"I've never been in this section of the city," said Anna. "Are we safe here?"

"Yes, Anna. They know me here."

It was a small neighborhood café, just off Florianagasse in the Eighth District. As Amalia and Anna sat down at one of the four empty tables, a small figure wrapped in a grey shawl waved a greeting to Amalia and came to their table.

"Good evening, Amalia. How are you on this spring night?"

"Quite well, Regina, quite well. Let me introduce you to my new friend, Anna."

"Hello Anna. What would you like tonight?"

"Just a small coffee, please."

"And you, Amalia?"

"Warm punch."

"I will be back with your drinks," said Regina as she walked to the kitchen with the order.

"And so, Anna, how do you like this café?"

"It is very different from Café Griensteidl."

"Yes, it is different, and here you will not be washing dishes, will you?"

"No, I will not. But remember that I cannot stay too long. I must catch the tram at Schottentor."

"And so you will, my dear, so you will."

Regina returned with their warm drinks and wished them well. Anna slowly sipped her coffee, taking care not to spill on the saucer. Amalia held her warm wine punch, letting the steam rise to her lips before she took a drink.

"Good health to us all," said Amalia.

"Yes, good health."

But Anna looked at her watch and knew that she must hurry to finish her drink and then walk quickly to Schottentor.

"I am sorry, Amalia, but I must leave now, or I will miss the last tram. Thank you for your kindness."

"I understand," said Amalia. "I am glad we met tonight. Perhaps we might soon see each other again."

"I hope so," said Anna. "Good night and thank you again."

Anna was not sure if she should find a tram that connected to the #41 or if she should hurry to Schottentor. She decided it was best to walk as quickly as possible through this district which she only knew well enough to head down toward the Inner City. Anna reached Schottentor just as the #41 pulled into the end station, in time to board the last tram of the night.

For the next two weeks, Anna returned to her daily schedule, from her morning ride on the #41 to the First District, then to her walk through the Inner City and her hours at the Café Griensteidl kitchen. Each day, she hoped to see Amalia, but each day she was disappointed. Like some beautiful vagrant butterfly, Anna walked the sidewalks of the Inner City, as she did every night, on her way to the State Opera House, waiting for the crowd to emerge. She stood just outside the opera house, near the entrance to the U-Bahn. She knew the beggars and the newspaper vendors, and they took no notice of her. On this night, she stood for fifteen minutes, waiting for the final aria and the final applause to release the women of beauty. On this chilly April evening, she watched them and listened carefully to them. "...a wonderful voice, but too large..." "...tenor overpowered..." "...death must be convincing..." "...lovely..." "...nuisances..." "...*che gelida* ..." "...yes, damp... where?..." "...Martin, your eyes are glowing..." "...yes, thinner..." "...Musetta was...."

She remained until the lights of the State Opera House were turned off, and then she walked to the Ring, hoping she might again meet Amalia, but finally content to ride the strassenbahn home, once again alone.

And so, Anna boarded the #41 each morning that April, and washed the cups, saucers, plates, glasses, knives, forks, and spoons at Café Griensteidl each day.

As Anna washed her days away, Amalia carefully wove her intricate rugs, offering them for sale at the Saturday bazaar at the Naschmarkt. Amalia sold enough to pay her rent and buy what few groceries she needed, but she had no time to walk the streets of the Inner City, until one night at the end of the month.

"Anna? Isn't it Anna?"

Amalia's lips seemed even brighter, her skin even paler, and her hair even shorter; and Anna smiled for the first time in weeks.

"Amalia! It is so good to see you! Where have you been?"

"Have you looked for me, Anna?"

"I have been looking ... I ..."

"I understand. How are you?"

"I am well. And you, you look wonderful."

"Thank you. I have been well."

"Have you finished your rugs?"

Amalia laughed, and assured Anna that she never finished her weaving. "I do come to the City at times just to walk, and watch."

"I do as well, but … isn't it strange…?"

University students costumed in imperial confidence promised authenticity for only three hundred schillings:

MOZART AS MOZART ONLY DREAMED!
HISTORY COMES ALIVE
IN THE SPLENDOR OF A PALACE!

Anna politely declined and turned to ask Amalia if she would go for a coffee.

"Anna, I am sorry, but I must meet a friend. Won't you call me? We must see each other soon."

"Yes. Of course. You must be busy. I will call you. Of course."

Amalia wrapped her arm tightly around Anna, and, for a moment, a few people nearby believed that they were lovers. Amalia quickly jotted down her telephone number and pressed the torn sheet into Anna's hand.

The next evening, Anna abandoned her nightly walk to the opera house and instead went directly home, where she called the number Amalia had given her.

"Hello? Is this Amalia?"

"Yes, of course, Anna. I'm so glad you called."

"I came home early."

"You must have neglected the opera tonight. Are you neglecting those fashionable women?"

"No. I don't think so, but I wanted to call you."

"And it's good you did. Now, shall we meet in person soon?"

"I would like to do that."

"Good! Do you remember Regina's café, in the Eighth District?"

"I do. Should we meet there?"

"Yes, we should. Are you free on Saturday afternoon, after I finish my work at the Naschmarkt?"

"I am scheduled to work then, but perhaps I could ask the supervisor."

"You must do that. Ask and then call me only if you cannot come."

"I will do that. Thank you, Amalia."

"Good night, dear Anna."

Anna could not get to sleep that night for several hours, but she did not know what kept her up. The next morning, she missed the early tram and had to rush through the First District to get to Café Griensteidl on time. The cups, saucers, plates, glasses, knives, forks, and spoons, however, were precisely on time: they welcomed Anna's embrace as they moved slowly through the warm water, lingering perhaps a bit longer than on previous days, as Anna rubbed each dish until each was again smooth and ready for the next hands, lips, and mouths which would be waiting at the café tables.

Anna was not yet ready to ask the supervisor to leave work early on the next Saturday. As she cleaned and gently scrubbed the dishes, she tried to invent reasons why she should have the day off and reasons why the supervisor would refuse. She imagined the supervisor becoming larger and larger as he grew more and more irate.

"Saturday? This Saturday?" he thundered in Anna's imagination, "No! No! No! this cannot be. Hannah, how dare you!"

"It's Anna, sir," she imagined she would say. "My name is Anna."

"Of course it is. But no, you cannot be gone on Saturday. No! This is impossible. No! We are too busy on Saturdays."

Anna then imagined herself taking a knife still warm from the cleaning tray and striking at the supervisor's heart. She would wait for the police to come, thought Anna, and she would proudly admit that she had struck the fatal wound.

"Anna," the supervisor's voice called out. "Anna, you are getting behind in your work."

"Yes sir, I am sorry."

"Is there something bothering you today?"

"I do have a question, if you have the time."

"I do, but please be quick."

"Sir, could I leave work early this Saturday, perhaps immediately after the lunch time?"

"It could be arranged. We do not need you this Saturday."

"Thank you, sir."

"Of course."

The following Saturday, as she had done for many weeks, Anna waited for the 6:37 at the Gerstoff stop for tram #41. When she got off at Schottentor, she walked to St. Michael's plaza, then through the Hofburg to the Heldenplatz, and then to the Ring and the State Opera House. From there she took Kärtnerstrasse to Stefansplatz and then the Graben to Kohlmarkt back to St. Michael's plaza and Café Griensteidl, where she entered through the back door. She hung her coat on the hooks, put on the grey apron, and began her work. Today, however, she checked the kitchen clock each hour so that she would know when she could leave.

The supervisor passed through the kitchen at half past each hour, ensuring that the dishes were clean and ready to be used again for the next table of beautiful people. He glanced at Anna's work, nodded, and moved on, saying nothing if no reprimand needed to be made. At 12:30, Anna hoped to leave, but the supervisor again said nothing. When he returned at 1:30, Anna coughed gently as he passed her station: he paused, looked at his watch, and simply waved Anna away, as if she were a temporary interruption to his daily routine.

Anna took off her apron, retrieved her work tunic on the hooks, put on her overcoat, left through the worker's door, and quickly walked toward the Ringstrasse and into the Eighth District. But she could not remember the street or address of Regina's café: she only knew that it was somewhere off Florianagasse. Just as she was about to pass Schönborn Park, she saw the street sign for Langegasse and knew that the café was toward her left. Two blocks down Langegasse, she saw the sign for Café Regina.

At the second table to her right, Amalia sat smiling as Anna approached. "I wasn't sure you would come," she told Anna. "I was afraid you had forgotten or had found a better rendezvous."

"I have no one else to meet," said Anna. "I just was held late at the café."

"But you are here now. Good. Shall we have some warm drinks?"

"That would be very good. I got a bit lost walking here, and it is still cool outside."

Regina noticed Anna as soon as she entered the café, and she came to their table and welcomed Anna.

"Hello again, young lady. It is good to see you have returned to my café. What would you care to drink?"

"Could I have a small coffee, please?"

"Of course. And Amalia, what for you?"

"A small glass of red wine."

"Excellent."

As Regina slowly walked to her kitchen, Anna looked first at Amalia and then at the other six tables. Two or three women sat at the tables to her right; directly behind Amalia, a man and woman dressed as if they had just left their Saturday morning work sat sharing bowls of goulash. To the left of Amalia, an elderly man sipped a cup of tea, as his golden-tipped cane rested against one of the vacant chairs. His eyes caught Anna's gaze, and he smiled and seemed gently to embrace both Anna and Amalia. Anna blushed, returned his smile, and turned back to Amalia, who asked, "How was your work today? I hope there were not too many dishes."

"It seems there are always too many dishes, but at least I have a job. My family does need the money."

"Tell me more about your family, dear Anna."

"My mother and my father live where they always have and where I used to live, a small village in Burgenland."

"But now you live in Vienna. Do you like the city?"

"I really don't know the city. I only go to work and sometimes walk through the First District."

"Perhaps you would like to join me some day at the Naschmarkt, where I sell my rugs."

"I've heard of the Naschmarkt, but I've never been there. Is it far?"

"Not so far; just outside the Ring. I am there every Saturday morning for the flea market. Thousands of people come to shop there."

"I'm not sure I would like that—and I must work every Saturday morning."

"You would be with me, and perhaps we might find you a better job."

"Is that possible?"

Just then a young woman with a white apron over a blue and orange tunic came with the coffee and wine. Anna thanked her, and Amalia called over to Regina: "Regina," Amalia asked, "do you need some additional help at your café?"

"I might, Amalia, if the person is a good worker and a good person."

"Anna here is just that sort of person–aren't you, dear Anna?"

"I am a hard worker, and I cause no problems. But would I have to wash dishes?"

"As Amalia knows," said Regina, "at my café we all wash dishes, and we all serve food and drink.

"What do you say, Anna? Would you like a new position?"

"I suppose so, but I must speak with my supervisor at Café Griensteidl."

"Of course. We should both go there this afternoon. Come, let's finish our drinks and confront that man."

As Anna drank her coffee and Amalia her wine, the elderly man with the golden cane rose from his seat and put on his overcoat and top hat. He smiled and tipped his hat as he walked past Anna and Amalia. Just before he reached the door, he turned to Anna. "Memory," he said softly above the sound of whispered conversations, "connects us to the past, young lady, but it must not bind us to a particular future." The sound of his golden cane on the café floor slowly receded until the café door closed behind him.

Anna rose from the table and told Amalia that she was ready to leave Café Griensteidl and join Regina.

"Excellent," said Amalia. "Let us go to put Café Griensteidl behind you. Regina, you have a new partner!"

Regina smiled as the two left her café and walked toward the First District. When they reached Café Griensteidl, Anna told Amalia to wait outside the worker's entrance.

"This is something I should do by myself," she told Amalia. "If I can't, then I'm not ready."

Anna slowly walked through the entrance and on to the workers' locker room, but this time she did not take off her coat and did not reach for the apron awaiting her on the hook. No other workers were present, and neither was the supervisor. Anna looked at the clock and knew that she must wait at least thirty minutes before he would likely appear. She looked again ten minutes later, and then fifteen minutes, and ten more, before the supervisor came through the manager's door and walked past her.

"Sir?" she said. "Sir?"

"Hannah. You should be ready for the dishes by now. Don't dawdle; there was a heavy lunch crowd."

"Sir, I have something to say."

"Don't waste my time. Tell me, quickly."

"I am leaving Café Griensteidl, sir.'

"You are? Well then, don't stay here any longer. Collect what pay you might have remaining and then simply leave.

No need to speak with anyone else. No need at all. No need."

"Yes sir, thank you," said Anna.

Anna went to the payroll office, asked for her week's pay, and then left without another word. Amalia was waiting outside the workers' entrance.

"Well, did you quit?"

"I suppose so. But it didn't seem to matter."

"Of course not; it never does. Let's celebrate. Come join me at my apartment for a glass of wine."

"I'm not sure I should. I better go home."

"Anna, then you should come with me to the Naschmarkt on Saturday, but you must stay at my apartment the night before: we must be at my stall by 6:00 on Saturday morning." Amalia lived in a small apartment in the Fifth District, just two blocks from the market. She told Anna that she had a small cot which Anna could use.

"Thank you, Amalia. I will first speak with Regina to see if I may have Saturday morning off work, and then I hope to join you."

On the first day of Anna's work, Regina helped Anna learn the café menu and the ways in which the kitchen was organized. She would begin by washing dishes, as she had at Café Griensteidl, but, Regina assured her, Anna would soon wait on tables and greet the customers. Those customers were mostly workers from the café neighborhood and a few students from the University. Regina had only three other helpers—Markus, a student who worked only in the mornings, Gabriella, a mother who worked only in the evenings, and Eva, who came whenever Markus or Gabriella needed a day off. Anna would attend to the hours between breakfast and dinner and would not work every Saturday.

"Of course, you may join Amalia this Saturday," Regina told Anna. "She is a dear friend and someone I trust entirely."

After her Friday shift, Anna met Amalia outside Regina's café, and the two again walked to the First District, but on this occasion they did not stop at Café Griensteidl.

When they arrived at Amalia's apartment, Anna thought she had walked to a wonderland of colors and shapes. On the floor were red, blue, green, gold, and silver rags, scraps of sheets, yarn, all carefully organized. A wooden frame was mounted on the wall, with strings hanging from nails and poles on each side.

"Ah, you've noticed the tools of my trade. Here's how I gather them: I use whatever I find at the flea market on Saturday morning. During the week, I interweave three ropes of fabric on the frame until I finish the rugs. Sometimes I work on the floor to braid circles and squares and designs I invent."

In one corner of the room, Amalia had placed the week's work: blue, red, purple, green rugs; fanciful shapes and combinations; rainbows and mandalas of color and fancy.

"How is it possible for you...?"

"Ah yes, my useless arm. I don't know how I learned: my mother simply taught me to weave and braid with what I had, however I could. I've never known any other way."

Amalia's soul had ample room for love and kindness, and so she gave Anna her cot for the night. She told Anna that she often slept on piles of cloth on the floor, to be near her most precious rugs.

The next morning, Amalia woke Anna at 5:00 so that they could carry the rugs to her Naschmarkt stall in time for the early shoppers. After small cups of coffee and slices of yesterday's bread, the two worked together to prepare for the Naschmarkt sales. Amalia showed Anna how the rugs must be folded and placed in three large leather satchels so that they would be ready for display. Amalia put on her light grey sweater, Anna her blue jacket, and they walked the two blocks to the market and Amalia's stall. Anna placed the rugs as Amalia instructed, and they were ready for the morning shoppers.

At first, few people strolled through the flea market, but

each hour more and more people stopped to admire Amalia's rugs. Most were dressed in workers' clothes, and nearly all looked intent. A few made offers well below what Amalia asked; Amalia only shook her head and gave a price only slighter lower than what she had posted. The haggling continued several minutes—some would shake their heads and walk away, only to return with yet another offer. Amalia accepted those which she thought fair.

"You see, dear Anna, the flea market makes all of us negotiate—there are no discounts for the beautiful people."

"It's something like the Saturday market in my village, but there are so many, many people here."

"Indeed there are, and today seems like a busy day. But Anna, you need not stay with me. You must explore the Naschmarkt for yourself. Just come back later and tell me what you have discovered."

Anna slowly walked through the crowd of Saturday morning shoppers in search of bargains at the flea market and inspiration at the food stalls. In the stalls opposite Amalia's, Anna looked on jackets, coats, cloths of every size and color, childrens' games, televisions, dresses, skirts—red, blue, brown, black–all of which could have been worn in Mariahilferdorf the week before. She saw wedding dresses and tuxedos and imagined the beautiful women and men who once wore them on their finest day. The knives, spoons, forks, plates, saucers, cups, and serving trays in the next stall only reminded her of long hours and tired hands, and so she did not pause. But the used bicycles, wagons, toys for infants and toys for men, board games, rosaries, medals, cookbooks, Bibles–those all seemed to merge into dreams of her childhood in Burgenland. So many fashion magazines, thought Anna, and crossword puzzle magazines, sweaters, glasses, binoculars, gloves, hats, shoes—and the bugles, Italian military helmets, swords, shields from battles won and battles lost.

Anna reached the end of the flea market and was carried

into the narrow confines of the food stalls. The force of the crowd pushed Anna to the fruit stand, where she gazed on red, yellow, and green apples, pears, oranges, melons, and mangos. ("How did they get mangos? Where do they come from?" she thought.) She felt herself floating past stalls with dates, figs, stuffed peppers, pineapples, wines, ciders, jellies, pickles, almonds, walnuts, cashews. When she passed the men selling gyros, hummus, curry, falafel, and curry, Anna imagined wonderful meals served by exotic women from the Orient. The smells of garlic, seafood, cinnamon, vanilla, and vinegars created for Anna aromas she could not identify nor separate. She passed lamb on skewers and sausages of every size and flavor, green, black, and red olives, magically rolled candies and breads as big as a tablecloth, cinnamon rolls, bird's nest pastries.

But more than anything, Anna was enraptured by the cheeses, so many cheeses, cheeses her mother might have told her of and ones whose tastes she could only imagine and enjoy. She stood before the cheese stall and read the magical names: Alpine cheese, Emmenthaler, Amadeus cheese, Beer Cheeses, Kaiser Max cheese, Quargel, Camembert. She imagined how each would taste and on what tables each would be served: Bergbaron with a sharp taste, the cheese vendor told her, served at the palace of a duchess; Grossglockner, which must be strong and hearty and found on the tables of mountain men. Lűneberg, Mondsee, Drautaler, each, imagined Anna, could be exotic cheeses served by beautiful young girls; Tirolean cheese, Alpzirler—too many cheeses to choose from but so many to dream of....

Men and women who seemed to know each of the cheeses, and seemed intent on purchasing desire, pushed past Anna who now was again in the middle of the aisle, again carried forward toward the end of the food stalls and restaurants. The current of shoppers dropped Anna at the far end of the Naschmarkt, seemingly miles from Amalia and her rugs. Anna walked to the outer aisles so that she could find her way back to Amalia and tell her of the wonders of the Naschmarkt.

When Anna at last returned to the flea market, Amalia was packing up the unsold rugs and sweeping the floor of her stall.

"Amalia, the markets have so much, so many clothes, so many foods. I have never seen such fruits, so many kinds of bread, and the cheeses, Amalia, the cheeses from lands I have never heard of."

"Yes, Anna, the Naschmarkt is a paradise of bargains and enchanted foods. I am so glad you came."

"And I am so glad you asked me. What a wonderful place—and so many people, such crowds. At times I thought I might never be released from the crowd and might never see you again."

"But you have returned safely, dear Anna. And now we should plan a celebration—of your new work, of my good day selling my rugs, and of the magical Naschmarkt."

"Yes, we must celebrate. What should we do?"

"First I must count my money, gather my rugs and tools, and then we shall return to my apartment and plan our festival."

Anna helped pack the rugs and finish cleaning the stall. She and Amalia walked the two blocks to the apartment and carefully placed the rugs in the corner of the room.

"And now, dear Anna, you should rest while I prepare for our meal."

"Can I help in any way?"

"No. Just lie on the cot and try to sleep."

Amalia left the apartment and returned to the Naschmarkt to buy what food and drink she believed Anna would enjoy and which she could afford. Anna quickly fell asleep and dreamed of mango palaces and pineapple kingdoms, a dream she had failed to dream in her home. A beautiful girl, dressed in a purple and silver tunic, emerged from the palace and gave Anna a tray on which lay slices of golden cheeses. Just as

Anna was about to taste the cheese, she heard Amalia close the apartment door and quietly walk to the cot.

"Ah, you are awake. Did you have a good sleep?"

"Yes, and I dreamed of a magical world."

"That sounds like a wonderful dream, dear Anna. You should accept the dream as we have accepted our world. And look here, I have returned with some wonderful food and drink from the magical Naschmarkt. Come, let us prepare the feast! First, Anna, could you please remove the cloths from my table and put them in the corner, the corner opposite my rugs."

"Of course, dear Amalia. And then what should I do?"

"You may just sit at the table. I will be your waiter tonight."

Anna sat at one of the two stools in the apartment, as Amalia unwrapped her purchases and brought them to the table, carefully holding first a bottle of wine with her arm. Amalia placed the wine in front of Anna and returned to her small kitchen for the glasses. Next, she brought the bread and then a fruit Anna had never seen, and finally a half-round of a pale-yellow cheese.

"Madame, is there anything else you might need tonight?"

"My goodness, Amalia, what have you found?"

"Tonight, we have a fine red wine from Burgenland, bread from the warmest oven in Vienna, slices of papaya from the tropics, and, of course, a soft and creamy cheese from the Tyrolean Alps–Contessa Paola, selected especially for you."

"Amalia, this is too much but it is so wonderful."

"We have much to celebrate, dear Anna, and so we must have a special meal."

"And this cheese, what did you call it?"

"Contessa Paola, for your pleasure."

"What does it taste like?"

"I don't know. I've never tasted it. The woman at the cheese shop said it was delicate but tart, and should go well with bread and fruit. Come, let's try it!"

Amalia cut a small wedge of the cheese and then sliced a small piece of bread. She gave Anna the first pieces and then prepared a serving for herself.

"So, Anna, do you like the royal Contessa?"

"I've never tasted any cheese like this. It's wonderful."

"Good. Now have some wine."

"I'm not sure. I don't often have any wine."

"Have as little or as much as you like. If you prefer, I will get you some water."

"Yes. Could I please have water and a very small sip of the wine."

Amalia poured a small glass of wine for Anna and a larger glass for herself. They toasted the good day, Regina's café, and the Naschmarkt. Anna slowly sipped her wine but had only that one taste. She preferred the cheese and the bread, and Amalia understood. They shared the food and spoke of the glories of the market and the future at Regina's café. Amalia showed Anna how she began to weave a rug with only one arm. "You must try yourself, Anna. Come, it's not so difficult." Anna tried to follow Amalia's instructions, but finally she gave up, telling Amalia that she would need years of directions and practice. "Yes, it has taken me since my childhood to learn the craft, but it has made me so happy."

The wine from Burgenland joined Contessa Paola to slowly close Anna's eyes and she drifted into a hazy sleep at the table. "Anna, I believe you should return to your cot."

"Yes. I think I am tired."

Anna lay on the cot, and Amalia placed one of her unfinished rugs over her. "Good night, sweet girl. I hope you sleep without dreams."

But dreams did come to Anna, dreams of crowds of people embracing her and dreams of Amalia holding her hand as she walked through the Naschmarkt, dreams dissolving into further dreams, a light reflected in the mirrors of Amalia's apartment, and mirrors themselves reflecting the light, endlessly.

On Sunday morning, Amalia looked into the mirror, proudly ran her hand across her head, and smiled at her gleaming reflection. Her pale face merged into her pale scalp; only her ebonied eyebrows and brightly scarlet lips added color to her wondrous image. She slipped her black shirt over her shoulders–her right hand working for both, her left arm awaiting instructions. Together they joined Amalia as she left Anna, sleeping quietly on a sunny April morning.

Later that day, Anna walked to the statue of Maria Theresa and laid a single rose at the feet of the Mother of Austria. On that same spring evening, a rainbow bridged the sky above the museums, bathing the city in a serene light and reflecting a world of beauty and perfection which Anna knew to be real because she herself could now imagine it. Maria Theresa rose to her feet, looked down on Anna, smiled, and accepted the rose. Anna turned away, faced across the Ring toward the Naschmarkt, and said yes . . . yes . . . yes.

About *Screening Vienna* (2016)

Conley's *Screening Vienna: The City of Dreams in English Language Cinema and Television* is the first thorough survey of the cinematic image-forming of Vienna and its historical aspects [and] culture in Anglo-American media.... Meticulously researched, rigorously analyzed, and cogently written, ... it utilizes literature, operetta, drama, and even Austrian film to make conclusions [about] the formation of the image of Vienna that shapes its past and present. ... Conley underscores the odd, the curious, and the downright erroneous "creations" of Vienna on the English-language screen.... The reader can conclude that the Vienna we think we know is the result of a strong dialectic of its history and creativity and the fantasy [which] that creativity has spawned.... This is essential work.

–**Robert von Dassanowsky,** Director, Visual and Performing Arts—Film Studies at University of Colorado and author of *Austrian Cinema: A History*

Timothy Conley's massive 2016 *Screening Vienna: The City of Dreams in English-Language Cinema and Television* covers nearly every extant English-language film set in Vienna, grouping them into quintessentially Viennese themes: the imperial past, science and medicine, immigration, music, theatricality, love and death.

–**Maxfield Walker Fulton** in *The Melodramatic Unconscious* (Yale PhD Dissertation, 2022)